Praise for Life, Death and Cellos

'A **very enjoyable read**.' Marian Keyes

'*Life, Death and Cellos* **is a witty and irreverent musical romp**, full of characters I'd love to go for a pint with. I thoroughly enjoyed getting to know the Stockwell Park Orchestra and **can't wait for the next book in the series**.' Claire King, author of *The Night Rainbow*

'*Life, Death and Cellos* is **that rare thing – a funny music book**. Rogers knows the world intimately, and portrays it with warmth, accuracy and a poetic turn of phrase. Sharp, witty and richly entertaining.' Lev Parikian, author of *Why Do Birds Suddenly Disappear?*

'With its **retro humour bordering on farce**, this novel offers an escape into the turbulent (and bonkers) world of the orchestra.' Isabel Costello, author of *Paris Mon Amour*

'**Dodgy post-rehearsal curries, friendly insults between musicians, sacrosanct coffee-and-biscuit breaks, tedious committee meetings: welcome to the world of the amateur orchestra**. Throw in a stolen Stradivarius, an unexpected fatality and the odd illicit affair and you have *Life, Death and Cellos*, the first in a new series by Isabel Rogers.' Rebecca Franks, *BBC Music Magazine*

ISABEL ROGERS

CONTINENTAL RIFF

THE *Stockwell Park Orchestra* SERIES

This edition published in 2021 by Farrago,
an imprint of Duckworth Books Ltd
13 Carrington Road, Richmond, TW10 5AA, United Kingdom

www.farragobooks.com

ISBN: 978-1-78842-267-3

Stockwell Park Orchestra

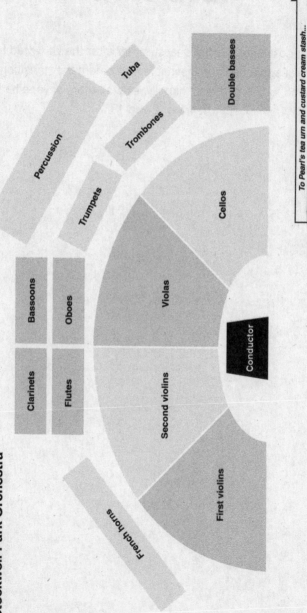

To Pearl's tea urn and custard cream stash...

Author's note

This book is set in a fictional summer after the UK voted for Brexit and it became inevitable, but before the transition period runs out. It also, happily, exists before anyone had heard of Covid-19.

1

London sweltered under a glare that was softening tarmac. In a shabby school south of the river, Stockwell Park Orchestra perspired through an August Saturday afternoon rehearsal in a hall with no air conditioning. Although Sunbridge was officially an academy and not a comprehensive, the perks of this transition hadn't trickled down past a lick of new paint, vast expanses of glass-walled offices and clumps of brightly coloured bean bags scattered in 'friendship corners'. It was the summer holiday: Sunbridge had emptied itself of students and refilled with musicians for a few days. The windows at the top of the hall remained mostly stuck shut.

Eliot Yarrow finished the first movement of Bruckner 7, laid his baton on the music stand in front of him and reached into the pocket of his shorts for a handkerchief. He mopped his face and neck. He was in his thirties and in fairly good shape, but even so his T-shirt was sodden in patches under the arms and down his back. While Bruckner can be a pleasant aerobic workout in midwinter, in oppressive heat he isn't a forgiving composer to conduct. Eliot wished he had paid more attention when the committee was putting together the summer programme.

'Well done – great start,' he said, smiling. 'Let's rehydrate and come back in twenty minutes. Pearl, do we have anything cold as well as the urn?'

Pearl stood up from her seat at the back of the violas and bustled out of the hall first, nodding. 'Lime cordial and orange squash,' she said. 'Give me a minute.' She walked through to the foyer making little tacky noises as her sandals unpeeled themselves from her feet at every step, her sundress billowing behind her as only seersucker can.

Players reached for water bottles and took swigs of lukewarm contents. On the back desk of the cellos, Ann fanned herself with her Bruckner part, wafting a breeze back to Kayla in the basses.

'Keep going, Ann, that's lovely,' she said.

Ann turned and gave her a few determined flaps before giving up. 'That's your lot. I'm too old for this. I can't.'

'Nobody can,' said Erin, walking past to put her cello in its case for the break. 'It's just as hot for us twenty-somethings.'

'And thirty-somethings. I can't take any more clothes off,' said Charlie, also putting his cello away.

'And we don't want you to, Charlie,' said Ann.

'God no,' said Carl, walking through the cello section from his place in the trombones. 'Man up, man. Sweating is alpha male stuff.' He grinned at Kayla. 'Isn't that right, darling?'

'If you "darling" me when you're this sweaty, I'll dump you,' said Kayla.

'Love's young bloom fades so quickly,' said Ann.

'So damply,' said Kayla, laughing. 'Come on, big boy. I'll buy you a lime cordial.'

They walked through to the foyer, where Pearl was dispensing large jugs of cold drinks with ice cubes in, much to everyone's relief. A few traditionalists asked for their usual tea, but Pearl had set up her urn further away from her table than usual so she wouldn't have to stand next to its radiating heat for long.

Charlie took an ice cube out of his drink and put it on top of his head, letting the meltwater trickle through his hair and down his neck. He looked as if he was having an almost religious experience. 'This is *the business*,' he said, his eyes closed. 'Everyone, do this. I can feel my brain re-solidifying.'

Soon there was a circle of people standing round him with ice cubes on their heads, grunting happily.

'Good god, I've broken the cello section,' said Eliot, wandering up with a drink and all his ice cubes more conventionally still in their cup. 'Is this a new meditation to drill down into Bruckner's psyche?'

'Ice hat,' said Charlie. 'New invention. S'brilliant.'

'Eliot, is it going to be this hot on the continent?' said Erin. 'Has anyone heard the forecast for next week?'

'Afraid so,' said Eliot. 'Apparently this high pressure's not going anywhere. At least we're not going too far south. We can cling to the North Sea coast and pray for sea breezes.'

'Oh blimey,' said Erin.

'We're not built for these temperatures,' said Charlie. 'We're a British orchestra. Shouldn't have to play in anything higher than "comfortable slacks weather", and even that's pushing it for some people here who never take their tank tops off.'

'Don't be such a wuss,' said Ann. 'I've been on more tours than you've had hot rehearsals. Our coach will have air con. We'll be playing in either churches (naturally cool) or concert halls (again, air con), so that just leaves a bit of sightseeing, and you can cope by wearing flip-flops and floaty tops like the rest of us.'

The mental image of Charlie in a floaty top caused some of the ice cubes to fall off people's heads.

'Do you go on tour every summer?' asked Kayla, who had recently been persuaded to join the orchestra because she happened to be the bass-playing Head of Music at Sunbridge Academy.

'No,' said Eliot. 'I don't think so. I mean, I've only been here since Christmas but I got the impression it was an occasional thing?'

'Yeah,' said Ann. 'Tends to happen every few years, I guess, depending on how generous Mr and Mrs Ford-Hughes are feeling. We couldn't afford it otherwise.'

'I wondered how it was so cheap,' said Kayla. 'Gotta love a bit of subsidisation.'

'And believe me, we worked hard to keep it,' muttered Erin.

'This time,' Eliot carried on, 'I gather from David we've been invited to take part in some Bruckner festival going on in Cologne, so we're building the tour around that. Amsterdam, Cologne, then Bruges.'

'Sea breezes; hot as fuck; sea breezes,' said Charlie. 'Right?'

'Probably,' said Eliot.

'A week of drinking and extra brass players,' said Carl.

'What could possibly…?' said Ann, innocently.

'Don't,' said Eliot. 'It's all going to be fine.' They laughed at him.

'Of course it is,' said Carl. 'All six nights of it.'

They finished their drinks, wiped up the spilled ice cubes before anyone broke their leg slipping on them, and went back into the hall to rehearse.

The orchestra was spending the weekend in intensive rehearsals before setting off to Dover early Monday morning to catch a ferry to Calais. Their committee – David (Orchestra Manager and fourth horn), Rafael (Financial Director and second bassoon), and Pearl (Administrator, Tea Urn Queen and back desk of the violas) – had indeed received an invitation to take part in the Cologne Bruckner Festival. This didn't have the superstar pull of the annual International Bruckner Festival in Linz in Austria, where every autumn Bruckner fans gather by the Danube to hear most of his music in some form or another. The city authorities in Cologne, on the Rhine instead of the Danube, wanted to fill a lot of its churches and performance spaces with various ensembles from around Europe for a more relaxed two weeks in August, offering less stratospheric ticket prices. Stockwell Park Orchestra was bringing Bruckner's monumental Symphony No. 7 to the party.

2

They were all back at Sunbridge the next morning to rehearse. At half past nine the occasional bells of London churches mingled with Sunday blackbird song and the chirruping of a few sparrows, who were putting in the bare minimum of territorial defence before the summer heat grew too oppressive and London's traffic noise drowned them out anyway. The temperature was still only pleasantly warm, but with a shimmer at the edge of things that promised another sweltering day before long.

Eliot was there early, in a fresh T-shirt and shorts, sorting through his scores on the music stand in front of him. Around him, players opened instrument cases, chatted and twiddled up and down arpeggios to warm up.

'We're doing the Strauss first today, so some of the wind and brass will be coming along later,' called Eliot, as people sat down. 'Alexander should be here... anyone seen him around yet?'

'I'll wait in the foyer for him,' said David. 'Keep a look out. See if he's on the way.'

Eliot nodded. Strauss's first horn concerto used a slightly smaller orchestra than the Bruckner they had been playing the day before: only two of each woodwind and brass instrument instead of three. David, as fourth horn, wasn't needed, and could loiter for soloists in his capacity as Orchestra Manager without having to miss anything.

'We'll crack on anyway,' said Eliot to the orchestra. 'Let's start at the top. Do people know this? Played it before?' There were loud cheers from Neema and Ryan (first and second horns), followed by laughter from everyone else. 'Anyone *except* our esteemed horn players, who obviously will have been brought up humming this at their mother's knee and thus have an unfair advantage?' A few nods. 'Well, it's great. And not just because we get to cross-fertilise from the Wagner tuba imports.'

Eliot looked round to see if Alexander had arrived, shrugged, and decided to go on anyway.

Strauss's first horn concerto starts with a single full chord from the whole orchestra, including timpani, that gives a solid bed for the soloist to bounce off with an exhilarating solo hunting call. If any music can encapsulate the essence of an instrument, it is this opening: confident, almost brash, an absolute declaration that *this* is what being a horn is all about, the thrill of the hunt and a quickening pulse. Richard Strauss was eighteen years old when he wrote this concerto: the testosterone-fuelled adolescent bravado shows. This first call races up an arpeggio and then immediately batters itself downwards again in looping flight, ending the short introduction with a splatted octave drop, as if to announce: 'I am here. This is what a horn does. Do not mess with me.' It is a calling card. In the space of four and a bit bars, a horn-shaped gauntlet is thrown down with all the panache of a master swordsman, and all the orchestra can do is listen in silence.

Eliot brought the orchestra in for their initial chord and, as he took them off, was about to skip to their next entry instead of beating silent bars, when Neema and Ryan spontaneously started to play the solo part together. This horn call is something all young horn players learn – a kind of shibboleth into the grown-up world. They turned to each other as they played, eyebrows working overtime, and coordinated their arrival at the bottom note with perfect aplomb. Eliot cheered, and carried on with the whole orchestra as it took up the theme. The music may have been written by an eighteen-year-old, but Strauss was surefooted around an orchestra, and conjured a mature texture that belied his inexperience. When it was time for the solo part to come in again, instead of Neema and Ryan there was a far-off ringing baritone voice singing the melody. It had an echoing quality of reverb that can only be produced when a voice bounces off an empty school foyer's lino. Several string players were laughing as they played their quiet accompanying quavers, and twisted in their seats, looking round for the singer. Eliot half-turned but carried on conducting as the voice approached. As a tall figure strode through the doors from the foyer the voice suddenly boomed into the hall, and the second half of the phrase seamlessly sprouted words: 'I knoooow I'm late, I'm really truly sorry. The tube… gets… on my' (he incorporated a crescendo to his top note which he had to do falsetto) 'WICK! I know that now I owe you aaaaall a pint.'

The orchestra collapsed into giggles and Eliot stopped conducting to greet the singer, who was carrying a horn case. David, following him into the hall, gestured to Eliot.

'Eliot Yarrow, our conductor. Eliot, this is Alexander Leakey.'

Alexander shook Eliot's hand. 'I'm so sorry I'm late. Unforgiveable.' At six foot four, Alexander towered above Eliot, and with his mane of shoulder-length blond hair and beard, looked like some elemental life force had been compressed into human form. His accent was Scottish, more towards Glasgow rather than Morningside, but somehow not of the city either.

'Don't worry,' said Eliot. 'We were enjoying your singing.'

'Let me get the horn out and I'll do it properly,' said Alexander, taking his case over to the side of the hall and opening it quickly. He put his mouthpiece in and blew warm air through the instrument to warm it up, though the ambient temperature of the hall meant it didn't take much. At a nod from Eliot, Gwynneth gave another A for Alexander to tune to, and then he was ready. He was playing by heart, so didn't need to set up any music stand.

Eliot and the orchestra gave their kick-off chord again, and Alexander bounced around his first call with a level of flexible confidence combined with subtlety of tone that made Eliot relax. He could tell from these first few bars that Alexander was a superb musician, and that they were going to have fun with this concerto. After the first arpeggios, Alexander turned to look at the orchestra while they replayed their first phrases, smiling and nodding at various players as they came in while he had a rest. When he reprised the tune he had sung on his way in, Eliot noticed again how similar the horn was to a voice, and how natural Alexander made it sound.

The horn melody wound through the orchestral texture like a walker through Alpine scenery: indeed, Alexander wandered around the hall beside Eliot, playing from various places and sidling up to different musicians as the tune developed. There was a moment when he and a solo cello struck up a musical conversation, as if they had met while out on a walk and were discussing the weather or how lovely the top of a nearby mountain looked. Alexander had walked round the back of Eliot and played directly opposite Erin, who grinned and played her answering phrases straight to him. Alexander leaned in and then away, moving around, never static. It was infectious music-making, and Eliot grinned too. Alexander's eyebrows waggled his appreciation as they finished their little duet, and he wandered, still playing, back to his place in front of the first violins as they joined in again. Charlie, sitting next to Erin, felt a proprietorial twinge about Erin's friendship. Alexander was obscenely good looking, if you liked the hairy Viking vibe, he thought. And everyone knew about horn players. He tried, as usual, to tamp down the feeling he refused to call his burgeoning… something for Erin, and concentrate on sitting next to her and playing Strauss.

3

The following morning, Monday, dawned far too early, given that in early August night barely gets going before the sun appears again. David had emailed all the orchestral players over previous weeks, detailing exactly where and when they had to be with their instruments and luggage. It was part of his job as Orchestra Manager to deal with the boring stuff: he accepted this. Knowing his musical colleagues as he did, however, meant that he had also scheduled an automatic text and WhatsApp to everyone at half past four that morning, in the hope of scooping any slugabeds into action. He knew it wasn't going to be his most popular idea. They couldn't miss the ferry. The thought of getting to Amsterdam without all the players was worse.

The sun was well and truly up when bleary musicians straggled towards the front door of Sunbridge Academy at 5.15 a.m.

David greeted each one with a smile and a tick on his clipboard list, before waving them over to the double-decker coach and the truck parked next to each other on the turning circle in front of the school doors. The truck was painted with a huge treble clef, a stave and the words *NOTE PERFECT TOURS* on the side.

Charlie nodded at the truck. 'Who drew the short straw then? Bit less plush than the coach, isn't it? Or are we taking a horse?'

'Instrument lorry,' explained David. 'We can't fit everything in the coach, so Note Perfect always sends along a specialised truck as well. Go and see Keith, our coach driver, and he'll sort you out.'

Keith, a substantial man in his sixties, wore a navy tank top over a white short-sleeved shirt and tie. It was a warm morning, hinting at the furnace of the approaching day, but Keith's demeanour indicated he would wear a navy tank top and short-sleeved shirt even if it had been snowing sideways. His grey trousers were clean and pressed, but the crease had the fragile look of one not long for this world. He too had a clipboard. When not in active use, his biro lodged above his right ear. It shared this perch with one arm of Keith's glasses. They had dark shades clipped to them in the 'open, horizontal' position, ready to be flipped down over the lenses when required. Keith, with a driving career spanning four decades, knew something about time and motion efficiency.

Charlie wandered over with his cello, pulling his wheeled suitcase.

Keith reached for his biro and hovered it over his clipboard enquiringly. 'I can see you're a cello,' he said. 'Any more clues?'

Charlie grinned. 'Charlie.'

Keith marked three different boxes on his sheet with squiggles decipherable only by himself. 'Right you are, lad. Now, give your instrument to Jörg here, and he can get it settled in the truck. Your big luggage can go there,' – he indicated a row of bags waiting by the open coach baggage doors – 'and anything small you can take on board yourself.'

'Jörg?' Charlie looked round for someone who was approximately like Keith.

'There he is,' said Keith, nodding towards a figure leaping out of the back of the truck. Jörg was a wiry twenty-something with a shaved head, interesting tattoos and a roll-up tucked behind one ear. Early morning sunshine glinted off a variety of eyebrow, nose and ear piercings. The coach driver uniform standards didn't seem to apply to him: he wore ripped jeans and a vest, revealing sinewy arm and shoulder muscles that came from tough manual labour, not evening sessions at the gym, the way Paul Newman's laconic strength looked effortless beside Arnie Schwarzenegger's contours. Charlie reckoned his must be more of a roadie type job, with less emphasis on customer interface.

'Oh, right,' said Charlie.

'For me?' said Jörg, frowning at the cello. His accent was German and precise.

'Yep – do you need a hand?'

'Not necessary.'

He took it from Charlie and stepped up into the truck, using the tail lift fixed in its halfway position as a staircase. Charlie got the distinct impression that Jörg would regard actually letting the tail lift move him up and down as a loss of face. He peered into the truck. Jörg was wrapping Charlie's cello case in a thick blanket before slotting it between wooden arms that protruded from the truck sides. The whole interior was festooned with webbing straps.

Everything already loaded was secured with at least two buckles. There was a comforting order to the space: a couple of double basses were in the far corner, with room for a third between them and what looked like a tuba. The cellos were starting to colonise one side. Opposite them were deep shelves, some of which were full of blanket-wrapped shapes that could have been violas, trombones or bassoons. It looked like a mummified catacomb of instruments. Underneath the shelves, a couple of horn case shapes were unmistakable despite their blankets.

Jörg tightened the second strap holding Charlie's case in place, checked the case was secure, and jumped down to the ground again.

'Thanks,' said Charlie, impressed.

Jörg nodded at him briefly before turning his attention to the next instrument case to stow, which happened to be Ann's cello.

'Morning, Charlie,' she said, handing her case to Jörg. 'I think.'

'It is. And a lovely one,' said Charlie.

'Christ, you sound chipper.'

'Come on, Ann! Nice weather. A week away.'

Ann almost laughed. 'Yeah. I'll be OK in half an hour when this coffee's kicked in.' She lifted a travel mug and took a long swig. 'And I'm going to need a fag before we get on the coach. Save me a seat. Erin's back there somewhere.' She flapped a hand in the direction of the coach as she walked over to the other side of the turning circle to light up.

'Hi, Charlie!' Charlie turned to see Erin waving at him from the steps up into the coach. 'Come on! Do you want to sit with us?'

He walked over, climbed the steps and followed her along the coach gangway. 'Depends – ooh! This is swanky. A little sink! Are we eating sweets on the back row upstairs or sitting under the teacher's eye down here? Oh, hi, Eliot.'

Eliot turned from stashing his small bag on the overhead shelf halfway along the coach. 'I think you know me well enough by now, Charlie, to know I'm not the strict teacher type of conductor.'

'Thank god,' said Charlie, walking past the first couple of rows. 'You're not pulling rank and going for a table seat, then?'

'Well, since there are only those two I thought I'd let David and Rafael get down to some serious spreadsheeting on them.'

'Ann and I can go here,' said Erin, tucking herself into the seat behind Eliot. 'We can flick Eliot's ears when we get bored.'

'Oh yeah, Ann said save her a seat,' said Charlie. 'She'll be here in a minute – just lung-cancering up.'

'This one's free,' said Eliot, sitting down by the window and patting the seat next to him. 'Come on, Charlie. You can cope.'

'As long as you're not going to do any weird conductor limbering,' said Charlie, sitting down. 'I lean into the aisle for no man.'

'Good luck, Eliot,' said Erin from behind. 'I have to sit next to him all the time. Nightmare.'

Charlie was about to shout 'oi!' but, before he could, the light levels inside the coach dimmed as Carl's bulk filled the doorway and a shout of '*BUNDLE!!*' boomed in. It was answered by an echoing '*BUNDLE!!*' from Leroy upstairs on the back row, and thus the trombone and tuba called to each other repeatedly like a pair of returning migratory birds locating each other after six months apart.

Erin smiled up at Kayla, who followed Carl towards the stairs.

Kayla made a face. 'Does this carry on all week? I get enough with the kids on school trips. Thought grown-ups might be more civilised.'

Erin laughed. 'They're just excited. You can sit with us if you like?'

'Better not,' said Kayla. 'I think Carl wants to relive his nookie-filled teenage years at the back of the top deck. I'll see how it goes. And frankly, I'm looking forward to a week not being either teacher or mum.'

'Where's your teenager?' asked Erin.

Kayla grinned. 'At my sister's. She said she wanted to train him out of his nocturnal habits. She likes a challenge.'

There was a shout of 'where's my woman?' from upstairs.

'Pipe down,' called Kayla. 'I'm my own woman, and don't you forget it.'

The rest of the coach joined in a loud '*oo – OO – ooh!*'

'Oh god,' said Eliot. 'They've all regressed. I don't want to take a youth orchestra on tour. I've done that. It didn't end well.'

'It'll wear off before we get to Dover,' said Ann, walking up behind Kayla. 'They just have to eat their packed lunch early and feel sick, then it'll all be OK and out of their system. That my seat? Cracking.'

'Hurry up,' called Carl. 'I'm lonely!'

Kayla giggled and walked on. Ann sat next to Erin with the soft 'oof' befitting a woman of her age who had woken far too early.

The coach filled up with sleepy musicians. Jörg packed instruments efficiently and Keith stowed luggage in the cavernous hold of the coach when he had marked off everyone's bags on his list. Players of small instruments like oboes or flutes carried them onto the coach with them. Larger instruments were with Jörg. David climbed onto the coach and did a final headcount, cross-checking both decks with his list of names.

'Right,' he said, looking at his watch. 'That's everyone. And not too bad, time-wise.'

Rafael smiled from his seat at one of the front tables. 'Excellent. Well done.'

'Hang on,' said Eliot. 'Where's Max? Haven't seen him yet. We can't play Bruckner without timps.'

'There won't be room on Jörg's truck,' said Charlie. 'It was looking pretty snug earlier.'

'Max is taking his own van,' said David. 'He prefers it that way. He's used to transporting them. He'll meet us on the ferry.'

'Do we know if he's on the road yet?' asked Rafael. From long and expensive experience of balancing his spreadsheets, he knew exactly what could go wrong with a tour, and all the pre-emptive steps to take.

'Yep, had a text from him already this morning,' said David. 'So,' he raised his head and addressed the whole coach via the microphone Keith handed him, 'hello everyone. Thanks for getting here so early.' There were varied muffled groans and a few cheers. 'This is – well, most of – Stockwell Park Orchestra off on our European tour. As you might have heard, we're meeting Max and his timps at Dover, together with Mr and Mrs Ford-Hughes, without whom this trip could not happen.' Cheers all round. David continued. 'Then when we get to Amsterdam, we'll hook up with the four Wagner tuba players – one of whom you've already met: our Strauss soloist, Alexander Leakey. They're also making

23

their own way there.' Riotous whoops ricocheted down the stairs from most of the brass section.

Keith retrieved his microphone, started the engine, flipped his dark lenses down over his glasses and swung the coach out of the school grounds in a smooth arc. Jörg jumped up into his cab and followed.

It isn't often brass sections are joined by the rare Wagner tuba, which looks like a perkier, smaller version of a tuba that has been on a diet, with a bell reaching skyward like an excited daffodil. Wagner invented them to achieve a sort of cross between the sound of a French horn and a trombone. They are unusual instruments, and bring with them many mysteries and arguments, not least because of their name. It is a tuba that is actually a horn, sometimes known as a Wagner horn or Bayreuth tuba, and hardly ever used. Wagner was working on *Das Rheingold* in the summer of 1853 and, knowing Wagner, had a headful of Nordic myths and probably wanted to recreate something like a Bronze Age *lur*, which to be honest would look perfectly at home in a brass band illustrated by Dr Seuss. Wagner wanted a sound that was deeper than the horn and mellower than the trombone, with the same indirectness that comes from a horn, which plays with its bell facing away from the audience.

Bruckner, who was a huge admirer of Wagner, decided to be a thorough fan and use Wagner tuba quartets in some of his own symphonies. They are played by horn players – sometimes not very well, because hardly anybody owns their own – and they often are hired out by opera companies or large professional symphony orchestras, if you promise not to dent them or forever pay your insurance premium. They are famous for being difficult to tune. Love them or hate them, they lend a peculiarly haunting melancholic quality to any music.

As Keith's coach trundled towards the Dover-bound A2, an old estate car containing four Wagner tubas and the men to play them was pulling into a Dartford service station for breakfast.

4

By mid-morning, both coach and instrument truck were safely locked on the ferry car deck, and the orchestra was upstairs indulging in either a second breakfast or coffee and pastries. Or both, in Carl's case. David and Rafael sat together consulting David's trusty clipboard, waiting to confirm that Max with his timpani van had made it. Mr and Mrs Ford-Hughes were flying business class straight to Schiphol, because they felt the experience of going on tour with musicians and having the full immersion in artistic life they craved didn't necessarily include tedious coach journeys and ferries.

Carl spotted the clipboard and called over his laden plate to David. 'Where are the Wagner tuba guys? Not like them to miss a meal.'

'No. They're coming separately,' said David, lifting the top piece of paper and peering underneath at another list. 'One of them has a big estate car apparently that can fit all of them plus the tubas. They're on the next crossing, I think.'

Carl laughed. 'So sometime between here and Amsterdam our coach will be overtaken by an estate caning it down the outside lane? We'll keep an eye out. Hear that, Keith?' He turned to their coach driver, who was making his way through a full English nearly as big as Carl's on the next table. 'We've got a race on.'

Keith sniffed and folded some egg on top of his fried bread. 'Route's plotted and timed for my hours. The rest of the traffic can play silly buggers if they like.'

Jörg, drinking a black coffee next to Keith, nodded. He was young, but took his job very seriously indeed. It was too expensive not to.

'Amen to that,' said Kayla. 'Thank you, Keith.'

'Quite right,' added Erin. 'Dial down your brass player testosterone and behave.'

Carl laughed.

'Never mind, Carl,' said Charlie. 'If you hang about with us string players enough, our chilled élan will rub off and you won't even miss the childish racing games you used to play. Ow!' He removed a toast crust from his hair where Carl had thrown it.

'Ah! Excellent. Hello, Max,' said David, visibly relaxing as he ticked him off the list. 'All well?'

Max nodded as he walked over from the car deck stairs. 'Fine. Now I just need a coffee.'

'We've got a whole convoy,' said Ann. 'Coach, instrument truck, timp van and tuba car.'

'And that's before Mr and Mrs Ford-Hughes join us,' said Eliot. 'David, when do we expect them?'

'Tonight,' said David. 'We'll meet up with them in Amsterdam, after we get to the hotel.'

'And then,' Eliot went on, 'am I right in thinking they'll be joining us on the coach for the rest of the trip?'

'Excellent,' whispered Charlie.

David nodded. A ripple of eyebrow-raising went round those players who had experienced Mrs Ford-Hughes's first concert with the orchestra a couple of terms before. 'They wanted to save time on their outward journey,' he said.

'That'll be it,' said Ann. 'Nothing to do with hours on a coach and a ferry crossing watching Carl setting the sausage-eating record over water. Oi – don't you dare!'

Carl sheepishly put another toast crust corner back down on his plate.

'Well, they're missing out,' said Eliot, grinning. 'I can think of no finer company. I intend to enjoy this week.'

Ann, Erin, Charlie, Carl and Kayla raised their coffee mugs to him in salute, and the ferry sailed towards Calais on a mirror-calm sea. All was well.

Forty feet below them on the car deck, next to the wrapped French horns on the truck floor, one of Jörg's blankets started to move.

5

Keith settled himself into the driving seat as the orchestra climbed aboard and filed past David, who clicked them off on a hand-held tally counter. As the ferry doors lowered to reveal a Calais that was even hotter than the Dover they had left behind, the vehicles around the coach began to start their engines.

David frowned. 'One short!'

'Who's missing?' said Rafael.

'Did you count yourself?' said Keith. He'd seen more trips delayed because of daft punters then he could remember.

'Yes,' said David.

Keith sighed and handed over the microphone.

David raised his voice anyway. 'Um, everyone? We're missing one person.'

There were groans from both decks of the coach.

'Desk partners,' said Eliot.

'What?' said David.

'Seat partners. Like desk partners in orchestra. If we're all sitting in the same seats as before, who's missing their seat partner?'

'Ah,' said David. 'Yes, of course. Quicker than a register.' He called down the coach. 'Who's missing their seat partner?'

Marco, a rather shy, nervous violin player on the lower deck, raised his hand. 'Pearl was sitting here before. And now she's not. Unless she's moved?'

After a moment's discussion, it appeared that Pearl was indeed missing. David confirmed that over the PA system for the benefit of the top deck.

'Do we need her?' shouted Carl. 'I mean, this trip is catered already.'

There was uproar.

'Carl, take that back!' called Eliot. 'You know as well as I do that Pearl is our mascot, our beating heart, the very soul of this orchestra. Nobody can rehearse without tea and biscuits!'

Loud cheers greeted the end of his speech, which had impressed even Eliot himself with its fervour. Everyone took it for granted he hadn't mentioned her contribution to the actual sound of the viola section.

'Is this your missing lady?' said Keith, nodding towards a figure hurrying to squeeze herself between the lines of cars on her way to the coach door.

David turned to look. 'Yes. Good. I wonder what kept her.' He absentmindedly kept the microphone on so the whole coach enjoyed the forthcoming explanation.

Pearl reached the steps and pulled herself up, puffing slightly. She was already too hot and the day had barely begun. 'Sorry, David,' she said. 'I suddenly realised I hadn't brought any reserve biscuits, and they do these lovely triple variety packs in the café, look!' She pulled open her canvas bag to reveal a pile of mini packets slithering about, as if she were a proud fisherman showing the catch in his net. 'You never know. And we've got this lovely hot and cold drinks tap here,' she gestured to the tiny sink, 'so we could have refreshments on the way, if we need them.'

'Hurrah for Pearl and her biscuits!' shouted Charlie, and the entire coach erupted into cheers.

'You did pay for those, didn't you Pearl?' called Carl from upstairs. 'We can't start our European tour with an Interpol warrant out for your biscuit rustling.'

Pearl smiled, and made her way to her seat next to Marco.

David clicked his counter with a decisive nod, ticked another column on his clipboard, returned the microphone and sat down.

Keith sighed. He leaned over to push the coach door closing button, flicked his dark lenses down over his glasses, and soon the coach was rolling onto French tarmac and out of Calais. He was in radio contact with Jörg, who in any case had a copy of the trip itinerary.

'OK, folks,' said Keith into the PA system. 'Settle down, settle down.' He waited for the noise level to drop below five on the Excited School Trip Scale, where one was the entire coach asleep and ten a weaponised food fight. 'Quick rundown of today's plan. Total journey time to cover three hundred and eighty-five kilometres to Amsterdam is approximately four and a half hours, travelling through France, Belgium and The Netherlands, with attendant documentation faff possible. On the way we'll be taking in the sights of cities such as Dunkirk, Bruges—'

'Shall we do our Bruges concert quickly, as we go through,' shouted Carl, 'to save time on the way back?'

Keith eyed him in the mirror to the upper deck, and decided to let this one pass. 'Bruges – without a concert this time – Ghent, Antwerp and Utrecht. We're not stopping in each one or we won't get there 'til a week next Wednesday. Now, theoretically, I could do the whole thing in one go: my hours let me. But I tend to find a journey is more pleasant if we have a convenient stop along the way. What do you say to a spot of lunch around Ghent?'

The coach wholeheartedly agreed.

'Right you are, then. Oh, and one more thing, seeing as we're at the start of our week together and some of you might be new to this game. The toilet on this coach, while perfectly up to the task required of it, can be – shall we say – sometimes overwhelmed. And believe me you do *not* want that to happen. 'Specially in these temperatures. Our air con can cope with so much and no more. Buy me a beer and I could tell you the story of a week I spent driving a rugby team round Toulouse in '93 and their unfortunate brush with a dodgy tandoori chicken. May I recommend that you avail yourselves of any and all facilities at our stop in Ghent, as required? Over and out.'

He received the round of applause this speech garnered with a contented sniff and a long look in his wing mirrors. He'd always found laying out the ground rules at the start of a trip saved him a load of hassle later. And he reckoned musicians weren't that different from schoolkids, underneath. Or rugby players for that matter. He shook out a piece of chewing gum from the pot in his dashboard cubby hole, and drove smoothly east-north-east.

Just beyond Dunkirk, crossing the border was uneventful. Even though everyone carried their passport in case an official needed any ID, the road wound its way out of France and into Belgium without so much as a toll booth.

'We got this tour in just in time,' said Erin. 'This time next year – who knows?'

Ann snorted. 'Bloody idiots. Brexit will kill a lot of musicians' careers.'

Charlie turned round from his seat in front. 'Do you think this'll be our last one?'

'The paperwork to move sixty of us through four countries in a week will be terrifying,' said Ann. 'Do *not* get me started.'

'Why aren't you running things, Ann?' Eliot called round his seat. 'I'd vote for you.'

Ann laughed. 'Because I'm too long in the tooth to be diplomatic enough. As you know.'

'She's right,' said Charlie. 'You should hear some of the comments from the back of the cello section that don't quite make it to the rostrum.'

Erin stared out of the window and sighed. 'It's all bollocks.'

'It is,' agreed Charlie. 'But let's ignore that for a week and enjoy ourselves. Put bollocks on the back burner.'

'There's an election slogan for you, Ann,' said Eliot. 'Nice and alliterative too.'

'When's lunch?' said Charlie. 'I'm starving.'

'Go and see Pearl,' said Ann. 'She can sort you out an emergency biscuit.'

The coach skirted Bruges, with Keith announcing the turning to it on their left so they would, in his words, be able to find it again by the end of the week in case they missed the coach because of their drunken musical shenanigans. They heard him check Jörg's location over the radio: the confirmation came through that the instruments were a couple of kilometres ahead of the coach, all was well and he would check in again at Ghent.

And so, a little over two hours after leaving Calais, they pulled into a diner just past Antwerp. Jörg was waiting for them in his truck. He had parked beside one of the lime trees that were dotted about the car park between rows, trying to mitigate the oppressive temperatures. Jörg's cab door was open, and he was leaning back on his seat in the shade with his boots resting on the window frame, trying to catch what little breeze there was. A small plume of smoke wisped out of the cab and drifted up to join the shimmering heat haze. As Keith parked in the next bay, Jörg stubbed his roll-up out in his ash tray and jumped down to the tarmac, locking his cab after him.

'I shall take a comfort break, get food and water, then return,' he called up to Keith's open window. 'Ten minutes maximum. OK?'

'Right you are, lad,' said Keith. 'It'll take me that long to sort this lot out.'

Jörg nodded and walked toward the diner.

'OK, folks,' said Keith into his microphone. 'Lunchtime. It's nearly two o'clock now – remember we've gone forward an hour. Shall we say, back at the coach in forty-five minutes? Two forty-five local time?'

He looked at David, who nodded his agreement, and everyone started to file out of the coach. As they streamed towards the diner, David and Rafael hung back with Keith by the coach door, in the shade of the lime tree.

'I gather Note Perfect Tours has an "on guard" policy, so we don't leave all the instruments unattended?' said Rafael. Although fully insured, Jörg's truck represented an insurance claim that made him nervous.

'That's right,' said Keith, pulling his tank top off over his head. It had reached critical temperature for even the stringent Keith Wardrobe Rules to be slightly relaxed. 'I'll wait here 'til Jörg gets back, then I'll pop in for a bite myself. Nobody's going to get near them, and they're not going to move by themselves.'

'Excellent,' said David, laughing the nervous laugh of a man standing next to a Treasurer who never joked about money. 'Thank you.'

He and Rafael wandered slowly over to the diner, trying to stay under the intermittent lime tree shade as much as they could.

Under the tree Jörg had found, the temperature in the instrument truck was fairly stable: warm, certainly, but not stifling. The blanket that had moved earlier was now folded neatly next to the French horns on the floor of the truck, and the small figure, curled into a tight ball on top of this makeshift bed, appeared to be asleep.

6

Later that afternoon, Keith pulled the coach off the road into the access drive at the front of the hotel in Amsterdam's Nieuw-West district, practically next to a tram stop and train station. It was a squat-looking utilitarian building, three floors high and very wide, promising acres of straight carpeted corridors inside and untold opportunities for wheelie suitcase racing. A woman stood beside the open front doors under a plastic awning that was grimy round its edges and spattered with bird droppings on top. She was in her extremely trim fifties, with long blonde hair twisted into a French pleat. Her trouser suit was impeccably pressed, and her neat shoes gleamed despite drifts of dust and rubbish on the surrounding steps. As the bus slowed to a halt, she adjusted a clipboard that had been nestled against her chest so she could see her paperwork, and drew a silver pen out of her jacket top pocket, clicking it open.

David climbed off the coach first, glancing up at the hotel doubtfully. The artistic slanting of evening sunlight didn't imbue the building with any more beauty than it undoubtedly lacked during the rest of the day. The woman stepped towards him, down the hotel steps and across the pavement.

'Good afternoon. Stockwell Park Orchestra? I am Ingrid Bauer, of Note Perfect Tours.' Her voice spoke beautifully modulated English with a hint of a German accent.

David shook her outstretched hand. 'Yes, good afternoon. I'm David, Orchestra Manager.' He felt dishevelled in contrast to her elegance, and was at an immediate social disadvantage. As an automatic response, his hand went up to his eyebrow to feel if his long-standing tic was trying to return. It usually joined in when he got stressed.

The rest of the orchestra spilled out of the coach behind him, stretching the journey kinks out of their spines. They regarded the hotel with about as much enthusiasm as David had.

'Not exactly your top-flight Hilton experience,' said Charlie to Erin.

'It never is,' said Ann. 'Give me clean sheets, hot water and no cockroaches, and we'll be OK. Anything else is a bonus.'

'Oh, don't come over all blitz spirit,' said Charlie. 'You're not that old.'

'Since that's about as close to a compliment as I'll get from you, I'll take it.'

Carl and Kayla were among the last off the coach.

'Aw, you old romantic,' said Kayla. 'Our first minibreak abroad and you bring me here!'

'We'll just have to turn the lights off,' said Carl, pulling her into a kiss.

'Oi!' shouted Charlie. 'Can you at least wait 'til we get in?'

'Do we know how the rooms have been allocated?' said Erin. 'Did Mr and Mrs Ford-Hughes budget for single occupancy, or are we going to YHA dorm it, d'you reckon?'

'Singles, I think,' said Eliot from behind them. 'Don't you read any emails?'

'I leave that to you and the committee,' said Charlie. 'Just do as I'm told.'

'Really?' said Eliot. ''Cause you don't strike me as a "just do as I'm told" kinda guy.'

Ann was looking up at the hotel roofline. 'Are Mr and Mrs Ford-Hughes booked here too, do you think? Because it doesn't look like this is a hotel with a penthouse suite. I doubt these rooms are quite what they're used to.'

Their debate on this was cut short by David raising his hand and attracting everyone's attention.

'Hello? Everyone? This is Ms Bauer, our rep from Note Perfect Tours, who will travel with us this week and is now basically in charge.'

Applause and cheers, which Ingrid accepted with a graceful smile.

'Good afternoon – please, call me Ingrid. Yes, I represent Note Perfect Tours, and will be your guide this week. I shall endeavour to make your trip run smoothly, and have much experience in this field. My colleague has already arrived,' she said, gesturing to Jörg's truck further along the drive, with Jörg himself standing by the cab, smoking. He raised his hand in a sketchy salute. 'If any players want to take their instrument with them into their hotel room, Jörg can assist you with retrieval. The truck will, naturally, be secured in a locked garage overnight so it is perfectly safe, and insured, to leave them if you prefer. I shall meet you in reception to coordinate check-in and allocation of rooms. We are booked here for two nights, so after tomorrow's concert we return here before leaving for Köln on Wednesday morning.'

'Thank you, Ingrid,' said Eliot, offering his hand. 'I'm Eliot, the conductor. Hello.'

Ingrid shook his hand. 'Welcome to Amsterdam. I'm sure we shall have a pleasant week. Any issues, please bring them to me and I shall try to resolve them promptly.'

Eliot fought the urge to bow. He recognised true leadership when he saw it.

Pete, the viola player who shared the back desk with Pearl, joined the drift towards Jörg and mused to nobody in particular, 'I thought we were going to Cologne next? Where's Köln?'

'Never change, Pete,' said Charlie, slapping him on the back. 'Köln *is* Cologne. Only more umlauty.'

David overheard this and the subsequent guffaws, and felt the stirrings of his tic come to life, like an old friend whom you weren't pleased to see but had to let sleep in your spare room for a few days until they got themselves straightened out. He acknowledged that it really wouldn't be a Stockwell Park Orchestra concert season without it.

Jörg ground out the stub of his roll-up on the kerb and went round the back of the truck, unlocking the doors and, as was his custom, letting the tail lift down halfway. Glancing back at Ingrid, he followed the direction of her pointed stare. Acknowledging his error, he quickly stepped back to the kerb to pick up his cigarette stub and disposed of it in the ashtray in his cab. Ingrid nodded slightly at him and bestowed a small smile, holding her clipboard with the reverence of a holy book. She knew the reputation of a tour company rested on the absolute integrity of its employees and the impression they gave to clients, in matters both small and large. A tour masterminded by Ingrid Bauer was the gold standard. With nearly sixty musicians on the coach and extras to come in two more vehicles, not even counting the instrument truck, she was vibratingly alive to the possibility of mishap. Musicians were even more random than children, in her experience. And far more often drunk.

Jörg swung himself into the truck and started handing down instruments to their owners, while Keith checked them off his list. As Jörg bent to give Richard, the orchestra leader, his violin, people standing around the back of the truck gasped. They were staring at something behind Jörg. He turned to see what they were looking at and started, muttering, 'Was zum Teufel?' He put his arm out to steady himself.

A slight girl stepped up to the door next to him. She wore dirty jeans and a T-shirt, and carried a battered rucksack slung over one shoulder. Screwing up her eyes in the bright sunlight, she raised a hand to her face for shade while squinting out over the crowd gathering around the truck.

She glanced at Jörg. 'Alright?'

Richard, who was still reaching up for his violin, took hold of it out of Jörg's frozen arms. 'What are *you* doing here?'

'You know this girl?' said Jörg. His face was a perfect storm of anger, outrage, intrigue, and dismay about breaking one of Ingrid's rules. Probably a lot of them. He was already wondering where the buck was going to stop.

'Well, yes,' said Richard. 'But—'

'What the hell are you doing here?' Carl's shout from over by the coach made anyone who hadn't already seen what was happening, turn to look.

'What's going on?' said Kayla. 'Who?'

Carl pointed. 'Look who's turned up.'

Kayla looked. 'Oh. Fuck.'

'Yeah,' said Carl.

Kayla walked over to Jörg and the girl in the truck. 'Hello, Tracie.'

7

Tracie Scott looked down at Kayla. 'Hi, Miss.' She jumped down onto the tail lift, and from there to the ground, turning to Jörg. 'Left my trombone wrapped up on the floor there by the horns, in one of them blanket things. Plenny of room. It'll be fine there, yeah?'

Jörg looked from her to Kayla helplessly, and said, 'I must speak with Ingrid.' He leapt down beside Tracie with light-footed ease and strode over to Ingrid, who was staring at the tableau, clicking her pen in readiness. She and Jörg proceeded to have a rapid conversation in German. Sibilants cut through the muted volume, leaving those overhearing it in no doubt as to its forensic analysis and apportioning of blame. Every so often a stray *Scheiße* would fly out of the vortex. People wisely shuffled away and towards what promised to be just as entertaining an argument by the instrument truck, but in their own language.

Carl was already interrogating Tracie. 'Were you in the truck all the way? On the ferry too? With the sodding *instruments*?'

'I can't believe this,' said Charlie.

'I can,' said Kayla, darkly. 'Tracie, are you OK? Here, have a drink.'

'Nah, I'm good,' said Tracie, but took the water bottle Kayla insisted on giving her and drank most of it down in one go.

David made his way through the crowd and came to a halt in front of Tracie. His eye twitched. 'Young lady, do you want to explain exactly how you got here?'

Tracie stopped drinking and wiped her mouth with the back of her hand. 'Hi. Well, I thought, seein' as how I'm in the orchestra now, I could come on tour too.'

'But you're—' David was lost for words. 'In the truck? On the *car deck*?' He rammed his hand over his eyebrow. 'You're only – what? – fifteen?'

'Sixteen,' said Tracie. 'Birthday coupla weeks ago.'

'Oh, that's OK then,' said Charlie, deadpan. 'What are we worrying about?'

David tried again. 'Have you any idea how many laws you've broken?'

'Nope,' said Tracie, remarkably cheerfully. 'I'm here now though. Who's to know?'

Kayla groaned. 'Just stop there, Tracie.' She saw Ingrid and Jörg approaching across the tarmac, looking equally stern in their different ways. Jörg's piercings gave him extra menace somehow, but Kayla didn't fancy her chances with an irked Ingrid either. She looked at David and grimaced.

Ingrid stopped walking to regard the group in silence. Her French pleat had emerged completely intact from the recent discussion with Jörg. She took in Tracie's grubby appearance with a slow down-and-up stare, her neck appearing to rise on ramrod tendons like a coldly outraged cobra. She consulted one of the pieces of paper on her clipboard, glancing back to Tracie and letting her pen hover over the end of a list.

'Allow me to record your details, junge Dame,' she said. 'Jörg informs me that he was unaware of your presence in this instrument truck. Kindly tell me your name, and when exactly you boarded, so we may inform the appropriate authorities.'

'Police?' said Tracie. 'No way.' She glanced sideways, to the edge of the slip road, as if looking for escape.

'Tracie, you must see that we can't just let you join in as if nothing has happened?' said David. 'Your parents will probably be going spare.'

Tracie shrugged her rucksack strap further up her shoulder and curled her lip. 'Parents? You're joking, ain't ya?'

Kayla tried to help. 'Tracie's home life isn't the, er, most stable.'

Tracie snorted and turned to David and Ingrid. 'Yeah. Mum's gone off to Tenerife for three weeks with the new boyfriend. She didn't exactly stock up the fridge. You can send me back to an empty flat if you want.'

David looked horrified at this snapshot of Tracie's situation. Even Ingrid began to look doubtful. Kayla took a deep breath and a quick decision.

'Look, can we talk about this inside? Ingrid, I'm a teacher at Tracie's school, and can confirm her story is probably true. Maybe there's a way we can sort it out?'

'She's not bad on the trombone,' said Carl, winking at Tracie. 'She could help bolster up our Bruckner.'

'Could I be responsible for her?' Kayla went on. 'In loco parentis, like on a school trip or something?'

Carl's relaxed attitude fastened on this in an instant. 'Hold on,' he muttered in Kayla's ear. 'We were going to share a room, weren't we?'

Tracie's ears caught this aside, and she made a face. 'Don't let me get in the way of you old people's fun.'

Ingrid sighed, and indicated she might be persuaded to relent. 'Let us discuss paperwork issues. Perhaps inside, as you suggest.'

They moved towards the hotel door, while Jörg resumed handing out instruments to whoever wanted theirs.

As they walked, Tracie dug around in her rucksack and one hand triumphantly waved a folded, dog-eared piece of paper in Kayla's face while the other flashed her passport. 'Got everythin' I need here: parental letter to go with my passport... for Belgium innit.'

'Your mum signed that before she went?' said Kayla, eyeing her with open disbelief.

'Well, she woulda done if she'd known about it. Did my research.' Tracie winked at Carl in her turn.

'You, my friend,' said Carl, 'are something else.'

As David and Ingrid shepherded Tracie into the hotel, followed by Kayla and Carl, a screech of tyres made everyone's head snap round. A filthy Skoda estate car came barrelling into the slip road, coming to a jerky stop beside the coach and skittering a few loitering viola players out of the way. It had a couple of St George flags fixed to the rear corners. They must have been mainly white once but now fluttered a defeated, crumpled sort of grey. Half a dozen Union Flags bristled along both sides of the roof box. The displaced viola players could see the back of the car was plastered with bumper stickers shouting various messages endorsing the greatness of Britain. The car somehow tried to convey the view that anything red, white and blue (the right kind of blue) was inherently superior to anything suspiciously European that sported a circle of gold stars and was emphatically the *wrong* shade of blue. Wavelengths of light were, apparently, suspicious and an enemy of patriotism.

'Blimey,' said Eliot.

'Quite an entrance,' agreed Erin.

'Are they with us, do you think?'

'That "with" is doing some heavy lifting,' said Ann.

Eliot nodded. 'Something tells me they are English, though.' He made flappy, flaggy motions with his hands. 'And that makes me nervous.'

'Oh great,' said Charlie. 'It's Alexander Leakey and friends.'

'I thought Alexander was Scottish?' said Ann.

As she spoke, Alexander unfolded himself from the back seat, cracking his spine and stretching out his great height.

'Why are you being so mean about Alexander?' said Erin to Charlie. 'It's not his car.'

Ann shot a quick look at Charlie, who was busy trying to obscure from Erin any possible reasons he had for resenting Alexander, because that was a whole other conversation he hadn't had with her. And wasn't sure he wanted to. Who was asking, anyway? Can't people just sit next to each other in the cello section as friends? Does everybody's life have to read like the script of *When Harry Met Sally*?

Ann let this conversation play out across Charlie's forehead wrinkles for a moment before taking pity. 'Nobody's being mean. Are they, Charlie?'

He frowned at her. 'No.'

Alexander saw them and waved. 'Hello! We made it.'

'Excellent,' said Eliot. 'And I see you brought your Wagner tuba posse.'

'Oh, yes,' said Alexander. 'Tom, Lamar and Julian.' He pointed vaguely at each of the other three men getting out of the car in turn as he said their names, and called to them. 'This is Eliot, the conductor.' He turned back to Eliot. 'Julian kindly gave us all a lift, to save us the coach journey. Which was going to take much longer than the coach. Apparently.' There was something urgent and slightly alarming Alexander seemed to be trying to telegraph to Eliot but, before he could explain, Julian ambled round from the driver's door and shook Eliot's hand.

'Julian Talbot.' It was almost bellowed into Eliot's face. His handshake was firm to the point of physiotherapy. 'Christ, this continental driving is a bloody nightmare. Frogs all over the shop, and not much better in Tintin country. They all drive on the wrong bloody side of the road, that's the problem. And in this heat!' He laughed at a barking foghorn decibel level, expecting to lead a chorus of merriment but drowning out any other evidence. Or silences.

Eliot disentangled his hand, massaging it discreetly and hoping it would still be able to wield a baton in the morning. Julian flapped the neck of his short-sleeved rugby shirt to direct a breeze inside, and the aroma of baked bean fart mingling with ripe sweat wafted over the car park.

Charlie and Erin looked at each other, gagging slightly. Eliot coughed and met Alexander's eyes. There was a pleading element to Alexander's gaze that prompted Eliot to try to help.

'Julian, our tour guide has just this second gone inside the hotel,' he said. 'You'll probably find her in the lobby. Ingrid. Lovely lady. She's with David, our orchestra manager. Why don't you go on in and get your rooms sorted?'

'Ingrid, eh?' said Julian, grinning a grin that was more of a leer, to be honest, and walked towards the door.

'Christ alive,' muttered Ann.

'I'd like to see him try anything with Ingrid,' said Erin.

'She'd snap his spine,' said Charlie.

Eliot turned to Alexander. 'Um… eventful trip so far?' No amount of upswing in his diction was going to gloss over what had clearly been the road trip of several lifetimes.

Alexander closed his eyes and covered his face with his hands, shaking his head. They could hear a muffled 'oh god oh god oh god' coming out from between his fingers for quite some time.

The other two Wagner tuba players, Tom and Lamar, walked up behind him. Tom gave him an encouraging slap on the back.

'Buck up, mate,' said Tom. 'It wasn't that bad.'

'It was quite bad,' said Lamar, looking as if he knew to the millimetre how much more he had to go on his tether.

Like Alexander, they were in their late twenties: all wore shorts of various lengths and pockettage, and loose T-shirts to try and keep cool. Being driven across northern Europe by a man if not technically old enough to be their father then at least a wayward uncle, in a vexillologist's dream car with dodgy air con and on-board flatulence, had been an experience none of them would ever forget.

'Well, you're here now,' said Eliot. 'And I'm delighted. Our Bruckner would sound very odd without you.'

'Come on,' said Ann. 'Let's go and sort our rooms then find a drink.'

'This is Ann,' said Charlie, conversationally, to Lamar and Tom. 'She's been on more tours than the rest of us put together. I'd let her have a few beers before asking her about thongs in the Trevi Fountain, but other than that, let's do exactly what she says.'

Alexander laughed. 'Sounds good. As long as we can give Julian the slip.'

Eliot led the way indoors towards Ingrid and the Clipboard of Room Allocations.

8

Tuesday morning started as clear and blue as Monday's, and promised to be just as hot. In the hotel breakfast room, knots of musicians began to arrive and help themselves to food from the buffet table. Soon after seven o'clock, Ingrid and Jörg were among the first downstairs: they sat at a small table in the corner, Jörg methodically spooning fruit salad into his mouth while Ingrid spoke and indicated items on her list. He nodded and carried on chewing.

The orchestra's rehearsal for their evening's concert was at ten o'clock, and the plan was to spend three hours polishing their programme before having the afternoon free for any sightseeing they wanted to do. All Ingrid had to do was arrange for Jörg's truck (repacked with all the instruments) to arrive at the venue (a church in the centre of Amsterdam) in time for all the musicians (who would have arrived by coach, car or van) to unpack, sit in the right place, and play. Then make sure everyone returned on time to perform at seven o'clock that evening. On paper, it was a simple matter of logistics. In a city of delights, distractions and temptations like Amsterdam, Ingrid knew exactly how much could go awry. She let Jörg load up on breakfast. There was a lot of work ahead.

Erin was already sitting at a table when Ann arrived, who went over to join her.

'Morning,' said Erin, buttering toast. 'Sleep OK?'

'Yeah, fine,' said Ann. She sat opposite Erin and started on her large mug of coffee, looking around. 'Ingrid's already on the case, I see. Do you think Jörg likes his job?'

Erin smiled. 'He seems very good at it.'

'Except for the bit where stowaways sneak into his truck.'

'Yeah. Good point. Where did Tracie end up last night? Do you know?'

Ann arranged slices of ham and cheese on her rye bread, took a mouthful and talked round it. 'I gather Ingrid put her in a twin room with Kayla, since Kayla had practically offered to be her guardian in return for not clapping her in irons, or whatever Ingrid had threatened.'

'Carl won't have been happy about that.'

Ann grinned. 'Probably not. But he's youngish and inventive. We are on tour. Love will find a way.'

Erin giggled.

Eliot and Charlie came to sit with them, each balancing a buffet-tastic amount of food on their plates.

'Morning!' said Eliot. 'May we?'

'God, you sound chirpy,' said Ann, making room for them.

'He didn't stay for that last beer,' said Charlie. 'Something about having to be up in the morning for work?'

'Well, he does have to chivvy us along,' said Erin, 'so it's probably best that he's the chirpiest.'

'Thank you!' said Eliot, lifting a tall glass of juice. He put it down after a gulp, looking quizzical. 'What is that? Looks orange, but tastes a bit… rubbery.'

'Mine was alright,' said Ann.

'I had apple,' said Erin.

Eliot shrugged and got stuck into the pile of eggs and toast on his plate.

'So, what's the plan today?' said Charlie.

'Don't you ever read David's emails?' said Erin.

'Of course,' said Charlie. 'I mean, I know it's music-lunch-loll-music, but I wanted to, you know, drill down into the granularity of the lolling.'

'Christ,' said Ann from behind her rye bread. 'Keep your granular lolling to yourself.'

'I'll only let you out at lunchtime if we can play things well enough,' threatened Eliot. 'Speaking of which, has anyone seen Max? I hope he turned up last night. Would be a shame doing all this without timps.'

'Go and ask Ingrid,' said Erin, nodding to where Jörg was still patiently nodding at the latest instructions. 'There'll be a Max-shaped tick somewhere on her lists.'

'And what about Mr and Mrs Ford-Hughes?' asked Charlie. 'When are they supposed to join us?'

'Can't imagine this is their kind of place,' said Ann.

'What – you reckon they're in some swank joint and we're slobbing it here?' said Charlie.

'Well, they are paying for most of it.'

'Even so.' Charlie drank his tea bristling with a sense of socialist fair play.

Eliot had finished his juice and was sitting very still with an expression of perplexed alarm on his face.

'Eliot, are you OK?' said Erin.

He seemed to roll something around in his mouth before spitting it discreetly into his napkin and peering into it. 'Oh. Well, that was unexpected.'

He picked up something about two centimetres long between his finger and thumb, lifting it above the table so they could all see. He squeezed it flat, then released, and it sprung back to its original shape.

'Thought my juice tasted rubbery,' he said. 'Turns out I wasn't having a stroke after all.'

'Eliot, have you been eating the juice machine?' said Ann. 'That looks like the connecting hose from the dispenser thingummy.'

'Ah. Might be.' Eliot put it on the side of his plate, where it looked like an incongruous bit of calamari.

'This hotel is shite,' said Charlie. 'No wonder Mr and Mrs Ford-Hughes aren't here.'

* * *

Despite logistical challenges, Ingrid managed to coordinate three out of four vehicles to the rehearsal on time; most of the Wagner tuba players wouldn't be required until later. She stood at the entrance to the church like a calm radar beacon, guiding everyone inside to where David and a few helpers had already set up orchestral chairs in the space in front of the altar. Pearl had put music stands out, and was walking through the seats distributing parts from the huge pile in her arms. It was pleasantly cool inside the church: a welcome contrast to the street outside, which was already uncomfortably sticky, even before ten o'clock.

Jörg managed to park the instrument truck close by, leaving the players just a short walk over a canal bridge to get to the church. When Tracie arrived for her trombone, he glowered at her.

'Woss matter?' said Tracie, all glottal stops and teenage allergies to morning appointments. 'Look, I didn't dent anything. I even folded your blanket up, so gimme a break.'

Jörg's face, although not forgiving her entirely, seemed to soften. After all, they were not so different in age.

Carl was behind Tracie in the queue for instruments. He watched Jörg look at Tracie's back as she walked over the bridge, round-shouldered and awkward. 'She's OK,' he said. 'By the end of the week, she might even apologise to you for sneaking into your truck.'

Jörg gave a small tight-lipped smile. 'Perhaps.'

Carl and Kayla walked across the bridge together. 'And if *I* can be that nice about Tracie, Jörg certainly can,' he said. 'I thought we might have to put up with a twin room, but didn't factor in you might be sharing it with somebody else.'

'Hmm,' said Kayla. 'And I was so looking forward to a week of *not* being mum to a teenager.'

Carl put his arm round her shoulders. 'Shall we try to have fun anyway?'

Kayla laughed. 'Deal. You never know, I might not have to share a room with Tracie all week.'

In the church, Max had wheeled his four timpani in from his van and was tuning them, tapping each one softly with a stick while his head bent close to hear them above ambient chatter and squawks from the wind and brass players.

Eliot and David chatted to each other while Eliot sorted out the scores on his music stand and got his baton ready.

'Alexander will be here soon,' David was saying, 'so can we do the Mozart first, and then the Strauss? Then we've got the other three Wagner tuba players along later for the Bruckner. Our trombones, and Leroy on the tuba, will just have to sit the first two out.'

'Right-ho,' said Eliot. 'Hey – there are loads of posters for us up around the place, aren't there? Ingrid's lot did us proud.'

'Note Perfect Tours always does a good job. There will have been local press ads too, I should think. Depending on the budget Rafael managed to squeeze out of Mr and Mrs Ford-Hughes.'

'Speaking of whom,' said Eliot, looking round, 'where are they? No sign of them last night. I was half-expecting to be on call for pre-dinner cocktail entertainment and schmoozing.'

David actually smiled, which was progress from the previous evening. 'I think we'll see them tonight, and from then on, of course, they're travelling with us.'

Eliot raised his eyebrows. 'Blimey, yes, I'd forgotten. They're actually coming in the same coach, aren't they?'

'Yes. Though not, perhaps, in precisely the same hotels.'

'There are limits, I suppose, for even the most enthusiastic thrill-seeker.' Eliot nodded. 'That chemical toilet isn't for everyone.'

Charlie and Ann, on their way to their seats in the cello section, caught up with Eliot's last remark.

'That chemical toilet shouldn't be for *anyone*,' said Charlie. 'We all heard Keith.'

'I don't trust Pete to comply,' said Ann. 'If Pearl provides any fig rolls, don't let him have any.'

'Oh god,' said Eliot, faintly.

9

Soon after ten o'clock, everyone was more or less sitting down ready to play.

'Let's keep things simple,' said Eliot, 'and rehearse in the order we'll play them in tonight. So: Mozart, Strauss, then Bruckner. Technically we have three hours, but we'll see what we need.'

'We'll need a coffee halfway through,' called Gwynneth from the oboes. There were several murmurs of agreement. Not everyone had achieved the early night that perhaps they should have.

Pearl bobbed up from the back of the violas into her meerkat announcement position. 'I haven't travelled with the urn, unfortunately,' – disappointed groans all round – 'but there are quite a few coffee shops round here. If we spread out, I'm sure we could all get some in just a few minutes. If Eliot says that's OK, of course.' She sat down again and settled her duster over her left shoulder, ready to play.

'I wouldn't dream of getting in between this orchestra and their coffee,' said Eliot, smiling. 'Let's see how it goes, shall we? So: *Figaro* first.'

The orchestra had decided to start their concert with one of the most loved amuse-bouche of pieces: the overture to Mozart's *The Marriage of Figaro*. It lasts less than five minutes, previews tiny snatches of some of the great tunes of the opera, and is a concentrated capsule of good humour in musical form.

'Now, of course I'd prefer to do this fancy-pants period instrument style,' said Eliot, 'with the second violins and cellos swapping places so we can give the audience a true classical stereo experience, but frankly for five minutes it's not worth it.'

'Good,' called Kayla from the double basses. 'Because we'd have to go too and, well, just no.'

'And she's contractually obliged to sit next to me anyway,' said Carl. 'If I have to read a book through Mozart and Strauss, at least give me my woman to look at.'

Eliot laughed. 'And I wouldn't want to upset Carl. Right.' He lifted his arms and checked the strings and bassoons were ready to go. Pete, sitting next to Pearl on the back desk of the violas, blinked a few times and shifted forward on his chair. He was never going to make it through all his bars of quavers, but Eliot mentally applauded his optimism.

Eliot gave an energetic upbeat and realised, as all the strings and both bassoons came in enthusiastically, that they had interpreted his energy as volume not speed. It was supposed to be *pianissimo*. He brought them to a halt straight away.

'OK, good. Shall we try that again, only *pianissimo* this time?'

There were some half-embarrassed smiles from people who should be able to play quavers quickly *and* quietly at the same time, and they set off again. This time, Eliot gave just as energetic an upbeat, but from a crouching position behind his stand. No orchestra can resist the Literal Dynamic Scale: the smaller the conductor can make themselves, the quieter the orchestra must play. It's the law. If the baton itself is too near the floor to be seen by anyone, that's when the players have to listen to each other to find out if they're in the right place, and therefore they must shut up enough to hear. Bingo.

Seven bars later, Eliot allowed himself to peek over his stand to bring in the oboes and horns, then the flutes and clarinets, and then four bars after that he was completely upright inviting everyone to let rip in the *forte* together, including Max banging out the beats on the timpani. Mozart only allowed them their fun for six bars before it was quiet again.

Eliot was enjoying himself tremendously. There was a thrumming energy in the bass line from the cellos and double basses that fed up through the orchestra which, to give it credit, was attacking the *presto* tempo with verve and enthusiasm. Mozart can sound boring if played sloppily, with his four-square harmonies and sometimes predictable developments. If the ensemble and dynamics can be both crisp and responsive, that's when it comes alive.

By the time they got to the *forte-pianos*, Eliot was employing the full reach of his body language: practically doing a star jump to get them to land on their chord with a loud thump, only to fall off the note almost immediately as if someone had put their hand over their mouths while they were shouting. Eliot tucked his hands into his chest and conducted the rest of the bar with the tiniest beats imaginable, before leaping up again. Three of those and Eliot's pecs had received their full workout for the day.

When they reached the section where the cellos and basses had a brief but sweeping tune as a soli with the violas, Eliot walked round in front of his stand and lunged in between the two sections, encouraging Charlie and Erin to lean towards the viola front desk as their phrase curled over the bar lines. Pete and Pearl, at the back, were trying their best to join in with the dynamic bulges, which since it meant playing relatively slow notes all on one bow, they could actually do. From behind the cellos, Kayla played the phrase on her bass with great musicality, and even Carl noticed and turned round from his book, nodding appreciation.

The phrase passed to the violins, and out of this suddenly intimate, string quartet-like texture, the first bassoon rose to prominence on *staccato* accidentals like a water bird running over uneven ground towards a lake on ungainly legs, only to glide off a moment later with the *legato* tune all to itself. Rafael, playing second bassoon, was as usual very happy to slot back into the *tutti* passage after his colleague had done all the nerve-racking solo work. In Rafael, the nature of a second bassoon and accountancy dovetailed nicely.

Strictly speaking, Eliot didn't have to play the whole thing, but he reckoned since it was probably too late to do any meaningful work on awkward corners and it only took five minutes, he might as well let it run. The second time the violas, cellos and basses had their swoopy tune, they entered into the spirit of it so much Eliot had to dial it back down a bit, laughing. By the time Max joined in again it was the home straight, and the whole thing barrelled towards the finish line with Eliot treading a dangerous path between encouraging the orchestra's enthusiasms and reining in any excess sprints for the tape. The final chords were accidentally augmented by a viola splat as the music halved its speed three bars before the end and Pete, head down and blinking fast, fell into the minim rest with the confidence of Wile E

Coyote's anvil splashing into a silent pond. Naturally Pete spent the final two bars too terrified to play anything.

Eliot beamed at them. 'Cracking. Well done. And if Pete does that tonight, the drinks are on him.'

The orchestra erupted into cheers. They knew a good bet when they heard one.

Eliot looked round to see if Alexander had arrived and saw him walking over, cradling his horn under one arm.

'Sounding great!' he said. 'I thought I'd come along from the start to see what was what.'

'Thanks,' said Eliot. 'Apart from Pete. But now he'll be too scared to play at all in the last bit, so I think I've knocked that one on the head.'

Alexander laughed. 'Sometimes I think most of the work of a conductor is managing the back desks of the strings.'

'Oi!' called Ann from the back of the cellos. 'I'm old but I'm not deaf.'

'And we all know she should be leading the section, but she won't,' added Erin.

'You've met our cello section, haven't you?' said Eliot conversationally. 'They're all nutters.'

'I like nutters,' said Alexander, twinkling at the cellos in general and perhaps Erin in particular.

'God, you'll fit right in,' said Eliot, turning back to the orchestra. 'Right. Let's top and tail the Strauss.'

Players leaned forward to sort music on their stands.

'Do you want me to stand facing out to where the audience will be?' said Alexander.

'Yeah, probably, thanks,' said Eliot. 'David can wander down to the back to check the acoustic. You're doing it from memory, aren't you?'

'Yep.'

'David?' called Eliot. David hurried over from where he had been sitting with the horns. The Strauss, like the Mozart before it, was scored for only two horns, so David as fourth horn was not needed until the Bruckner. 'When we get going, could you check the sound down at the far end?'

David nodded. 'Will do.'

'Great.'

Eliot gathered up the orchestra and let Alexander fill the church with his first exuberant horn call. It ricocheted off the stone walls and high ceiling, producing a far fuller sound than the Sunbridge Academy hall could ever achieve. David, who was by this time standing at the far end by the main door, knew that when the space was filled with an audience it would dampen the reverberations, but even so, playing in a hundred-year-old church was always going to be more satisfying than a patched-up school from the 1980s.

Eliot let the orchestra play into the horn's first solo melody, then stopped: no point tiring Alexander's lip unnecessarily before that evening. He turned to David, who gave a thumbs-up.

'Sounds great from here!'

They spent a while playing round some awkward corners, dovetailing when Alexander and Eliot wanted to move the tempo on or slow it down, until they were both happy.

'OK, that'll be great tonight, thanks,' said Eliot. 'Thank you, Alexander!'

The whole orchestra shuffled and kicked their feet on the floor in a hands-free musician's version of applause for their soloist.

Maureen, a dour woman who sat on the outside of the first violin second desk, removed her earplugs.

'Everyone's a critic,' said Alexander, smiling.

Marco, who sat next to Maureen, made a face at Alexander, but it was too late. Maureen was infamous for lacking any semblance of humour, and had frequently reduced people to desperate measures if they had been unlucky enough to be trapped next to her in a pub.

'I am perfectly within my rights to protect my hearing, given your bell points directly at my right ear in your current position,' she said, clipping shut the small plastic container holding her earplugs.

Alexander looked horrified. 'Ah. Yes. Of course you are. My apologies.' He looked over to Eliot for guidance of how to proceed.

Eliot winked at him quickly while Maureen's attention was still on her earplug box, and said smoothly, 'Of course you are, Maureen. Quite right too.'

Maureen was not to be deterred. 'The Musicians' Union states that a symphony orchestra can be anything up to 94 decibels, and as such—'

'Perhaps this evening Alexander might take a step or two towards the audience?' said Eliot mildly. 'I'm sure I can crane my neck around a bit more?' He raised his eyebrows at Alexander to gauge whether this might be possible.

Alexander nodded. 'Sure.'

'Well, then. Good,' said Eliot. 'Now, coffee? Shall we all race to the coffee shops and see if we can be back for some Bruckner in twenty minutes?'

'What about the instruments?' called Max. 'We can't all go.'

A voice called from the other end of the church. 'I shall remain. I can also direct you to the nearest suitable places for your coffee.' Ingrid rose from where she had been sitting near the door.

'Oh, hello, Ingrid,' said Eliot. 'I didn't know you were there. How kind.'

Ingrid smiled and inclined her head slightly in Eliot's direction. 'It is a pleasure.'

'Right then,' said Eliot. 'Back here in time to play by half past? Go!'

The players filed out into the heat, which was easily ten degrees warmer than inside the church. Ingrid stood on the porch step, pointing out the three or four cafés in turn, like a member of aircraft cabin crew indicating exits. Players streamed away from her with the urgency of caffeine-seeking missiles on a deadline.

10

Tracie walked over the canal bridge with Carl and Kayla. 'Buy you a coffee, Miss?' she said, grinning, her steps light. 'To say thanks for dinner last night. And, y'know… ev'rythin'.' She sniffed and glanced down at the canal. 'Not sending me back.'

'I wasn't going to send you back to an empty flat with no food,' said Kayla. 'And I know you don't have any money – don't worry. This week is on me. We can sort things later, if they need sorting.'

'I can get money,' said Tracie.

'Do *not* steal anything,' said Carl. 'That really would fuck things up.' He looked defiant as Kayla widened her eyes at him. 'What? She swears more than I do!'

Tracie laughed. 'Fuckin' right.'

'Stop it, both of you,' said Kayla. 'God, it's like having *two* kids. And I'm supposed to be on holiday.'

They bought takeaway drinks and loitered on the way back in the shade of a canal-side tree. The glistening water certainly cooled the street, but also added its distinctive smell of wet, slightly algaed stonework tinged with a whiff of sewage.

'Wouldn't want to swim in that,' said Carl, nodding at the dark water.

'I wonder how many shopping trolleys are down there,' said Kayla.

'Bikes, probably, here. More bikes than people.'

Their attention was diverted from the water by a shout of 'Hi guys!' from the bridge.

Erin, Charlie and Ann came to join them under the tree.

'It's too darn hot,' said Charlie, then started clicking his fingers rhythmically.

'You what?' said Tracie.

'Oh child,' said Ann, not unkindly. 'You have so much to learn.'

'*Kiss Me Kate*,' said Carl. Tracie looked unenlightened. 'The musical? Cole Porter?'

Tracie shrugged.

Charlie leaned in on one side of Tracie and sang a line, clicking his fingers. Erin joined in with the second line on her other side.

'Oh god,' said Carl, but Charlie and Erin were on a roll and could not be stopped.

They sang the rest of the verse and chorus together, both clicking fingers with their free hand and stepping in time in an impromptu almost-dance routine that didn't upset any coffee.

'I'd applaud but I'd have to put my cup down,' said Ann. 'Lovely. Now shut up.'

Tracie was looking at them all with incomprehension.

'Basic musical theatre band knowledge, mate,' said Carl. 'You gotta know this stuff. You'll be playing it soon enough.'

'At Sunbridge, you reckon?' said Kayla. 'Not very likely.'

'Aye, aye,' said Charlie quietly, nodding to the church door on the other side of the canal, where Julian, Tom and Lamar were approaching, carrying their Wagner tuba cases. Julian carried a second case for Alexander in a proprietorial manner.

Ann drank some more coffee as she watched them go in. 'That Julian. I didn't… didn't take to him.'

'Don't think Tom or Lamar took to him either,' said Erin.

'Can't see his car anywhere close,' said Charlie. 'Thank god.'

'It's not exactly subtle,' agreed Kayla.

'Imagine driving across Europe, as a guest, looking like that much of a plonker,' said Charlie. 'I mean, I know we're officially about to leave and all that, but he's just taking the piss.'

'If he gets through the whole week without his car being keyed, I'll be amazed,' said Ann. 'And that's without him even opening his mouth.'

They wandered back towards the church. Julian was discussing with Eliot where the Wagner tubas should sit.

'We've put your chairs in a block there, behind the horns,' said Eliot. 'Alexander's already around, somewhere. He was here earlier for the Strauss.'

'I'll find him,' said Julian, looking around. 'He's on fourth tuba of course. To save his lip, apparently.' He smirked, and jerked his head for Lamar and Tom to follow him over and sit down. They trailed along as the short-sleeved rugby shirt strutted to the back of the orchestra. It was a different colour from but identical in style to the one Julian had worn the day before: collar still up at the back. Neema and Ryan, the first and second horns, looked at each other with apprehension. They would be sitting directly in front of Julian, bearing the brunt of his opinions.

Eliot asked Gwynneth for an A, and the orchestra tuned as the stragglers sat down. Alexander slid into his seat on the end of the Wagner tuba line, nodding to his section with a smile. Julian did not return it. Alexander shrugged and tuned anyway, getting used to the different feel of the instrument after playing his horn earlier. They all used their regular horn mouthpieces anyway, so note production was essentially the same. Playing the fourth part, Alexander was indeed likely to save his lip as much as possible for the Strauss solo part, since the fourth part was at the lowest pitch.

'I don't intend to crash through the whole symphony or we'd all be dead before this evening,' said Eliot, to approving cheers. 'Let's take a few of the corners, and a lot of the stuff with the Wagner tubas, to let them get their bearings, as it were. Why don't we start with the second movement? Trombones, you're up. Leroy, ready? Thanks for waiting, guys.'

Leroy nodded and balanced his tuba on his lap, ready to play. Carl, sharing his part with Tracie, made sure she knew where she was starting: the trombones were to come in after the first phrase on the Wagner tubas.

Eliot gave a couple of slow beats into the *Adagio*, which is marked *Sehr feierlich und sehr langsam* (very solemn and very slow). At the Leipzig premiere at the very end of 1884, it was the first time anyone had heard Wagner tubas used in a symphony, with their mournful sound. They start the slow movement, together with a tuba and the lower strings, with the top Wagner tuba line sharing the tune with the violas. Eliot gave a quick smile of encouragement to Pearl and Pete at the back of the violas before they set off. There is nothing so nervous as a viola back desk just before a section solo.

Quiet chords swelled from the orchestra and filled the church. They were chords that play over a final panoramic scene of a devastating film, where the shot will track over fallen dead and invite us to reflect on the utter waste of life and uselessness of death. These are the chords any film composer will seek to emulate. Bruckner got there first. It is said he wrote this movement in anticipation of Wagner's death, who was in poor health at the time, which seems to be an unbelievably crass move although, if you want to impress your idol with how sad you're going to feel when he croaks, you have to get cracking while he's still alive or you won't have time to make it good enough.

Four bars into this existential heft, the violins joined in. The firsts were instructed to play their phrase entirely on their lowest string, the G string, even when it went up in a register they would normally switch up to a higher string. Playing it on the low string but having to move their left hand far up the fingerboard gave the melody an intensity unachievable on the upper strings: the timbre was dark, moody and electric. This was enhanced by some players teetering on the edge of their skill, wondering if they had the strength in their fingers to reach up the fingerboard and still play in tune. Only the sixth bar into the movement, and already Bruckner had dialled the pathos up to eleven simply by telling them to play it on the G string. The first violins had most of that bar entirely to themselves. It was an extraordinary sound.

Of course, even a sad Bruckner couldn't maintain that level of angst, and the movement does lighten up further in, with a section sounding as if it were at a carefree waltz, but soon enough the Wagner tubas nose back in with the same mournful chords they had at the start, and the melancholy starts all over again.

That one slow movement alone lasts more than twenty minutes, so Eliot didn't slog the orchestra through the whole thing, bringing them to a halt once everyone had got their ear in and knew what to expect with the new acoustic.

'That's going to be great,' he said. 'How are our Wagner tubas?'

'I just wish we didn't have all these perky tunes,' called Alexander, to laughter.

'I know!' said Eliot. 'Bruckner skipping through the daisies, Bruckner turning carefree backflips… crazy stuff, man.'

'We'll try to dial it down,' said Alexander, smiling.

Julian frowned down the line of his section. 'We're a bit bottom-heavy, but the ensemble's not bad, considering,' he said to Eliot. 'Balance OK for you?'

Alexander looked contrite and mimed zipping his mouth, causing Eliot to fight to keep a straight face. 'Um, yes, thanks, Julian. You are all sounding very splendid. In fact, the whole brass ensemble is excellent.' There were foot-shuffles throughout the orchestra and murmurs of agreement. Julian was placated. Neema, directly in front of him, rolled her eyes at Eliot.

Eliot cleared his throat and spent the next hour dipping into the other movements, making sure nobody was going to come across a hidden corner they weren't expecting that evening.

As the final chords of the rehearsal died away and Eliot was thanking the orchestra for their attention, a small outbreak of applause made its way towards them from the main door of the church. Mr and Mrs Ford-Hughes approached: she smiling broadly and clapping with great energy, he a couple of steps behind but still looking extremely genial. Mrs Ford-Hughes wore cream linen trousers with a billowing silk top that looked as if it was competing to see how many species of vibrant flower could fit on one garment. Her wrists and neck were festooned with clinking bangles and gold chains, which were ideal for applauding purposes. Whether they would also be ideal for sitting-quietly-listening-to-a-concert purposes remained to be heard. She had finished the whole ensemble with an enormous brimmed straw hat the size of a giant lily pad.

'Marvellous! Just marvellous!' she cried in her fruity Arkansas twang, approaching Eliot for a kiss. He had to stoop under the brim of her hat, but with some good-natured bending and plane-alignment on her part, the manoeuvre was achieved. He reappeared, coughing only slightly at the perfume density.

'Lovely to see you both,' he said and, turning to the orchestra, gestured to them both. 'A round of applause for our most stalwart supporters and, crucially this week, sponsors!'

Mrs Ford-Hughes accepted the warm thanks with a beaming smile. 'It's just peachy to see y'all here. Gonna be a great week. We'll see you at tonight's concert!'

As the orchestra rose to put their instruments away, David and Ingrid both approached Eliot from opposite ends of the church. Mrs Ford-Hughes looked delighted to see David, and he submitted to her proffered cheek with gallantry. Mr Ford-Hughes stood a little back, wisely leaving his wife to deal with performative social duties for them both.

Trying to stop the catch in his throat, David croaked at Eliot, 'I think we're OK to leave instruments here – is that right, Ingrid?'

Ingrid nodded. 'Yes indeed. I was about to suggest I make a small announcement to the players?'

'By all means,' said David, and turned to quieten the chatting players who were milling about behind him.

As Ingrid outlined plans for the afternoon, involving Jörg being stationed in the church until they returned for that evening's concert and therefore guarding their instruments if left where they were, Mrs Ford-Hughes leaned in towards Eliot to whisper.

'Such an efficient woman, Ingrid. She really is excellent. A credit to the company. As you know, we just flew in this morning and she has arranged everything without a hitch:

transfers, hotel, hospitality... which reminds me, Eliot darling, my husband and I are having a small soirée before the concert this evening at our hotel—' (she mentioned the name of a significantly more plush hotel than the one currently housing the orchestra, just a short walk away from the church venue) '—and we would be delighted if you could come? And David and Rafael, of course, as representatives of the orchestra committee.'

Eliot nodded and thanked her: he had been expecting this. Ingrid was explaining that those people who wanted a lift back to the hotel with Keith in the coach should meet directly outside.

Mrs Ford-Hughes continued, 'Do you think Pearl would want to... I mean, I know she's technically part of the committee, but...' She trailed off, not quite knowing how to phrase her judgement that someone who did the teas and coffees from an urn might perhaps not be the kind of person who enjoyed a pre-concert soirée.

Eliot, knowing full well that Pearl much preferred social gatherings if she was the one providing hospitality, preferably with a trestle table between her and any conversation, said he was sure Pearl wouldn't want to go but perhaps he could ask her anyway on Mrs Ford-Hughes's behalf? Mrs Ford-Hughes dipped her hat brim gratefully.

Ingrid was concluding her team talk to the orchestra. 'So, you will depart from the hotel by coach at six-thirty this evening, in concert dress. Keith will drive you here. I shall represent Note Perfect Tours at the soirée with Mr and Mrs Ford-Hughes, and accompany them and their guests here myself. The concert will start at seven-thirty. So: until six-thirty, you have a free afternoon. Please enjoy Amsterdam.'

11

The orchestra scattered itself over a heat-haze shimmering Amsterdam, breaking apart for the afternoon into its constituent elements. Ingrid had to trust they would reassemble that evening in the correct order, as if summoned by Eliot's baton. She left Jörg at his post in the church and stood with Keith by the coach door, marking off who boarded on her clipboard.

'What shall we do, then?' said Erin, as she walked over the bridge with Ann and Charlie.

'Food first,' said Charlie. 'I'm starving.'

'How can you be hungry in this heat?' said Ann.

'My rapacious appetite for life?'

'Maybe it's worms,' said Erin.

'If we have to eat together,' said Ann, 'can we at least not talk about worms?'

'OK – look, let's grab something at that café,' said Charlie, 'and we can plan. I definitely want to buy some clogs. Preferably with tulips painted on them. If we insist on arriving at the wrong time of year for real tulips, I can at least combine them with tourist tat and feel as if I've made the most of my trip.'

'You're a cultural colossus,' said Ann.

'He's got a city guide, look,' said Erin. 'With a checklist. I think we're going to be bustled around tourist attractions if we're not careful.'

'My afternoon was going to feature sipping a cold beer in the shade by a pleasant canal,' said Ann. 'You two young things can bustle all you like.'

They found an empty street table at the café and ordered cheese *tostis* and, in Charlie's case, *bitterballen*, together with three Aperol spritzes and enough water to rehydrate after their rehearsal. Charlie carried on reading his city guide, enthusing about things he wanted to do.

'We need to go to Jordaan!' he said. 'Looks like we're just on the edge of that here. I bet I could find some clogs there. Then there's a Cacaomuseum, for all your chocolate needs. Of course. Wait! Oh my *god*! There's a *cheese museum*! Can we? Please? Can we?'

Erin and Ann looked at each other.

'Did you spike his Aperol spritz?' asked Ann mildly.

'Heatstroke, maybe?' said Erin. 'Charlie, calm down. We'll find you some clogs, and you can fill them with cheese. OK?'

'There's always art,' said Ann. 'The Rijksmuseum is amazing. And probably air-conditioned.'

They ate, bickering good-naturedly about the ideal temperature to enjoy high art and how much cheese you could fit in a clog.

* * *

A couple of blocks further down the same canal, Julian was leading several brass players into a bar. His fellow Wagner tuba players, Tom and Lamar, had decided they could bear Julian's company when diluted by Leroy (tuba), Ryan and Neema (horns) and a few other trumpet and trombone players.

'Pint of your finest,' barked Julian at the bar tender, before turning round to smirk at his colleagues. 'They won't have pints, of course. Bloody litres or some such.'

Indeed, the woman behind the bar was trying to clarify, in perfect English, exactly what size beer Julian required.

'Oh, just... yea big,' Julian said, holding out his hands to show roughly the size of a pint glass. 'You got Amstel?'

'Of course,' said the bar tender, pouring a half-litre glass and putting it on the bar in front of Julian. '€4.50, please.'

'Christ,' he said. 'That's just taking the piss.' As Julian sorted unfamiliar Euro notes out of his wallet, the others exchanged looks behind his head. Their afternoon plans might have to be changed.

* * *

Pearl was boarding a Metro, holding a guide to the Anne Frank House in one hand and a portable electric fan in the other. She moved the fan constantly over different parts of her face and neck like a man shaving at a distance of six inches from his skin. What she didn't know was that her serious cultural itinerary could well intersect with Charlie, geographically if not philosophically, as his cheese museum was just over the Prinsengracht from the Anne Frank House: close enough to lob a Gouda or two.

* * *

Carl was trying to persuade Kayla to return to the hotel with him on the coach.

'We can't,' protested Kayla, knowing exactly what Carl had in mind. 'What about Tracie?'

Tracie was on Carl's side. 'I don't need babysitting. You gave me a map – our hotel's not that far.'

'I'm not letting you wander round a strange city on your own,' said Kayla.

'I live in Stockwell,' Tracie pointed out. 'I'll be fine.'

'And we know she can look after herself,' said Carl.

'That would be all we need – she gets herself into a fight and arrested,' said Kayla, then sighed. 'OK, look. Take this money and get yourself some lunch before you go wandering. And remember to drink water – this weather is crazy. Got your phone?' Tracie nodded. Kayla sent a text to lodge her number in Tracie's phone. 'Right. Be back at the hotel by half five, in time to get ready. Call me if you need to.'

'Sure,' said Tracie. 'Thanks.' She sketched a wave and walked over the bridge.

Carl put his arm round Kayla. 'They grow up so fast.'

'Hope I'm not going to regret this,' said Kayla, and they went to board the coach.

* * *

Eliot also decided to return to the hotel on the coach for a few hours' rest and a quiet look through the scores. On the way, he asked Ingrid about the party later with Mr and Mrs Ford-Hughes.

'So – who's going to be there? I guess Note Perfect Tours has arranged some top guests?'

Ingrid allowed herself a small smile. 'Yes of course. Naturally we wish the tour to be attended by some of the most well-connected music-lovers in each city we visit. We have already a good reputation in this.'

Eliot nodded, acknowledging Ingrid's professionalism and trying to damp down his natural mirth about the whole arrangement. 'Of course. Your name – your company name, I mean – is famous in Britain for organising great tours.'

Ingrid almost fluttered her lashes. 'That is gratifying to hear. Tonight we have—' she consulted another list underneath several sheets of paper on her clipboard, '—several players in the Concertgebouworkest, one of whom is married to a local politician. I believe a small group of conducting students from the Conservatorium van Amsterdam is also coming with one of their tutors. There will in addition be a number of people who regularly donate to the arts, in much the same way as I believe Mr and Mrs Ford-Hughes do in London.'

'Crikey,' said Eliot, under his breath.

'I beg your pardon?' said Ingrid.

'You have assembled quite the party!' Eliot could only imagine how dowdy his concert gear might look next to a roomful of conspicuous jewellery. He was glad Charlie didn't have to go as well: the wealth dissonance might have broken him.

'It is merely the first of three social events during this week,' Ingrid continued. 'The focus, of course, will be tomorrow night in Köln as part of the Bruckner Festival there.'

'Of course.' He stared absentmindedly towards Ingrid across the aisle, at the clipboard on the table in front of her. 'Do you ever use an iPad or tablet or anything, these days? I mean, I hate conducting from them so I understand if paper is your thing…?'

'These printouts are merely duplicates of my computer system,' Ingrid said, as if teaching the basics of tour planning to a small child. 'Every morning I print what I need. I have found in the past it is safer not to rely on electronic devices for everything when one is on the move.'

'Ah. Yes. At least you can mop spilled coffee off a paper list and no harm done.'

Ingrid's expression hinted that she had dealt with far more cataclysmic problems than spilled coffee in her career, but she returned to the current timetable. 'Tonight is a pre-concert soirée. Tomorrow, Mr and Mrs Ford-Hughes join many others at a gala evening, which will be a much bigger event. Then the following evening, on Thursday, you play your own concert as part of the festival.'

She sat with a naturally upright posture, her hair as neat as ever in the French pleat. Eliot found himself intrigued. 'Do you play any instrument yourself, Ingrid?'

She looked at him and smiled. 'My father taught me the accordion when I was a child. I don't get much time to play these days, but I do enjoy it when I can.'

'Underrated instrument, the accordion. You were never tempted by an orchestra?'

'You can't get an orchestra into a bar.'

Eliot thought about the pub after rehearsals. 'Oh, I don't know.'

'I mean, to play.'

'Well, no. Is that where your accordioning takes place then?'

'I grew up in a small town in Germany,' said Ingrid. 'We, as you say, made our own entertainment.'

Eliot laughed and nodded, trying to reassess the new image of a slightly drunk young Ingrid playing rowdy folk songs while tankards of beer sloshed all around her.

12

Ingrid kindly arranged a taxi for Eliot, David and Rafael that evening, since they had to be at Mr and Mrs Ford-Hughes's soirée earlier than the coach was going to leave. She told them she would see them later at the party once she had ferried all the musicians to the church. It would then be a short walk from Mr and Mrs Ford-Hughes's hotel to the concert, and they and all the guests could go together.

As the taxi drew up at the Waldorf Astoria on Herengracht, the men looked at one another.

'I vote we don't tell the orchestra where the Ford-Hugheses are staying,' murmured David, getting out of the taxi. 'We might have a riot on our hands.'

Rafael eyed the opulent frontage of the hotel that stretched across half a dozen seventeenth-century canal mansions. 'We can't really complain. It's their money. I'm just glad they want to spend some of it on us.'

'Spoken as a true financial director,' said Eliot, clapping him on the shoulder. 'I, on the other hand, wouldn't say no to a wallow in one of the roll-top baths I bet they've got in there. It looks a roll-top bath kind of place. Which door do we go in, do you think?'

There were several double staircases up to front doors along the row, rising above the semi-basement storey half under the street. Eliot tipped his head back to take in the two further floors above the front door. Over all of them, several winch and pulley systems common in Dutch houses cantilevered out over the pavement, to move furniture in and out of the tall narrow buildings. He whistled quietly. Amsterdam was thin but very tall, like an etiolated city built out of Stephen Merchants.

'There,' said David, pointing to one particularly imposing door. 'This looks like the right one.'

'Ah yes,' said Eliot. 'The one with the flag over it and the little plaque. Silly me.'

'Shh,' whispered Rafael.

'Sorry.'

They climbed the steps and were ushered in by a uniformed doorman wearing a splendid hat. Inside, even the air smelled rich: a combination of fine Paris scents wafting from ambulatory guests, fresh flowers, and a blend of floor wax and an ozoney sea-salt spritz particular to a certain class of hotel.

Eliot checked his jacket was done up and squared his shoulders. Undaunted, David led the way and asked an enquiring concierge where they might find the Ford-Hugheses' soirée. They were shown to a group of people on the terrace, which was lit by candles even though the evening light had barely dipped. A waiter offered them glasses of champagne from a polished tray and, since there seemed not to be any soft drinks available, Eliot shrugged and took one. He didn't have to drink it all. As he took the first sip, he nearly dropped the whole thing at a sudden cry from the other side of the terrace.

'Eliot, darling!'

He put his hand to his lips to catch any stray champagne that had been as startled as he was, and turned to see Mrs Ford-Hughes bearing down on him with the relentlessness of a steamer at full throttle, arms outstretched and a wide smile on her face as if she were being reunited with a long-lost close relative instead of a professional conductor she had seen barely five hours earlier. He braced himself for impact, both physical and perfumed.

She enveloped him in a tangled hug that involved a lot of jewellery and bits of her floaty dress sleeves. Happily, she had swapped her brimmed straw hat for a fascinator, but Eliot still had to dodge its manic bead-bobbing if he were not to lose an eye. He caught the scent of quite a few glasses of champagne on her breath.

'Maryanne, how delightful,' he said to the air somewhere above her ear, and helped her regain the vertical. 'Thank you for inviting us to your party.'

'Soirée, darling, soirée. We're on the continent now.'

Eliot glanced at David and Rafael, who were almost giggling and frankly being no help at all.

'Indeed, yes. Soirée. And a fine one it is.'

'You must come and meet our guests,' she said, tucking Eliot's arm into hers and pulling him towards a group of smiling people. 'Everyone! This is Eliot Yarrow, conductor of Stockwell Park Orchestra! I'm sure he's got a peach of a concert lined up for us tonight!'

Eliot prepared to make small talk with some of the most experienced musicians in Amsterdam while dodging Mrs Ford-Hughes's fascinator which kept pinging round his head like a terrifically hungry mosquito.

* * *

At six o'clock Ingrid stood in the lobby of the orchestra's rather less luxurious hotel with a fresh printout of her list of musicians to convey to the concert. Keith had brought the coach round to the door and was waiting there, engine switched off and door open, for the orchestra to embark.

In ones and twos, players arrived from their rooms upstairs, dressed in concert black. Kayla and Tracie came out of the lift together, Kayla clearly trying to reassure her about something.

'It looks fine. Stop fidgeting.'

Tracie lifted the back of her collar and tried to settle it more comfortably on her neck. 'It's itchy. Is there a label there or something?'

'No. Look, you'll just have to put up with it. I didn't have a huge selection of black tops.'

'How was I to know you wear all black, not white shirts like what we did last term?'

'That was a special concert, to fit in with your school uniform – you know that,' said Kayla. 'And, you know, if you'd actually *asked* anyone about this trip, we'd have told you.'

'You'da told me to stay at 'ome,' said Tracie sullenly.

'Well, perhaps.' Kayla smiled. 'Still, you're here now. And have a black top. I can wash them both through later and we'll get through the week. It looks great on you!'

Tracie was still trying to wriggle her way into a more comfortable position as they approached Ingrid.

'Good evening,' she said, ticking their names off.

'Alright, Ingrid,' said Tracie, regaining some of her chirpiness.

Ingrid pursed her lips and let them pass, acknowledging Kayla's apologetic expression. 'On the coach, please. We shall depart shortly.'

Max, the timpanist, walked through the lobby and was also ticked. His name was colour-coded on Ingrid's list, indicating that he was joining the coach for tonight but had his own transport between city stops. Ingrid's spreadsheets were nested things of beauty. She and Rafael, had they but known it, enjoyed similar passions.

Julian, Tom and Lamar cut it fine for the coach departure time, complaining they were going to have to wait around for ages at the other end since they were only in the second half of the concert. Ingrid bathed them all in the light of her benevolent administrative smile. 'I would prefer to convey the entire orchestra to the concert venue in good time,' she said. 'I am sure you will understand the logic of such a move.'

They did, though not without some resentment.

Shortly after six-thirty, after Ingrid had made two calls from reception to latecomers' rooms to chivvy them down, Keith closed the coach door and set off for the short trip into the centre of the city. Jörg's vigil was nearly at an end, and Ingrid carried the small holdall containing his change of clothes to transform him from casual tattooed roadie into her front-of-house assistant and Note Perfect Tours representative.

By the time Ingrid joined the Ford-Hugheses' soirée, the guests were merry and the conversations loud. Eliot saw her walk out onto the terrace and waved her over.

'Hi! Is my orchestra safely delivered?'

Ingrid sipped the glass of champagne a waiter had offered to her as soon as she had set foot on the terrace. 'Yes. I am glad you and the orchestra committee arrived here without mishap.' She looked round for David and Rafael, who were at that point enjoying an anecdote from a professor at the Conservatorium that involved him turning round and demonstrating conducting the start of Beethoven's Fifth Symphony upside down through his legs. 'Ah. I see.'

Eliot followed her gaze. 'Yeah. That's the fourth time he's told that story. I heard it first time round. He's got... um... much further into character since then.'

The professor staggered and almost fell into some of his students who were flanking him, but straightened up with a roar of triumph and delivered the punchline, to laughter and a ripple of applause from his small audience.

'Fascinating,' said Ingrid, and took another sip. She looked at her watch. 'We have forty-five minutes before the concert is due to start. I assume you, David and Rafael, would wish to go earlier than Mr and Mrs Ford-Hughes and their guests?'

'Yes, I should think so. We'll leave in about ten.'

'Understood. I shall ensure the rest of the party reaches the venue at the correct time.' She nodded and walked over to Mrs Ford-Hughes, who was giving an impromptu excerpt from Strauss's *Four Last Songs*. Eliot shuddered with what he suspected might be PTSD, and rationalised that he could leave as early as he liked. He was the conductor, after all. He lifted his glass to take one last sip, only to discover he had already drained it.

13

They arrived at the church before seven o'clock. Eliot almost
didn't recognise Jörg as he passed him just inside the main
door, taking ticket money and distributing programmes. He
wore a crisply tailored lightweight suit and had removed at
least half of his piercings; his one allowance for the stifling
temperature was no tie. Eliot wondered if he could suggest
to the men of the orchestra that they discard their jackets
altogether. It never seemed fair that the women players were
allowed any style of dress so long as it was black: they were
never burdened with jackets over shirts and ties. Somehow
orchestral tradition managed to be at once severely patriarchal
yet also less strict for women. He acknowledged that it was
just in this one narrowly defined area. All these thoughts
had fallen through Eliot's head like dominoes before he had
taken a dozen steps past Jörg. He decided to try to fix what
was in his control and let go, in a Zen-like waft, of the rest.

'Do you think it's too hot for jackets?' he asked David
and Rafael. 'I mean, this concert's just ours, isn't it? Not part
of the Bruckner Festival, which might have its own strictly
German rules about what to wear, I guess. But tonight?
Shirts?'

'It is very warm,' said David. 'We've done it before. What do you think?' He turned to Rafael, walking next to him.

'I can't see any reason why not,' Rafael said, after a moment's thought. He ran a finger round the front of his collar. 'Ties too?'

David smiled. This was a holiday-mood spontaneous Rafael he wasn't used to. But he liked it. 'Definitely.'

'Excellent,' said Eliot, as they reached the side room where the rest of the orchestra were getting ready with their instruments. 'I'll let them know.'

He opened the door onto a familiar pre-concert scene: around sixty people crammed into a room that was slightly too small, each getting their instrument out of its case and fiddling with what needed fiddling with: tightening bows and rosining them for the string players, playing a few duck quacks in the case of oboes and bassoons, and any number of warm up arpeggios and valve clearing from the brass. The heat was even more oppressive in that enclosed space.

'Hello everyone,' Eliot called. The noise quietened. 'Hi. Thanks. Last-minute change that might be quite welcome: no jackets and ties tonight. Not in this heat.'

There was an appreciative cheer from those currently wearing jackets, who then proceeded to remove them. Eliot, David and Rafael did the same.

Alexander Leakey approached Eliot, looking if anything more Thor-like in just his shirt. 'I guess we can let the other Wagner tuba boys know about jackets at the interval. If we're having one?'

'Um, yes, a short one,' said Eliot. 'Where are they now? Didn't they come in the coach with you?'

'Oh yes,' said Alexander. 'But after Ingrid had gone up the road to meet you at the party, Julian said he wasn't hanging round here and buggered off, and took the other two with him. They said they'd be back in time for the Bruckner.'

'Hell.'

'I did try and persuade them not to but, well, let's just say Julian had definite ideas.'

'I can imagine. Christ, do you think they've gone for a beer?'

Alexander shrugged. 'Either that or he's gone to buy a new flag.'

Eliot spluttered out a sort of stressed laugh. 'Great. Well, let's do your bit first and then worry. I suppose I could tell David and maybe he could have a quick look for them – he's not in the first half either.'

'He's over there,' Alexander said, nodding to where David was draping his jacket over a chair next to his horn case.

'Right,' said Eliot. 'If his tic starts up again, I'm going to give Julian even more of a piece of my mind than I was going to anyway.'

'What?'

'Oh, you'll probably see.'

Eliot walked with purpose over to David, who received the news with an increasing frown and, as Alexander watched, a twitch in the side of his face that he tried to stop with the flat of one hand. Shortly afterwards, David stormed past Alexander, out of the room and back into the main church, having whispered something to Rafael on the way out.

Eliot wandered back. 'That went well.'

'It'll be fine,' said Alexander. 'I'll play all four tuba parts in the Bruckner if you like.'

Eliot laughed properly this time, letting some of the tension escape. 'Knowing you, you probably could, you talented bugger.'

Mr and Mrs Ford-Hughes and their guests began to arrive at around a quarter past seven, shown to the church door by Ingrid, who was deftly avoiding being patted on inappropriate places by the conducting tutor. She peeled off to stand next to Jörg and gestured that they should all proceed into the church and await the concert. Their high spirits and excited level of chatter spilled into the church and spread out among those people already there. Mrs Ford-Hughes walked to the very front row, as she did for every concert, and settled herself just to the left of Eliot's stand, in line with where Alexander would play the solo in the Strauss. Jörg had not been idle during the afternoon, having removed a couple of rows of audience seats so Alexander wouldn't deafen the first violins.

Eliot, peeking through the side room door, saw them come in. He wandered towards the main door, eventually finding Ingrid sorting tickets and money with Jörg.

'Ingrid – hi!'

She raised her eyebrows at him over an elderly couple sorting their change. 'Yes?'

'A quick word?'

They stepped to the side, out of the way of more audience coming in.

'Is everything alright, Eliot?'

'Um – for now, yes. It's just that our last piece, the Bruckner, has extra instruments in. The Wagner tubas, you know? And three of them have gone walkabout.'

'Excuse me?'

'They've wandered off. Probably for a beer.'

'What? Everyone was accounted for on the coach from the hotel.'

'Yes, they came on the coach. Anyway, apparently they said they'd be back in time for the Bruckner, and David's gone out for a look around now to see if he can find them, but I thought I'd better let you know. You know, if you see them loitering outside.' Eliot trailed off, rather in awe of the sight of Ingrid visibly gathering her organisational strength before his eyes, like a superhero transformation powered by clipboards and a clicky pen.

She inhaled through her nose and appeared to grow taller. 'I see. Leave it with me.'

'Thanks. I'd better go back and rally the troops. I understand you're doing a small introduction for us – is that right?'

'Yes. Once you and the orchestra have taken your seats.'

Eliot went back to rejoin the players in the side room, and a few minutes later, at a sign from Ingrid, they filed out to applause and took their seats. Richard, the leader, then walked out and invited Gwynneth to play an A for them all to tune, including Max leaning over his timpani with his ear nearly touching the skins of the drums and twiddling the taps round the top edges. Temperature changes unfortunately make different instruments behave in opposite directions: brass and woodwind instruments go sharper in the heat, and strings on violins, violas, cellos and double basses stretch and go flat. The orchestra sorted out their micro-changes and ended up more or less on the same frequency.

When they fell silent, Eliot walked to his stand and bowed. The church was almost full. Mrs Ford-Hughes beamed at him from the front row, most of which was filled with guests from her soirée. Eliot sensed the warm second-hand alcohol fumes lap towards him, and tried to focus his mind on the professional end of the evening. This was what he was being paid for. Showtime.

Ingrid joined him facing the audience, having left her clipboard on the table with Jörg. She gave a warm welcoming speech, first in fluent Dutch, which raised a few chuckles from the audience, and then smoothly switched to a shorter one in English which was joke-free, before handing over to Eliot to start the concert. He tried not to worry about what she might have said about them in Dutch.

He locked eyes with both bassoons and all the strings, checking they were ready and prepared for the *presto* quavers. Pete was blinking himself up to a revved frenzy at the back of the violas. Ann winked at him from her place at the back of the cellos. He grinned, remembered to crouch, and off they went.

14

The *Figaro* overture went down extremely well, raising a genuinely appreciative cheer at the end, which Pete had managed not to balls up by simply miming the last three bars, as Eliot had predicted. In the event, he had mimed in time, but better safe than sorry.

Everyone was more relaxed now the concert had started. Eliot scanned the back of the church, but couldn't see either Ingrid or Jörg. He checked that Alexander was ready to come on for the Strauss concerto, and turned to the audience.

'Thank you for that lovely reception for our Mozart: you're very kind. Next tonight, we have one of the finest horn concertos for you: Strauss's first. Written when he was only eighteen! Honestly, Mozart only got around to *Figaro* when he was thirty. Slacker.' He paused while the audience laughed. 'Our soloist tonight is Alexander Leakey.'

Alexander came on, almost bounding, smiling and nodding at the applause. Eliot asked for another A from Gwynneth, and Alexander twiddled quickly up and down a few arpeggios to check he was in tune with the rest of the orchestra, then nodded at Eliot to show he was ready to start.

From the very first horn call, Alexander filled the church with his absolute conviction that the French horn was the best instrument of all, and he was the right man to play it. Unless a horn player believes that in their bones, their performance will never thrill anyone. He owned the space utterly, and the effect was electric.

He had thirty-two bars' rest after his final flourish in the first movement, which allowed him to gather himself into the wholly mellow mood of the second movement. Eliot smoothly negotiated the invisible line between the first and second movements, sliding the music evenly from three flats to seven, from four brisk beats in a bar to three slower ones, the change cunningly disguised by triplets in the wind and violas in the last few bars of the first movement. By the time the orchestra landed gently in the first bar of the second movement, it was as if they had passed underneath a waterfall and were through to a cave the other side, where the ripples were in a minor key and Alexander was playing from a different realm. The melody rose up a fourth on the second note: an easy slur on which to split the top note that catches out many a famous soloist. Alexander floated up to it as if merely an echo in the stillness of the cave, with no apparent breath or muscle movement. Eliot and many of the orchestra and audience felt the hairs lift on the back of their neck and their forearms. For such a large figure for whom extrovert movement came as a natural gait, Alexander seemed to produce this ethereal sound from a place of complete stillness. His diaphragm, from years of training, lifted the column of compressed air from his lungs and directed it into the bore of the horn like a focused blue flame.

It was impossible to tell if the audience held their breath for the entire slow movement, but it felt as if they did.

Alexander's last ringing *fortissimo* octave leapt out of the quiet texture before dipping back in again like a dolphin changing worlds briefly as it breathes above water, and he and the *pizzicato* strings rounded off the movement sounding as introspective as they had started it.

A pause over the last quaver rest was all Eliot got to gather himself and the orchestra into a wholly different speed and genre. Discarding the four extra flats together with the minor key they had dragged along, they hopped over the bar line together into the third and final movement, back into E flat major and a whippy *allegro*. Eliot grinned, energising his beat to kick things off. Max started a sustained roll on the timpani, the trumpets and orchestral horns started calling with a bouncing, infectious rhythm, and the wind popped in with some triplets, all winding themselves up for the big finish.

As Alexander set off with his exuberant tune, tipping it into 6/8 time, the orchestra galloped along beside him with obvious enjoyment. There is something infectiously happy about music written in triple time: perhaps we grew up dancing to it. Once he had finished his first scoot with the tune, and the orchestra had had their go without him, the trickiest twenty-two bars in the whole thing arrived, for ensemble in general, and the flutes in particular.

This section had fallen apart many times during rehearsals, even before Alexander had joined them. The horn part wafts a smooth melody that winds chromatically through thinned-out orchestral texture of only violas and cellos holding sustained chords. On top of that, the mischievous teenage Strauss had added two solo flute parts sounding like the perkiest birds in the world. Imagine a couple of blue tits on speed, and then wind it up even more. Brian and Amber had to play three fast quavers each, starting off the beat, interlacing with each other but never touching, *staccato*, but then halfway through pause on their top notes longer for a couple of bars before returning to the *staccato* repetitions. No matter how Eliot tried to conduct it, communicating to Brian where he wanted the third of his quaver pattern to land wasn't getting through. Brian either fell behind the beat so he squashed into some of Amber's quavers coming up behind him, or got so anxious about it that he played them faster and faster and he met Amber the other side too soon. Eliot had resorted to clapping beats in rehearsals, dancing it for them, asking them to play with their eyes shut just listening to each other, and finally tried it for as long as they could without actually taking any breaths.

Amber, of course, should have been playing first flute, but Brian had been in Stockwell Park Orchestra for over a decade and things like that had a certain momentum about them. Eliot made many mental notes after their Strauss rehearsals that some traditions might be about to get broken. Meanwhile, they had a tour to get through.

Eliot glanced ahead in his score to what he feared might be a car crash. It was just Alexander and the strings, coasting towards it. He could see Brian's lips move as he counted his bars' rest. Amber looked confident and committed, but she had to rely on Brian to come in first, *ppp grazioso* (quieter than *pianissimo*, gracefully). Eliot locked eyes with Brian and did a convoluted jerk with his elbow to indicate the silent first beat to launch Brian into his perky trampolining. It worked. Amber tucked herself in behind him, and Eliot's eyes didn't leave either of them for the whole section. Brian read his leger lines and accidentals right, Amber fitted her phrase in neatly too, and the whole thing was an unexpected triumph. Even Alexander, when he had four bars spare just afterwards, turned and flashed a grin at them in support. Eliot wasn't counting any chickens: the whole thing was coming at them as a repeat a couple of pages further on in his score, only a tone lower, with different accidentals waiting like unsuspected potholes in the road.

Whether it was Alexander's bravura performance pulling everyone along or simple luck, they made it through, and by the time the end was in sight the whole orchestra was unstoppable. Alexander ripped down and up the range of the horn effortlessly. Near the end, in the pyrotechnic display written as a sort of cadenza, he landed perfectly on an impossible-sounding low splat of a note and then immediately jumped up over two octaves to pin a laser-clear top F to the back of the church. Then, with him keeping Eliot in his peripheral vision at all times, they set off on the finale section, *un poco più mosso* (a little more movement) in which Alexander had to play a dizzying array of quavers even faster than Brian and Amber had been forced to earlier, with added *acciaccaturas* (extra tiny notes before the real ones) thrown in. He reached the final razzing arpeggio without splitting any of them, and Eliot brought everyone off their final crotchet absolutely together. The audience's involuntary whoop hit them before the clapping started, such was their delight.

Alexander grinned out over them, acknowledging the applause before standing to one side and indicating the whole orchestra behind him should share in the glory. He even gave a special clap of his own in the direction of the flute section, which made Brian and Amber beam with pride. Eliot shook his hand with huge pleasure, nodding his own congratulations. They were both drenched in sweat, despite no jackets.

As the noise died away and Alexander walked into the side room to swap his horn for a Wagner tuba, Eliot glanced at the door at the back of the church, hoping to see Ingrid and the other Wagner tuba players, or David smiling and giving him a thumbs-up, but there was nobody. He addressed the audience.

'Thank you so much. We'll have a short interval now, before we bring you our Bruckner symphony. I think there are refreshments over by the main door.'

He gestured to where Jörg was sorting wine and soft drinks on his own behind a trestle table. After a whispered suggestion from Eliot, Pearl went to help him, since Ingrid wasn't around.

The orchestra started to move from their seats into the side room, and the noise level rose from an audience in search of a drink and, in some cases, a toilet. Eliot and Alexander arrived in the side room first, where Carl, Tracie and the rest of the trombones waited, scattered about on chairs, together with an extra one player each of trumpet, tuba and horn. David, the fourth horn, wasn't there, and nor were any of the other three Wagner tuba players.

Carl looked at Eliot. 'Still no sign?'

Eliot shook his head. 'Ingrid and David must still be out looking. Where the hell have they got to?'

'There was that bar they went to earlier this afternoon,' said Alexander. 'He was banging on about it on the coach here.'

'Do you know where it is?' said Eliot.

'Vaguely, from what he was saying.'

'Show me?'

They were walking towards the door, when Carl called after them. 'Want a hand?'

Eliot nodded. 'Why not? As long as we don't lose each other and make it worse. I hope they're not pissed.'

'I'll sober them up,' muttered Carl, looking furious.

'Glad you're on my team,' said Alexander.

'Glad you're both on mine,' said Eliot, who was dwarfed by both of them. 'Let's go.'

15

Outside, they scanned the street for Ingrid and David, but saw neither in the genial crowds of people who were wandering about in groups of two and three, enjoying the beautiful evening.

'God, this is hopeless,' said Eliot.

'I think it's down this way,' said Alexander, crossing the bridge and carrying on along the canal on the other side. Carl and Eliot set off at a sort of dog trot behind him.

'We need to know where David and Ingrid have looked,' said Eliot, fishing in his pocket for his phone and calling David's number first.

David answered, and Eliot almost yelped at him. 'David! Have you found them? Where are you? Alexander reckons he knows which bar they might have gone to.'

From the wince on Eliot's face and the distance he held the phone out from his ear, Carl and Alexander gathered that David wasn't entirely happy either.

'Slow down!' called Eliot into his phone. 'I can hardly hear you. Where?' He waved at Alexander and Carl to stop. 'Julian's in a what?'

'A fight,' said Alexander, pointing up ahead, where the back of Julian Talbot could be seen wrestling awkwardly with a couple of men in the crowd spilling out of a bar. 'And yes, that's where I thought he might be.'

'David,' Eliot called loudly into his phone, 'we can see Julian – we're just up the street. Where are you? Oh.' He looked over to the other side of the canal, where David could be seen standing opposite the bar fight with a phone clamped to his ear. 'Look, I've got Carl and Alexander with me. We'll get Julian, and hopefully Tom and Lamar too if they're there, and get back to the church. Do you know where Ingrid is?' All three of them saw David shrug. 'You get back to the church, keep an eye out for Ingrid, and we'll see you in a minute.'

David waved and started walking back along his side of the canal towards the church. On their side, Eliot, Carl and Alexander approached Julian, who was trying to wriggle out of a headlock. The instigator of the headlock was younger and stronger, and was having none of it. A pile of rowdy people crowded round, clearly approving of any and all headlock action.

'Julian's made new friends, I see,' said Alexander.

'Come on,' said Carl. 'Let's break this up.'

'Careful, Carl,' said Eliot. 'We want to de-escalate, OK?'

Carl looked grim and walked straight up to the man holding Julian. 'Hi there. Can I borrow this piece of shit? I promise I'll hit him later, but right now we need him to play in a concert.'

The man turned to stare at Carl, taking in Alexander's bulk right behind him, and Eliot manfully bringing up the rear. Under his bicep, Julian's muffled voice could be heard stressing the need for him to regain his freedom, or vocab to that effect.

'Do you speak English?' Alexander enquired politely. He turned to Carl. 'We shouldn't assume.'

'Quite right,' said Carl.

They both smiled at Headlock Man.

'Yes, I speak English,' he said, breathing hard. 'This is your friend?'

'God, no,' said Carl. 'As I said, he's a piece of shit. But we're in the middle of a concert, and he's in the orchestra.'

Eliot chipped in from behind, 'And we're a bit late? We'd be so grateful if you'd let his head go and then we can, you know, get off.'

'It's just back there, along the canal,' said Alexander, pointing at the bridge they had crossed.

Headlock Man almost laughed. 'He said things, in there.' He jerked his head behind him to the bar. 'We do not like to hear these things.'

'I can imagine,' said Carl. 'His name is Julian and he is a horrible man. I agree.'

'You do not like your friend?'

'He's not our friend. Honestly. More of a colleague. A shit colleague.'

Julian tried again to struggle out of Headlock Man's grip, but was clamped even tighter.

Eliot tried again. 'Um, we are also missing two other people. They may have been here with Julian? Are they in the bar too?'

'They were,' said a firm voice from inside. 'I located them and we were about to return to the concert.'

Headlock Man turned round, and they all watched in silence as Ingrid led Tom and Lamar outside. They looked suitably crestfallen. Ingrid looked as if she could laser anyone who made a sudden move with one glance. She nodded to Headlock Man.

'I apologise for the behaviour of that man,' she indicated Julian, whose wriggles were becoming weaker. He had stopped trying to yell altogether. 'He will be reprimanded.' Headlock Man looked confused, so Ingrid said something rapidly to him in Dutch. Whatever it was, it resulted in Julian being released with a small push towards Carl and Alexander.

He immediately turned and tried to bristle with his usual antagonistic bravado, but Carl laid a hand on his shoulder that looked outwardly friendly but was as effective as a vice.

'Thank you,' said Ingrid, stepping round Headlock Man. Behind her, Lamar and Tom skirted him warily and went to stand next to Julian in disgrace. Ingrid addressed the small crowd. 'I am so sorry for the inconvenience. It will not happen again.'

Headlock Man nodded and turned to go back into the bar. Julian, with a flare of bravery that came from thinking himself safe, shouted after him.

'Yeah – retreat. You're good at that!'

With a sudden roar of anger, Headlock Man turned, his arms outstretched, and accelerated into Julian, Tom and Lamar. Caught by surprise, Carl lost his grip of Julian's shoulder. The momentum carried all four past him at surprising speed. Headlock Man, still yelling, managed to stop just in time, teetering on the brink as Julian, Tom and Lamar dropped into the canal below.

There was a small moment of absolute silence after Headlock Man's yell stopped. A moment later, shouts of fury and shock exploded from the water as three heads resurfaced, spluttering, flinging sprays of drips up over the wall and onto the pavement and the people standing there.

Ingrid moved first. With a restrained murmur of 'Scheiße' to herself, she stepped neatly to the edge of the canal and looked over. At the sight of her face glaring down, all three in the water stopped yelling immediately, treading water.

Suddenly it seemed to them they were in less danger if they remained in the canal rather than climbing up to face the Bauer wrath.

Headlock Man said something quietly to her in Dutch. She nodded, and he walked away towards the bar. Apparently the debt had been paid and he was calling it quits.

Carl and Alexander leaned down to offer their arms to the swimmers. While they hauled Tom and Julian up and out of the water, Eliot leaned towards Lamar. They caught each other's wrists, and Eliot heaved upwards. There was a small ripping sound. Eliot knew immediately what had happened but, to give him his due, he continued to lift Lamar until he was able to balance on the edge of the pavement on his own.

Eliot straightened up and felt round the back of his trousers with trepidation.

Carl laughed. 'Got your lucky concert pants on, I see.'

'Damn,' said Eliot. 'How big…?'

'Big enough to distract Mrs Ford-Hughes in the Bruckner, I'd say.'

Alexander glanced over. 'Ah. Pity you have to stand with your arse to the audience.'

'Look, never mind about that now,' said Eliot. 'We've had a successful fishing trip. Let's hoof it back to the church and carry on. You lot,' he pointed at the three Wagner tuba players dripping Amsterdam canal water all over the pavement, 'will have to play like that. You're at the back anyway.'

'There are paper towels in the toilet at the back of the church,' said Ingrid. 'And I have a comb. Follow me please.'

She led an odd-looking procession across the bridge: three bedraggled men in formal dress whose shoes squelched at every step, followed by three equally formal dry men, one of whom had a large tear in the back of his trousers that broadcast the news that today was Red Stripy Underwear Day for touring conductors. The remaining crowd outside the bar gave them a warm valedictory round of applause and returned to their drinks.

David was hopping from one foot to the other at the church door, waiting for them. He was about to express his relief at their return but decided to keep silent as he saw Ingrid's expression. Instead, he opened the door for them and she swept inside with the three squelchers.

He smiled weakly at Eliot. 'Well done. Audience is fine here – Jörg and Pearl are handing out refreshments.' He glanced behind him, through the door into the church. 'Are they – er—'

'Soaking wet? Yes,' said Eliot.

'But you're fine,' said David. 'And we can kick off again on schedule.'

'He's fine from *your* angle,' said Carl.

Alexander snorted with laughter.

'What do you mean?' said David.

'You don't happen to have a needle and thread, do you?' said Eliot.

'What? No. Why? Pearl might.'

'I bet Ingrid does,' said Carl. 'Why don't you ask her?'

'If you dare,' said Alexander.

'Split my trousers,' said Eliot. 'And since we're not wearing jackets – and I don't particularly want to put mine on in this heat – I'd rather not flash my smalls at the great and the good sitting next to Mr and Mrs Ford-Hughes in the front row.'

David's mouth twitched. It made a change from his eye. 'I see.'

They all went inside and made their way to the side room past the audience, who were busy discussing if they had really seen three orchestral players go past dripping wet. Eliot clasped his hands behind his back and tried to keep his back to the wall while Alexander and Carl followed close behind to block the view.

Ingrid was standing in the side room with Julian, Tom and Lamar, who were patting themselves down with paper towels. With silent disapproval, Ingrid handed her comb to each of them in turn. The rest of the orchestra watched in disbelieving silence. David broke into their trance by chivvying them back out in front of the audience for the second half.

'Um, Ingrid?' said Eliot. 'You don't happen to have a needle and thread, do you? Sorry.'

Ingrid turned her head like an owl. Eliot twisted his hips to show her a little of what had happened at the back of his trousers. She looked if anything more disappointed with the developments of that evening, and retrieved a small travel sewing kit from her bag on the table.

'We have no time for a full repair,' she said. 'Be quick.'

Eliot thanked her and turned to the players who were filing past out into the church. 'Can any of you sew?'

Ann stopped and nodded. 'Yes. I hate it though. Why?' She looked over at Ingrid supervising the combing. 'And what happened to *them*?'

'Ignore them,' said Eliot, turning round to show her why. 'This is urgent.'

'Ah,' she said. 'OK. Give me a needle and thread.' She laid her cello and bow down by the wall.

When most of the orchestra had left the room and there was more space, Eliot handed over Ingrid's kit, and soon Ann was kneeling behind him trying to do running repairs on a fidgeting buttock seam.

'Don't stick the needle in me!' said Eliot, trying not to wince in anticipation.

'If you keep still, I won't,' said Ann, getting the giggles. 'For god's sake, nobody take a picture.'

'Too late,' said Carl, putting his phone back in his pocket.

'Oi!' said Eliot. 'Go away.'

'Stay still!'

David cleared his throat. 'Shall we go and sit down?'

'Yes! Bugger off,' said Eliot.

'Won't be a minute,' said Ann. 'Eliot, stop jiggling.'

'I wouldn't jiggle if I trusted where you're putting that needle.'

Ingrid ushered everyone except Eliot and Ann out of the room, plus four Wagner tubas. A minute later they heard her making a short announcement in the church about the second half starting, which was met with a small round of applause.

'Thank god for Ingrid and her sewing kit,' said Ann, snipping a thread and standing up. 'You're all done. Sort of. It's a rush job. Don't lunge.'

Eliot grinned. 'Thank you so much. I owe you several pints. You go on and I'll be out in a sec.'

'I'll try not to look as if we were up to anything in here,' said Ann, smiling.

'They wouldn't believe it if we told them.'

Eliot was greeted by an enormous wave of applause, and for the second time that evening he wondered what Ingrid had told them.

'Thank you; you're very kind. We'll now play you Bruckner's Seventh Symphony.'

He turned and smiled at the orchestra. The four Wagner tuba players sat meekly behind the horns, three of them with a wodge of folded paper towels on their seat. Alexander gave him a thumbs-up.

Eliot checked Neema and Ryan and the cellos were ready: they shared the first melody over a shimmer of violin *tremolando*. Ann winked at him. He settled himself, and away they went.

16

Wednesday morning brought another slab of heat to the continent before it had cooled much during the night before, with a promise of still more to come. Jörg had already loaded the instruments directly from the evening's concert, including the Wagner tubas, and started the journey to Cologne straight after his early breakfast.

Alexander sidled up to Eliot in the breakfast room, bringing a coffee over with him. 'Could I have a quick word, Eliot? Sorry to interrupt.'

Eliot nodded, munching toast and waving him to a spare seat at the table.

Alexander glanced round the room before starting to talk. 'It's about travel arrangements.'

Eliot swallowed toast and took a gulp of his tea. 'Oh yes? Bet I can guess what you want.' He smiled conspiratorially.

'Well, I wondered if your coach was absolutely full to capacity.'

Eliot grinned. 'I have a feeling it isn't, quite. But you'd have to check with David. Why – is there something wrong with your existing transport?' Never were eyebrows raised more innocently.

It was Alexander's turn to grin. 'Honestly, the leg from Britain to here was bad enough. But the thought of having to share a car with Julian again is... too much.'

'Do you think your fellow passengers might feel the same?'

'I think there is no doubt of their feeling in this matter. I would go as far as to say that their feelings might perhaps be stronger than mine.'

'But you were elected spokesperson?'

'Yeah.'

'That's what you get for being a soloist. Which went completely brilliantly last night, by the way.'

Alexander looked out of the window, suddenly bashful. 'Thanks. It was fun, wasn't it?'

'It's a great piece. And all the better for being played while dry.'

They were laughing companionably as Ann and Erin came over holding their breakfast plates.

'What are you laughing about?' said Ann. 'It's too early for laughing. Can we—?'

Eliot nodded and they sat. 'Sure. Alexander was just asking if he could hitch a ride with us from now on.'

Erin giggled. 'Can you imagine the stink in Julian's car today? Farts plus rank canal water from his clothes.'

'Ah,' said Eliot. 'I think Ingrid might be waving her magic wand over those – the water, not the farts, I mean. She's promised to find a fast turnaround dry cleaner in Cologne for all their concert gear. And one that can do a more permanent repair on my trousers.'

'I did my best under very trying circumstances,' said Ann. 'Having said that, Ingrid is worth her weight in gold. Every tour should have an Ingrid.'

'She's quite scary,' whispered Erin.

'We have nothing to fear if we behave ourselves,' said Eliot. 'And probably fear itself, so maybe don't let it show.'

'What have we got planned today?' said Erin. 'Get to Cologne, then what? Concert's not til tomorrow.'

Eliot's eyes twinkled. 'We arrive in Cologne in the midst of their great Bruckner Festival, which – I gather from David – is the whole reason for our tour happening this week.'

'"Midst"?' said Ann.

'One does not simply turn up "in the middle" of a Bruckner Festival,' said Eliot, making a circle with his finger and thumb and trying to look like Boromir. 'It has a midst, and we shall penetrate it. At least, Mrs Ford-Hughes will be penetrating their gala evening. She was telling me about it last night. Apparently, soirées are mere foothills to the mountain range that is a gala evening.'

'OK, JRR Hartley,' said Ann, laughing. 'Stand down.'

Erin saw Alexander looking at the conversation with a bemused expression. 'Don't worry. They're always like that. Even before she sewed up his arse.'

'You're never going to let me forget that, are you?' said Eliot.

'Nope.'

'It *is* a good story,' said Alexander to Eliot, sympathetically.

'Do we all get to go to this gala evening?' said Ann. 'Or do the rest of us hoi polloi have to find our own entertainment? And planning ahead, do we have to be up early tomorrow morning for a rehearsal? I can't remember David's timetable – I know he's given us one.'

Eliot shook his head. 'No – lie-in tomorrow if you want. Rehearsal in the afternoon, then concert in the evening. And I think the gala is just for special people.' He expertly dodged the toast crumbs thrown at him by both Erin and Ann. 'I reckon Alexander will be on her list after last night.'

Alexander looked alarmed. 'Don't throw things at me. I didn't know!'

'Huh,' said Ann. 'We'll be having much more fun anyway.'

'Yeah. Stupid gala evening,' Erin mumbled into her cup.

'You're probably right,' said Eliot. 'Can I find you after and join you for a drink?'

'Can I come too?' asked Alexander, looking at Erin.

She smiled. 'I should think so.'

* * *

Keith stood at his usual spot for departure, stacking people's bags and checking their owners off his list as they boarded the coach. He had already cleared a significant space in the rear hold for the Ford-Hughes multi-part wheeled matching luggage set. They had arrived in high spirits by taxi from their hotel and were already installed in the front seats of the coach, at the table behind Keith. Looking at how much space was left for everyone else's bags, Keith hoped his loading tessellation skills wouldn't desert him.

Ingrid and David compared clipboard sheets. From around the corner of the hotel, Max's timpani van trundled from its secure car park and drew up next to the coach. He got out and approached David and Ingrid, not sure who should field his query and not wanting to upset either of them. He, like everyone in the orchestra, had seen Ingrid in full flight the evening before, and wasn't taking any chances.

'Morning, Max,' said David. 'All set for Cologne?'

Max smiled with relief at not having to make the first move. 'Morning, David. Hello, Ingrid.' Ingrid nodded at him, smiling, and gave a long blink for a greeting. 'I just

wanted to check I had the right hotel details for my satnav?'
Max proffered a folded piece of paper.

David moved his reading glasses down from the top of his head to his nose and cross-checked Max's paper with his. 'Yes, all good. I'm not sure if we're stopping en route this time, but usual arrangement: check in under the Note Perfect Tours booking. Ingrid, do you want to allocate him a room in case he gets there first?' He handed the paper back to Max.

Ingrid looked at a list a few sheets of paper down. 'No need. We each have a single room in the Cologne hotel. It is bigger than here.'

Max smiled. 'Thanks. See you there.'

A car horn tooted at close range, making them all jump, and Julian's estate swung in next to Max's van. Flags remained its most prominent feature. Julian got out and slammed his door.

'Oh heavens,' said David faintly.

'David, mate,' shouted Julian as he walked over, still not strictly speaking within conversation range but not letting that bother him. 'Wanted to confirm you're transporting the tubas before the lads and me crack on to Krautland, yeah? Still room in the old roof box if not!'

David had already spoken with Alexander after breakfast. He had agreed the coach did have space for three extra passengers, and had fervently hoped he himself would not have to break the news to Julian. It appeared that Alexander, not to put too fine a point on it, had dobbed him in it. He put his hand to his eye in preparation. The group of players waiting to get on the coach turned to watch, like a crowd at an awful tennis match where the shots were increasingly offensive insults. It was a rather one-sided tennis match, certainly. More like someone walking straight to the net firing tennis balls at a hapless line judge who had to either dodge or get bruised.

Ingrid inserted herself into the game with the authority of an umpire who had a microphone, forensic knowledge of the rules and a disdain for metaphor.

'Mr Talbot,' she said sharply, raising the flat of her hand towards him like a traffic officer. Julian halted, teetering with his stilled momentum. 'First, I would be grateful if you could give me your concert clothes that were… soiled last night.' The onlookers tittered. Ingrid ignored them. 'I have sourced a cleaner in Köln who requires delivery as soon as we arrive.' Julian opened his mouth to reply but Ingrid pressed on. 'I have a plastic bag here. Please seal it. Second, I would also be grateful if you refrain from calling my country "Krautland". Germany is my home. You will not abuse it.' This drew brief applause from the coach crowd. Julian glanced at them.

'Yes, miss,' he said, deliberately.

There was an audible intake of breath and all eyes were on Ingrid.

She didn't blink or lose eye contact. 'Third. I confirm all four Wagner tubas are in Jörg's truck and on their way to Köln.' She held a folded plastic bag and a piece of paper out towards him. 'The clothes, if you please. And here are directions to the hotel.'

Julian walked over to her and took them out of her hand, spun on his heel and went back to his car.

Ingrid clicked her pen and made a note on the clipboard, for all the world as if she were keeping score.

Keith recovered first, resuming the coach boarding. 'Come on, in you get, lads and lasses. We've got a fair way to go today.'

Some of the last to emerge from the hotel were Alexander, Tom and Lamar. As well as their normal luggage, Tom and

Lamar also carried clear plastic bags containing their still-damp clothes from the canal dunk, holding them away from their bodies at an angle. They handed them over to Ingrid, who propped a second bag open to save any possibility of contamination. The scent of canal water had, if anything, intensified overnight. Julian had found his bathing clothes too, and returned to Ingrid with his own plastic bag.

'Ah, great!' he said, spotting his fellow Wagner tuba players. 'Ready to go?'

'Oh shit,' murmured Alexander, looking at David but realising he had been overly optimistic to think David would take this one for him.

'Thank you,' said Ingrid, carefully zipping her outer bag closed around the three sets of clothes as if they were toxic waste. She ticked some more boxes and stepped towards the coach. Max decided it was a good moment to drift back to his van too. David stood rooted to the spot and wished he wasn't.

'Yeah, Julian,' said Alexander, 'about that lift.'

'Come on. Let's rev this baby up and hit the tarmac – another road trip with the boys!'

'Um... you go on. We'll be OK on the coach with the others. I mean, now Jörg's got the Wagner tubas anyway, there's no need...' Alexander trailed off.

'What? You'd rather go on that tourist charabanc?' Julian stood absolutely four-square, his paunch jutting over his shorts underneath yet another short-sleeved rugby shirt. The thinning hair over his crown wisped gently in the morning air. He laughed. 'Don't be an arse. Come on, Tom. Lamar?'

Tom and Lamar shifted uneasily, until Lamar said 'No, you're alright. Coach is fine, honest.' They edged towards Keith, gatekeeper of the non-Talbot travel atmosphere.

'Well, we'd better get a move on,' said David, making chivvying motions with his arms.

'You're bloody idiots,' said Julian. 'Sod off then. You're missing out. See you in Krautland.' He turned with one more deliberately aggressive look at Ingrid as he walked back to his car, spun the wheels reversing and kicked up a load of stones turning into traffic, blaring his horn. The flags of St George fluttered greyly as Amsterdam's morning rush hour swerved around him.

Alexander let out the huge breath he had been holding. 'Remind me again why we had to get him along?' he asked David.

David sighed the heavy sigh of one who had been forced to bargain hard. 'The Wagner tubas. He owns the whole set – something to do with an orchestra he used to play in? I'm not sure. Anyway, it was free tubas *and* Julian, or hugely expensive tubas without him. And – well, you've met our treasurer, Rafael?'

Alexander laughed and clapped him on the shoulder as he passed. 'Yeah. Understood. It'll all be fine.'

They climbed into the coach and Keith shut the door.

17

As the coach left Amsterdam for the three-hour trip south to Cologne, Keith came onto the public address system to take a straw poll to see if people wanted to stop for coffee on the way. He managed to phrase it so his subtext of never using the on-board chemical toilet was somehow prominent yet unarticulated. The vote was definitely for a coffee stop.

'Right you are,' he said, snapping his dark lenses down over his glasses. 'We'll hop over the border into Germany and find somewhere just after that.'

Mrs Ford-Hughes smiled and nodded, and then started as if remembering something. She leaned across the aisle to where David was sitting in the other front seat. 'David? Would you mind if I said a little something to the orchestra? I was so taken with their performance last night. I can't tell you how much we enjoyed it!' She clasped her husband's hand as she spoke, and he smiled at her indulgently.

'Of course,' said David. Ingrid gave her the microphone.

Mrs Ford-Hughes levered herself to her feet and turned round to face the rest of the coach, holding tight to the back of her seat to keep her balance. 'Good morning, Stockwell Park Orchestra!' she cried, beaming at those on the lower deck she could see. There were a few cheers, and some 'good morning's drifted down the stairs in return. 'My husband and I wanted to say how marvellously you played last night – it was truly a peach of a concert! And we're so excited to be joining you from now on for our itty-bitty tour.'

'And thank *you* – both – for your hugely generous support for our, er, itty-bitty tour,' Eliot called out from his seat, provoking a huge cheer which Mrs Ford-Hughes acknowledged with delight. She was clearly determined to enjoy everything that week with gusto. She sat down again. Mr Ford-Hughes squeezed her knee and nodded.

David turned to Ingrid across the table. 'Did you want to outline today's timetable, since we have them all together here?'

Ingrid nodded, stood and retrieved the microphone from Mrs Ford-Hughes. 'I add my thanks for last night's concert. It was extremely well received – especially, may I say, the Strauss played by Mr Leakey?'

There were whoops from everyone, which Alexander acknowledged by half-standing and bowing awkwardly to Ingrid.

'Hear hear!' shouted Eliot.

'I have received several messages from Mr and Mrs Ford-Hughes's soirée guests to that effect,' said Ingrid. 'I believe the concert will be reviewed in a local paper today. I shall pass it on to David when I receive a copy. Today, our timetable comprises travel and rest. We shall arrive in Köln for lunch, after which you have free time to view the beautiful city for yourselves.'

'Are there any canals though?' called Charlie, to renewed laughter.

'I'm steering clear if there are,' said Lamar.

113

'It's Julian we have to steer clear of,' said Alexander. 'Without him, we'll be fine.'

Ingrid waited for the noise to die down before speaking again. 'There is the Rhine, of course. But perhaps better viewed from above rather than from underneath it, yes?' She acknowledged applause for her good humour. 'Please note we are part of the Köln Bruckner Festival, which runs all this week. Our concert tomorrow forms part of their programme. We have a rehearsal scheduled for two o'clock tomorrow afternoon. You may wish to attend other festival events this afternoon, this evening, or perhaps tomorrow morning. I have programme details if anyone would like them. Some of you, of course,' she nodded towards Mr and Mrs Ford-Hughes, 'will be attending the gala evening tonight, and I shall speak to those attendees separately with our itinerary.'

There were muted teasing sing-song echoes of 'gala evening' from various unidentified members of the orchestra, immediately hushed by giggling hushers.

'You will have noticed,' Ingrid continued, 'that this coach is now full to capacity.'

'It's the tuba boys!' yelled Carl from the top deck back seat, to more cheers.

'Thank you for having us!' Alexander called up the stairs.

'I hope everyone is comfortable nonetheless,' said Ingrid. 'Please let me know if I can assist you with anything. Thank you.'

She switched off the microphone and sat down to warm applause. The orchestra knew a formidable talent when they saw it.

'Hey, look!' said Charlie, pointing out of the window. 'It's Max's van. No wonder he left ahead of us: he doesn't exactly cane it, does he?'

Indeed, as he spoke, Keith was easing the coach past Max. By the time half the coach length had pulled past, Max noticed everyone waving, and waved back, giving a thumbs-up.

Carl watched half the top deck waving out of the window and leaned into Kayla on the back seat. 'You know what this calls for?' he whispered.

'I dread to think,' said Kayla.

'Oh yes.'

'Oh no.'

'Oh yes.'

'Carl, *no*.'

But it was too late. Carl had already climbed up onto his seat as the coach finally pulled clear of Max's van, and the last sight Max had of his fellow musicians until he reunited with them in Cologne was of Carl's buttocks mooning at him through the rear window.

18

Shortly after noon, they arrived at their hotel on Mauritiuswall, a street flanked with pale boxes that had regular square windows all the way up, with the odd brightly coloured plastic handrail at street level every now and then to relieve the monotony.

Charlie peered out of the window. 'Another five-starrer, I see.'

'It's just the style round here,' said Ann.

'It looks like we've been shrunk into a flat-pack Legoland. I thought Cologne was old and pretty.'

'It *was* old and pretty before we flattened most of it in the war, remember. They had to completely rebuild.'

'Fair point. Reckon Mr and Mrs Ford-Hughes are staying here too?'

Ann laughed. 'We'll have to wait and see.'

They climbed down off the coach and helped Keith find their luggage as he was unloading it all from the cavernous hold. Ingrid had stationed herself on the pavement at the bottom of the steps up to the main door, matching people to rooms.

'Did you manage to get an extra one for Tracie?' asked Kayla, trying not to betray too much hope in her face. 'I mean, otherwise I can share again.'

Tracie stood next to her, for once not looking belligerent. 'Sorry, Miss.'

Kayla smiled at her. 'Don't worry. It's not your – well, it is your fault. But in a way I'm glad you're here now. Maybe we should have tried to arrange for you to come officially.'

Tracie flashed a brief grin.

'There is space for Tracie to have a single room,' said Ingrid to Kayla. 'I have allocated you two adjacent rooms, given your guardianship role.' There was only so much responsibility Ingrid was prepared to take, and it came to a very professional boundary in Tracie's case.

'Don't suppose there's a chance of a double?' muttered Carl just behind Kayla. She tried not to jump too much as he slid his hand in her back pocket.

Tracie laughed and walked into the hotel ahead of them, calling behind her, 'Carl, you're as bad as the Sunbridge boys.'

In time, all the players had filed into the hotel and were on their way to their rooms. Ingrid had told everyone who had signed up for the tour lunch to meet her in the lobby in fifteen minutes; otherwise, people were free to explore the city on their own. Mr and Mrs Ford-Hughes were standing next to the vast pile of their luggage on the pavement, as Keith balanced the last items on top.

'Ingrid, honey, did you call that cab?' called Mrs Ford-Hughes, fanning herself. She was keen to embrace much more expensive air conditioning than a hotel on Mauritiuswall was able to provide.

'Yes,' said Ingrid, walking over and looking at her watch. 'The driver should have been here five minutes ago – I shall call again.'

Before she could dial, however, a taxi pulled in behind the coach. The driver got out and said 'Note Perfect Tours?'

to nobody in particular while eyeing the Ford-Hughes pile of luggage with a resigned droop of his shoulders. He accepted the inevitable, and began loading with the brisk cheerfulness of one who knows a good tip can be earned if one tries.

'Excelsior Hotel, *bitte*,' Ingrid said to him as he held the door open for Mrs Ford-Hughes. He walked round to his own door and Ingrid leaned down to take her leave of the Ford-Hugheses. 'I shall meet you at the Excelsior at six o'clock, and we can go on to the gala together. Enjoy the beautiful city of Köln in the meantime.'

'Thanks, honey,' said Mrs Ford-Hughes. 'I sure am looking forward to this party.'

* * *

A lot of the orchestra ended up joining Ingrid at the Brauhaus she had arranged to go to for lunch, as they were all hungry: they had the rest of the day and the following morning to themselves to explore. They walked to it in a straggling line from the hotel, not quite holding hands in pairs to form a crocodile but definitely getting the feeling they might be asked to do so at any minute if they mucked about crossing roads. Ingrid led the way with David at the helm.

They were welcomed in and sat on huge farmhouse-style tables.

'Excellent!' said Alexander. 'Let the afternoon of Kölsch begin.'

Indeed, everyone was already being issued with a glass of local beer, brought round in deep metal trays that looked like the ends of metal beer kegs. They had circular holes in the top level to fit the beer glasses, and a handle on a stalk coming up from the middle that let the waiter carry many glasses without any chance of them sliding off.

'You will automatically get more Kölsch throughout your meal,' said Ingrid to everyone, while they were still sober. 'If you don't want any more, simply put your coaster on top of your glass.'

'This is going to be a great afternoon,' said Erin.

'We don't have anything else to concentrate on, do we?' said Charlie, next to her.

'I have to be ready to make extremely polite and possibly obsequious conversation with Cologne music-lovers this evening,' said Eliot, opposite. 'And so does Alexander.'

'Cheers!' said Alexander, on the other side of Erin, looking as if that were a problem to be dealt with later.

Ingrid was busy showing people the tradition of clinking their glasses at the base instead of the top.

'Oops, too late,' said Erin to Alexander. 'I think I've just given you seven years' bad luck.'

'Damn it, Erin!' said Eliot. 'We still have two performances of the Strauss to get through. If it falls apart, I'm blaming you.'

'Well, the first one will be difficult to top,' said Erin, smiling at Alexander.

'If it falls apart, it'll be Brian's fault,' said Ann. 'How he made all those quavers last night I'll never know.'

'Shh!' said Eliot, looking round to see if Brian was within hearing range.

Ann emptied her first Kölsch glass. 'He's three tables away, relax. And, as we know, hearing isn't his strong point.' She nodded her thanks for her second beer, which was delivered swiftly from a passing tray.

They happily ordered all sorts of recommended dishes: several people had a Halve Hahn (rye bread topped with

Gouda and raw onion); Alexander went all-out for Hämmche (salt-cured pork knuckle with sauerkraut and mustard); the rest tried Ähzezupp (pea soup).

'You know,' said Erin, licking butter off her fingers, 'we'd better split into Onion and Non-Onion groups this afternoon. Nobody will want to be stuck in a cable car with me after all this unless they've eaten it too.'

'You're doing the cable car?' asked Alexander.

'We thought we would – Charlie's got guidebooks for everywhere and he's been reading stuff out to me on the coach for the last three hours.'

'They were useful facts,' said Charlie. 'Everyone needs useful facts in a new place.'

Alexander leant over and nicked some onion off Erin's plate. 'There. I'm safe.'

Charlie leant in from her other side and took some as well. 'Me too.'

'Oi!' said Erin. 'This is as bad as nicking crisps in the pub.'

'Oh, you've done it now,' said Eliot. He turned to Alexander. 'The first thing I learned when I went for drinks with this lot was *always* buy your own crisps. They are very possessive.'

'Oi again!' said Erin, flicking a crumb of rye bread at Eliot, who carried on talking to Alexander as if nothing had happened.

'They also get quite violent.'

Ann watched Erin, squashed in the middle between Charlie and Alexander. Her lips twitched. The Kölsch kept coming.

When most of the food had been eaten, Charlie got out his guidebook. 'So, what *are* we doing then? I mean, unless we all want to go and listen to bits of Bruckner all round the city…?'

Apparently nobody was wild about that idea.

'We're doing our bit tomorrow,' said Eliot. 'They can't require us to do nothing but Bruckner while we're here. Plus I'm bound to have to talk Bruckner tonight, so let's have the afternoon off.'

'Excellent,' said Charlie. 'Well, apart from the obligatory cable car, there's another bloody chocolate museum—'

'Are you just taking us on a European tour of chocolate museums?' said Ann.

'Well, they seem very popular,' said Charlie. 'I don't make the rules.'

'Imagine a tour where he did make the rules,' said Erin, making a face at Eliot and Ann opposite her. 'We'd all have to drink four pints and march round socialist hotspots until we were worthy enough.'

'Just because you say I look like I sell the *Socialist Worker* when I wear my cap – which, by the way, is vintage,' said Charlie, 'doesn't mean you can cast petunias on my politics.'

'Focus,' said Ann. 'If not the chocolate factory, what else? Has anyone been here before? It must be one of the last European cities I haven't actually visited, with or without my cello.'

'Whistle-stop tour a couple of years back,' said Eliot. 'But no time for seeing anything.'

'Well, there's the cathedral. Obviously,' said Alexander. 'Very tall. Very gothic. Very spire-y.'

'Bet it's got a cracking acoustic,' said Charlie.

Alexander grinned. 'Flash mob?'

'We'd get arrested,' said Eliot. 'You need somewhere slightly less… iconic to get away with that kind of thing.'

'Well, David has asked me to do the Tour Tweets for the orchestra,' said Erin, looking mischievous, 'so if you want anything to go viral, you know…'

'What – you've been given the password and everything?' said Charlie.

'The power might go to her head,' said Ann.

'I don't suppose anyone wants to go on a boat cruise?' said Alexander. 'I wanted to in Amsterdam but we were too tight for time. We might be here, too. Dunno.'

'There are two-hour evening trips,' said Charlie, consulting his guidebook. 'They look amazing. Highly recommended. But you and Eliot have to go to the—'

'Gala evening!' chorused everybody.

Alexander sighed and said sadly, 'You go on without me. It's OK.'

Erin leaned against him and gave his arm a hug. Charlie flicked over a page of his guide quickly and said, 'There's loads of art. Famous paintings. Anyone?'

'Isn't there a zoo?' said Ann.

Charlie flipped more pages. 'Ooh!'

'What?' said Eliot.

'Oh, maybe not.'

'*What*?' said Erin and Ann.

'Bit dark,' said Charlie. 'There's a place here you can see where the Gestapo kept prisoners, and you can go into the dungeon cells and everything.'

'Maybe not,' said Ann.

'That's what I said,' said Charlie. 'I mean, it's a lovely sunny day and everything. You need to come here specially in winter for that kind of stuff, I reckon. Get properly serious and depressed about it.'

'You should start your own tour company,' said Erin. 'Classified by mood. People would know what to expect.'

'There's a botanical garden,' Charlie continued, turning pages. 'Or Roman stuff? Oh *god*! There's a theme park:

Phantasialand! It's one of the biggest theme parks in Europe. Can we? Can we? Please? Oh hang on – it's fifteen kilometres away.'

'And just like that, all our hopes were dashed,' said Erin.

'I suggest back to hotel for a freshen-up,' said Ann. 'Then cable car, maybe zoo, maybe botanical gardens, and see if we can get on a boat tonight. Those of us who don't have to schmooze, that is.'

Eliot and Alexander exchanged gloomy looks.

'Who am I kidding?' said Ann. 'I just want to flop in the shade with a cool drink.'

'Maybe the chocolate museum?' asked Charlie, putting his head on one side in what he hoped was a winning manner.

'Maybe,' said Ann, smiling. 'If you're good. Let's get cracking. We can all look at the cathedral as we go past, how about that?'

They agreed, and were soon walking back to the hotel.

'We'll have to come back and change in time to get to this gala thing,' said Eliot to Alexander. 'I think it's black tie. We can check with Ingrid.'

Faint cries of 'gala evening!' floated back from Charlie, Erin and Ann up ahead.

'Are they always that annoying?' asked Alexander.

'Yep,' grinned Eliot. 'You get used to it.'

19

By the time Ingrid met Eliot and Alexander in the hotel lobby at a quarter to six, she couldn't tell that half an hour earlier they had been running through Cologne's streets desperately trying to get back in time to have a shower and change. The flush on both their faces could well have been due to the heat of the day and not the late return of their cable car over the Rhine. If they hadn't managed to flag down a taxi near the train station to take them the final few kilometres, it would have been a very different meeting.

They had left Ann, Erin and Charlie about to board a cruise, and had tried not to sulk too much about it.

'Good evening,' said Ingrid, glancing over their clothes and apparently finding no fault. She herself was impeccable in a long, elegant, shimmering dress that caught the light every time she moved. Her hair was in its usual French pleat, but secured with jewels, and her neck and ears glinted with understated evening sparkle. Ingrid Bauer had risen to this occasion – as she did to every one – with magnificent ease, and produced it all from an uncrumple-able capsule wardrobe that unrolled from her suitcase in hotel rooms across the world.

'Ingrid! You look beautiful,' said Eliot.

'Thank you. I trust your trouser repair is adequate?'

'It's wonderful, thank you.' He smoothed the material over his buttocks as if to demonstrate the invisibility of the mend. 'I'm so grateful to you for finding such a prompt turnaround.'

Ingrid smiled. 'Yours was easy to expedite. The other three pairs of trousers and shirts will need until tomorrow afternoon, I understand, to regain their…'

'Aromatic friendliness?' suggested Alexander.

'Lack of pong?' tried Eliot.

'Pristine cleanliness,' said Ingrid gently. 'All will be well. Shall we?'

'Aren't David and Rafael coming too?' asked Eliot, looking around the lobby for them.

'They are attending one of the other festival events together, I believe, and said they will make their own way to the gala.'

Ingrid had arranged a car to pick them up and then collect Mr and Mrs Ford-Hughes from the Excelsior before going on to the gala. Eliot and Alexander exchanged raised eyebrows as the sleek limo drew up to the hotel, looking out of place in the decidedly ordinary district.

'Beats running about the streets like urchins,' murmured Alexander as they got in.

'I could get used to this,' said Eliot.

While they drove, Ingrid outlined the evening in more detail.

'Representatives from all the orchestras and choirs taking part in Köln's Bruckner Festival will be there tonight, as guests of the Festival Director and Board of Trustees. It is being hosted by the Hochschule für Musik und Tanz.'

'Really?' said Alexander. 'Friend of mine studies there. The Musik bit, not the Tanz. Maybe we'll run in to her.'

'I think it's quite a big place,' warned Eliot. 'And probably on holiday at the moment.'

'It is,' said Ingrid. 'The Hochschule is the largest music academy in Europe.'

'You should have told her you were coming,' said Eliot.

Alexander shrugged.

Ingrid carried on, undaunted. 'The festival runs all week, so this Wednesday gala is positioned to be midway through what they hope will be a successful celebration of Bruckner's music.'

'We can check out the opposition,' said Eliot, and then, at a rather sharp glance from Ingrid, 'I mean, I'm sure they're all lovely.'

'And equally good at playing,' added Alexander.

'And singing,' said Eliot.

They waited anxiously for Ingrid's face to soften.

She held it for a moment, before saying 'They might be bad. You never know.'

By the time the car drew up at the Excelsior, Ingrid had risen in Eliot and Alexander's estimation.

'Wait here, please,' she said to them and the driver, and stepped out of the car.

Eliot turned to Alexander. 'Do you think we'll know anyone there tonight? I mean, apart from your friend who might be loitering.'

'Maybe. It's a small world.'

They gazed idly out of the windows, and had to swivel their heads up a long way to see to the tops of the cathedral spires, directly opposite the Excelsior.

'Our hotel doesn't have this kind of view,' said Alexander.

'We don't have the Ford-Hugheses' kind of money. Mind you, there are drawbacks. Soirées and gala evenings and such.

I had to be nice to an awful man last night. He kept doing the same Beethoven 5 anecdote. With increasing... um, actions.'

'You're a pro. You can cope.'

Eliot sighed. 'Wish we could've gone on that river cruise.'

'Me too. But we're working. This isn't a wee holiday,' Alexander said, trying to convince himself as much as anyone. 'We're probably the only two on this trip who are actually being paid to do it.'

'True. God, you're bracing. Probably just what I need.'

The door opened to a waft of Mrs Ford-Hughes's perfume. She stooped to get into the limo, cleavage first.

'Hello, Eliot! Alexander, I'm so glad you could make it tonight!' She settled herself next to Alexander in one of the rear-facing seats and patted his knee. 'Honestly, after last night's Strauss I simply couldn't wait to introduce you to people. Did you know Strauss is one of my very favourite composers? Eliot will tell you – won't you, honey?'

Eliot smiled gamely. 'Indeed yes. I had the pleasure of conducting Maryanne last year in a performance of the *Four Last Songs*. Nobody who was there will ever forget it.'

Mr Ford-Hughes nodded. 'It was a triumph.' His wife beamed at him with uncomplicated pleasure.

'Though perhaps tonight we shouldn't go round saying we prefer Strauss to Bruckner,' said Eliot, 'even if it's true.'

When Ingrid was safely in and the door shut, the driver eased the limo into the northbound traffic along the west bank of the Rhine towards the Hochschule für Musik und Tanz.

20

The Hochschule's recital hall was decorated with tea lights and swags of satin draped over any available surface, giving it a delightfully un-Wednesday celebratory party feel. Waiting staff circulated with glasses of fizz on polished trays, keeping an eye on the covered grand piano on the stage at one end of the hall. A small notice was positioned on top of the cover asking guests not to leave their drinks on it.

Ingrid led her small party along the greeting line, where Eliot and Alexander were introduced to more members of the Cologne Bruckner Festival Committee than they could remember. There were gentlemen in crisp shirts and bow ties, and ladies in long dresses, some of whom even sported a tiara or white gloves. There was a bedazzling array of jewellery worn with the air of one who knows it is not fake and has the safe at home to prove it. Eliot felt he had stepped into the ball scene in *The Sound Of Music*, and glanced round nervously in case small children were about to pop up singing in harmony. At the other end of the line, once they had shaken every hand and possibly bowed once or twice, they were each given a glass and set free to twirl slowly and decoratively in the accepted Brownian motion of gala evenings.

'Cheers,' said Eliot, turning to his companions. 'Here's to the Stockwell Park Orchestra's tour, our sponsors, and our soloist!'

'And our conductor!' said Mrs Ford-Hughes, clinking her glass with his.

'Not forgetting our guide,' said Alexander, raising his glass to Ingrid, who smiled her appreciation.

'Crikey, of course not,' said Eliot. 'We all know we utterly depend on Ingrid. My trousers especially.'

'What?' said Mrs Ford-Hughes.

'Let's just say, Ingrid has already saved the tour, and the less you know about it the better,' said Eliot, grinning.

Mrs Ford-Hughes laughed, looking around the hall and sipping her fizz. 'Oh, darling!' she said suddenly, laying her hand on her husband's arm. 'Look! Isn't that the Schneiders? They said they'd be here.'

Mr Ford-Hughes turned his head to see. 'Yes, my dear. I believe it is.'

She leaned in conspiratorially to the others. 'It was the Schneiders who told us about this whole festival razzmatazz, back last year. They're patrons of some super orchestra over here in Germany – where is it, darling?'

'Hanover.'

'Oh, you're darn tootin'. So we saw them when we were all over in Bayreuth, it must have been July last year, and Jutta was gushing about this Bruckner thing in Cologne, and, well,' she spread her arms and grinned, 'here we all are!'

Ingrid smiled, perhaps at the vagaries of international arts sponsorship, perhaps at Mrs Ford-Hughes's colloquialisms. 'Herr Schneider is a most respected patron of the arts here in Germany,' she confirmed. 'I believe he funds not only the Hanover orchestra but also various promising solo artists. His name is associated with many good causes.'

Alexander laughed. 'I wonder if he wants to sponsor a penniless Scottish horn player trying to make his way in the cut-throat world of soloing?'

'Well then!' cried Mrs Ford-Hughes. 'Alexander, I just knew it would be good for you to come along. That's *exactly* what this kind of shindig is for. I'll introduce you.'

Alexander spluttered into his drink. 'I was joking.'

'Too late now,' murmured Eliot into his ear, and then louder, 'What a wonderful idea! Mrs Ford-Hughes, you could launch Alexander's international career.'

He laughed as Alexander was borne off by Mr and Mrs Ford-Hughes, looking back helplessly. Eliot raised his glass to him.

'So,' he said to Ingrid. 'Who else is here? With whom should I schmooze?'

'Schmooze?'

'Um, charm. Meet. Do my bit to enhance the reputation of Stockwell Park Orchestra.'

'Ah, yes of course,' she said. 'I can introduce you to a number of people connected with the festival. I believe we also have an address by the festival director scheduled for later, followed by a short performance.' She indicated the stage at the end of the hall that was currently empty save for the piano, which happily remained drink-free.

'Oh yes? What's that going to be? Jazz riffs on a Bruckner theme?'

'A motet. *Locus Iste.*'

'Ah – one of my favourites!' Eliot smiled. 'And nicely short. One doesn't want your gala to turn into a concert, after all.'

Ingrid nodded once, which could have meant she agreed with Eliot or merely acknowledged that he had spoken. 'It is to be performed by a chamber choir from Japan, who were given this honour because they had travelled the furthest to be here.'

'Excellent,' said Eliot. He looked at her closely. 'Are you kidding?'

She raised her eyebrows. 'I am not.'

Eliot exchanged his empty glass for a full one from a passing tray, and decided to make the most of the evening.

* * *

When David and Rafael got there, the festival director was mid-speech. She was also mid-drink, and took the audience up several anecdotal cul-de-sacs before getting to the point of the evening. She was one of the white-gloved, tiara-ed hostesses. Her consort wore a sash, and Eliot was delighted to discover that they were, as he had hoped, members of minor European royalty.

Gräfin Friederike von Dürr spoke in German, and Ingrid whispered a translation for Mr and Mrs Ford-Hughes, Alexander and Eliot.

'Gräfin von Dürr is thanking the Hochschule for their hospitality.'

'Hoch-hospitality,' whispered Eliot to Alexander. Their sniggers were cut short by a full-wattage Ingrid glance. 'Sorry.'

The white gloves were spread wide, as if she were waiting for an owl to land on each one, and Gräfin von Dürr embarked on what was clearly a list full of names with more than their fair share of consonants. Her tiara sparkled as she nodded for emphasis on each umlaut.

'She is thanking her festival committee members for their service,' Ingrid said, and paused. The pause lengthened. 'It is a large committee.'

Eliot and Alexander got the giggles but tried desperately to keep them under control. Their attention was caught by David and Rafael sidling towards them along the back of the hall, trying to avoid bumping into anyone who was standing motionless listening to the speech.

'Hi,' whispered Eliot when they made it.

David nodded his greeting, and Rafael smiled.

'You're just in time for the Japanese singers,' said Alexander. 'The wee princess here is just the warm-up act.'

Neither David nor Rafael appeared to be enlightened by this nugget of information. On the contrary, they seemed distracted.

'There's been a bit of a kerfuffle in the Old Town,' said David to Eliot. 'We got held up trying to get through it. Some kind of fight breaking out.'

'I think students were involved,' added Rafael.

'And now,' said Ingrid, 'she is telling us who some of the musical groups involved in the festival are. Who is here this evening – that kind of thing. And where we all come from.'

Small pockets of cheers sprang up around the hall as different groups were identified and welcomed. They all heard the words 'Stockwell Park Orchestra, London' when they were mentioned, and waved when the clapping turned in their direction.

Ingrid continued to whisper as the speech went on. 'She is saying that Köln is the equal of Linz and that just because a festival has been happening in Linz for over forty years doesn't mean there isn't room for another one, perhaps even greater. Ah, her husband comes to introduce the choir, I see.'

'It was quite alarming at one point,' said David, clearly shaken by his journey to the gala. 'A whole load of them started running off towards the river. I think they were chasing something.'

'Are you OK though?' asked Eliot.

'Yes. Glad to be here.'

'I think there are a lot of students in Cologne,' said Alexander. 'Maybe some high jinks going on? It could be the heat.'

At a signal from Graf Oskar von Dürr, they turned their attention to the stage, where an extremely neatly dressed Japanese chamber choir were filing on and arranging themselves in perfectly angled rows. Their conductor followed them, acknowledged the applause, and turned to his singers.

'By heart,' whispered Eliot. 'Impressive.'

Bruckner's beautiful motet *Locus Iste* rose from the stage, and the ever-present waiting staff circulated quietly among the guests. Their trays had now been augmented with piles of hors d'oeuvres in vast quantities. Clearly they had been tasked with delivering the calorific equivalent of a full sit-down dinner in tiny capsules at twenty-second intervals.

David and Rafael accepted a glass of champagne each and a small bacon-wrapped bratwurst, smiling their thanks.

The party got back to its previous level of chatter after the Japanese chamber choir had taken their bows to enthusiastic applause. Mrs Ford-Hughes worked the room like a pro with her husband, extending their network of art-loving money across Europe, with her husband exchanging discreet business cards with everyone he met. They were a formidable team.

When she circled back towards Eliot later, she was full of gossip.

'Have you heard about the riot?'

'I don't think we can characterise it as a riot, my dear,' said Mr Ford-Hughes, trying in vain to dampen her enthusiasm for an exciting diversion.

'But Jutta said she had heard it from those darling Italians who have come with their viol consort—'

'To a Bruckner festival?' asked Eliot.

'Did he write for viols?' said Alexander.

'Maybe they're playing arrangements of his chamber music?' Eliot guessed.

'No, listen!' said Mrs Ford-Hughes impatiently.

'Maybe the Italians were exaggerating?' said Rafael. 'You know what they're like.'

'About viols?' said Eliot.

'Oh, you pumpkin!' Mrs Ford-Hughes punched Eliot's arm playfully, although what with champagne and adrenaline and the possibility of civic unrest nearby, it was still hard enough to leave a small bruise. 'They were saying that there's been a riot down by the riverbank and people have fallen in, or were pushed in, or something, and there were some reporters there clicking away.'

'Just the kind of publicity the festival won't want,' said Mr Ford-Hughes. 'If it is true and not simply a rumour.'

'It won't be to do with the festival, though, will it?' said Alexander.

'They were heading towards the river when we came through earlier,' said David. 'And on a Wednesday!'

Eliot and Alexander looked at each other, perplexed.

'Who riots on Wednesdays?' asked Eliot.

'Not me,' said Alexander. 'Saturday night after the pubs chuck out or nothing.'

'Young people and the heat,' said Rafael, with an altogether disapproving air. 'Guaranteed to rile them up.'

Before they could analyse weather-related riot instigations, Ingrid approached to let them know their car was ready. They dropped Mr and Mrs Ford-Hughes back to the Excelsior and carried on to the hotel. Any crowds, rioting or not, were nowhere to be seen.

In a drab industrial estate warehouse on the outskirts of Cologne, the local newspaper, *Die Sonne*, was starting to put together their weekly print run. Unusually for such a small outfit, they had an exciting front page story. Coming out on a Thursday, they were seldom the first print media to break a story of social unrest, because who riots on Wednesdays?

21

Thursday breakfast at the hotel was sparsely attended. Ingrid and Jörg, obviously, were the first people of the Stockwell Park Orchestra party. Ingrid was a woman of routine, and Jörg worked for a woman of routine, so that was that. He had safely stowed the instrument truck the previous day, and they were running over their forthcoming logistics, with an afternoon rehearsal and evening concert.

Erin and Charlie were there, arriving separately but gravitating towards the same table with their coffee and croissants.

'I said I'd take Ann up a coffee after breakfast,' said Erin. 'She said if she didn't have to get up for a rehearsal there's no way she'd make it.'

'Well, she *was* enjoying the river cruise,' said Charlie, laughing. 'And why not?'

'Have you seen anything of Eliot? Or Alexander?'

'No.' Charlie looked at her sharply. 'Why?'

'I just wondered how the mythical gala evening had gone, that's all.' Erin sounded defensive even to her own ears.

'You could ask Ingrid – she's over there.' Charlie nodded towards where Ingrid and Jörg's heads were bent over Ingrid's iPad.

'Best not to disturb, I reckon.' Erin ate some more croissant.

The morning was already warm. Charlie leaned back in his chair and pushed his elbows over the adjacent seat backs. 'Can we play in shorts and T-shirts tonight, do you think? It's going to get too hot for trousers and socks and all that malarkey.'

'Socks are malarkey?'

'I don't like playing with sweaty feet.'

'The flip-flop king. Stylish.'

'We could all take a dip in the river and play soaking wet. It didn't seem to do the Wagner tubas any harm last time.'

'I don't think Ingrid will stand for that again,' said Erin.

Charlie glanced over at Ingrid. 'Perhaps you're right. Oh – watch out. Here comes our gala evening expert.'

Erin turned to see Eliot walk towards the buffet. He sketched a wave in their direction and concentrated on piling his plate up and pouring coffee.

'He doesn't look too bad,' said Erin. 'Maybe the gala evening wasn't all it was cracked up to be?'

Eliot came over, sat down at their table and grinned. 'Morning.'

'You're chirpy,' said Erin.

'Erin, you're sounding more and more like Ann these days,' said Charlie.

Erin stuck her tongue out.

'God, I've missed this,' said Eliot.

Erin looked contrite. 'Sorry.'

'Never mind about that. How was the gala?' asked Charlie.

Eliot took a big gulp of coffee and arranged a pile of cheese on rye bread. 'It had minor royalty doing the compèring. And a Japanese chamber choir singing *Locus Iste*.'

Charlie and Erin looked at each other.

'He's lost it,' said Charlie.

'Bloody haven't,' said Eliot. 'There was a Countess Something von Something with a sparkly head, who was tipsy, with a husband who looked like Baron von Trapp.' He waved his hand in Ingrid's direction. 'Ask Ingrid.'

'OKaaaaay,' said Erin. 'Well, we went on the boat trip. It was great.'

'Well, we had a Japanese chamber choir,' said Eliot belligerently.

'You've said that,' said Charlie.

'They were very good,' said Eliot. 'And short. Short is good.'

'Bit racist,' said Erin.

Eliot chewed and swallowed. 'The *music*. The piece was short. Which is unusual for Bruckner.' He shook his head and smiled.

'Oh,' said Erin in a small voice.

'She's a bit tired,' whispered Charlie. 'And maybe still drunk.'

'We dropped Mr and Mrs Ford-Hughes off at *the* most sploncy hotel you've ever seen, right next to the cathedral. It was all lit up and everything. You know, coloured lights from the pavement.' Eliot waved a piece of bread at them. 'Honestly, we have to slum it here and they get a penthouse suite next to gothic spire-yness.'

Alexander walked in dressed in sports gear, looking suspiciously as if he had taken exercise. He spotted them and came over. 'Hi. You're up early. Look what I found on my run.'

He threw a newspaper down on the table between them and walked off to the buffet.

The folded front page of *Die Sonne* showed a picture of a man being pushed into the Rhine. The photograph must have been taken from a bridge, looking back towards the bank. The man had been caught mid-fall with his limbs at awkward angles as he tried to save himself, but past the point of losing his balance. There was a crowd behind the figure, full of shouting faces with bared teeth and anger written all over their gestures. Scuffles were frozen mid-punch on either side of the falling man. Several faces had bleeding noses and ripped clothes.

'Blimey,' said Eliot, pulling the paper towards himself. 'I thought David and Mrs Ford-Hughes were exaggerating. They said something about a riot last night. I didn't believe them.'

'We didn't see anything,' said Charlie. 'Mind you, we were out until after dusk. This is still daylight.'

Erin was staring at the paper. 'Oh god.'

'What?' said Eliot.

'Look. Look at the man.'

Eliot and Charlie looked. After a moment, Charlie burst out laughing.

'Fuck me, not again,' he said, shaking his head.

'It is, isn't it?' said Erin.

'Yep,' said Eliot. 'I'd recognise that rugby shirt anywhere.'

'And just as voluntarily as last time, by the looks of it,' said Charlie. 'How's your German? What does it say?'

'Um…' Eliot unfolded the paper flat and concentrated. 'Something about a disturbance in the Old Town… god, it mentions Brexit… bad language, fighting, tourist argument… "the man who started the fight ended the evening drinking"? No – "nearly *ertrunken*"… Ah, yes. Means in the river, of course. Well, they don't name him, or why he is in Cologne. That's something.'

Alexander returned with his breakfast. 'So. Judging by how calm Ingrid is over there, I don't reckon she's seen this. Do we tell her, or not?'

Eliot pinched the bridge of his nose. 'How have we been saddled with a gammon racist Brexiteer for a European tour? Why would he have even wanted to come?'

'Something to do with him owning the whole set of Wagner tubas, I think?' said Alexander. 'From what I gathered via David. They would be really expensive to hire otherwise.'

'Well, it's not worth it,' said Eliot. 'Jesus.'

'Do you think he made it back to the hotel?' said Erin. 'I mean, should we check?'

'He might need bailing out of a police station,' said Charlie.

Eliot looked over at Jörg and Ingrid again. 'Our rehearsal's not 'til two. That gives us some wiggle room if we need to, um, actively *do* anything.'

'You mean like break him out of jail?' asked Charlie.

'Whoa there, tiger,' said Erin.

'No,' said Eliot. 'If he really has been arrested that'll be above our pay grade. But, you know, we could put out feelers before… escalating the situation.' He was still looking at Jörg with a pensive expression.

Alexander followed his eyes. 'You mean ask Jörg to find out before we have to tell Ingrid?'

Eliot nodded. 'What do you reckon?'

'Jörg does look frighteningly effective at doing pretty much anything,' said Charlie. 'I mean, he's kind of skinny but he's got those springy legs. I bet he can do karate or something. It's all in the balance. Like Bruce Lee. Wiry but devastating.'

The rest of them stared at Charlie demonstrating some karate hand gestures over his breakfast plate, not bothering to suppress their giggles.

'What?' he said.

'Well,' said Erin, laughing, 'first we need to find out if Julian's asleep in his room, or all this cloak and dagger stuff is a waste of time.' She glanced at Charlie. 'Springy karate notwithstanding.'

They filed out to the lobby and approached reception.

'*Guten Morgen*,' said the man behind the desk, smiling pleasantly.

Eliot smiled back in what he hoped was a winning manner. '*Guten Morgen. Bitte würden Sie Julian Talbot anrufen? Er ist ein Freund von mir.*'

'Of course,' said the receptionist, in perfect English. He consulted a screen, picked up the receiver and dialled.

'Is my accent that bad?' whispered Eliot.

'You've got a long way to go before you catch up with Mrs Ford-Hughes,' said Charlie, and they giggled. Alexander looked perplexed.

'Last year,' said Erin. 'The *Four Last Songs*. Don't ask.'

'You don't want to know,' confirmed Eliot.

'Ah,' said Alexander, nodding. 'The Strauss she mentioned last night? Gotcha.'

The man put the phone down and shrugged at them. 'No reply. I'm sorry.'

Eliot thanked him, and they walked a little distance away from the desk. 'Now what?'

Erin looked at her watch. 'Quarter to nine. I'll take Ann some coffee. We've got until – what did the schedule say? – one o'clock until we leave for rehearsal. He's got plenty of time to turn up.'

'Maybe he's just asleep in his room?' said Charlie.

'Well, I'm going to go for a walk,' said Erin. 'See if I can get some good pics to put on the orchestra Twitter feed. If anyone wants to come along I'll meet you here in the lobby in twenty minutes.'

22

Erin and Charlie wandered together round the Old Town district, before the heat of the day really wound itself up. The streets were shaded by trees in full leaf which grew at regular intervals in the pavements, lending their humidity and lowering the temperature. Every now and then they stopped to sit on a bench and appreciate the breeze coming off the Rhine.

Erin took pictures of narrow streets with their pretty semi-circular patterned cobbles, and of the wide town squares surrounded by cafés and bars, their tables covered with cloths spreading out from the edges like wide field margins, some gathered under green umbrellas.

They stopped in front of a fountain flanked by stone friezes of what looked like elves hard at work, while Charlie read from his guidebook.

'This is the' – he stopped and squinted at the page – 'Heinzelmännchenbrunnen. I think. Blimey. The pixies are all there, look. It's the Pixie Fountain.' He nodded knowledgably.

'Yeah, I gathered,' said Erin, smiling. 'Though, to be honest, it's more of a pipe than a fountain?' She took a picture anyway. 'Come on. Let's find a café under a tree and have coffee and cake. I've seen some people with amazing cakes. We deserve cake. And I need to get these pics onto Twitter while the orchestra's still in Cologne.'

'Let's go.'

They found a café and ordered a different cake each, neither really knowing what was going to turn up but trusting that it would be delicious. Erin logged into the orchestra's account and tweeted her pictures.

'I suppose I ought to follow it too,' said Charlie, getting out his phone. 'What is it? Then I can retweet to my vast following.'

Erin laughed and told him the orchestra's Twitter handle. 'Since I've started doing this, we've gained a few hundred followers, you know. We don't need your vast following.'

'Well, if you're going to be like that.'

'No, please retweet us. We do need it. Oh, I should stick all this on Facebook too, hang on.'

Charlie laughed and tried some of his cake. 'Mmmm – god! This is delicious. Can we do an exchange? What have you got?'

Erin ate a piece of her own cake and chewed thoughtfully. 'Something orangey. Wow. Tangy. Really good.'

They each took a forkful of the other's cake and ate that too.

'Mine's nicer,' said Charlie. 'I win.'

Erin rolled her eyes, shaking her head slightly. 'Keep it. I like my orange amazingness.'

Charlie was scrolling his phone. 'There are some more pictures of Julian being chucked in on the local news pages. I can't see any mention of the orchestra or the festival, so that's something. Maybe they think he's just a bog-standard tourist. My German's not great though.'

'There's nothing on the festival hashtag on Twitter,' said Erin. 'Or from the main Bruckner Festival account. So that's good.' She scrolled a bit more. 'Ha! I see Eliot and Alexander have found their own boat trip this morning – look at Eliot's tweet.' She showed Charlie a picture from Eliot, showing him and Alexander grinning wildly, with the railings on the boat and the river behind them.

She tapped out a few messages with her thumbs. 'Noel Osmar is keeping tabs on us. He says he wishes he could come to hear our concerts this week. I've told him he could probably do with a holiday and he should come out to meet us.'

'He needs to keep Stockwell safe from thieves and ruffians for us,' said Charlie. 'Anyway, he doesn't strike me as the kind of policeman who takes holidays.'

'Maybe. Would be nice to see him, though.'

'Are you morphing into a social media type now?' asked Charlie. 'Has that temp job corrupted you? I thought Ann was training you to be a professional cellist.'

Erin grimaced. 'Yeah, she's trying. I've got to get my application for music college in by the end of October. Went to a couple of open days last spring.'

'Brilliant! Oh, so hang on. October? So it's not for this coming year?'

'No – to start September next year. *If* I get an audition. And *if* I pass it. They would let me know by Christmas.' Erin sighed. 'A lot of ifs. A lot of practice.'

Charlie looked at her sideways. 'You're not planning on leaving London, are you?'

Erin smiled. 'No. Why? Would you care?'

'Bollocks to that. You'd better not leave Stockwell Park though. We need a leader who can play all the fiddly bits.'

Erin ate some more cake. 'I promise.'

'Is Fenella going to let you keep the Strad to go to college with, then?'

'Yes, I think so. Which is pretty bloody amazing.'

'She turned out not all bad, considering,' agreed Charlie. 'Despite being the most annoying person on the planet.'

The borrowed Stradivari cello Charlie referred to was at that moment safely locked in Erin's London flat; she had brought her own on the tour. She still wasn't completely comfortable with carrying a six million dollar instrument around in everyday life. It was strictly reserved for solo work, not workaday orchestral stuff. How she came to be playing a priceless cello inherited by their former section leader, Fenella, is another story entirely.

They finished their coffee, licked their fingers to dab up the last cake crumbs, and ambled slowly back towards the hotel in time to grab a quick Halve Hahn at another brewhouse with Ann, Eliot and Alexander before the coach left for their rehearsal. They had agreed that if Julian hadn't turned up by then, it might be time to activate Jörg, if not Ingrid herself.

23

By the time they met in the lobby, several people reported the story that Julian had been spotted returning to the hotel mid-morning. Everyone seemed to have heard it second- or third-hand, and it sounded more embellished with every retelling.

Carl and Kayla were passing the story on to Ann as Erin and Charlie arrived.

'From what I heard, he looked like shite,' Carl was saying. 'Dishevelled, stank, and apparently had a shiner too.'

Kayla nodded. 'Marco said he'd heard he looked as if he'd been in a fight. I didn't believe him. Surely not again?'

'That man is trouble,' said Ann.

Charlie and Erin exchanged glances.

'Um, yeah,' said Charlie, fishing his phone out of his pocket. 'Have a look at this.' He showed them *Die Sonne*'s website, with the front page picture. 'Front page splash. Of his splash. As it were.'

'Well, at least he's turned up,' said Erin. 'Otherwise we were going to have to tell Ingrid.'

'And she would probably kill him after last time,' said Ann. 'Lucky Julian.'

'Come on, I'm starving,' said Charlie. 'Anyone seen Eliot and Alexander? Can we text them?'

'There they are,' said Erin, pointing at the pair walking in from the street. 'Let's go.'

* * *

When Ingrid counted them all onto the coach at one o'clock, nobody was missing. If she had heard about Julian's evening, she did not betray it. Julian himself boarded the coach and found a seat opposite the toilet door, having left his car in the hotel car park until the drive to Bruges the following day. People stared at his swollen eye and nudged each other.

Before Keith started his winding progress towards the Hochschule für Musik und Tanz nearly four kilometres away, Ingrid reminded them they needed their concert clothes with them, as nobody was scheduled to return to the hotel until after the performance that evening. With a gesture that could only be interpreted as a small flourish, she produced three dry cleaning bags and walked along the aisle between the seats, delivering clean concert gear upstairs to Tom and Lamar, and then finally to Julian.

He accepted his bag with a small upward nod, which could have been simply a jut of the chin, and turned to look out of the window.

Eliot leaned towards Charlie next to him and said quietly, 'He is quite breathtakingly rude.' As Ingrid returned to her seat at the front, he called out, 'Three cheers for Ingrid!' and led a raucous appreciation of her service to the orchestra. Ingrid herself went slightly pink but she looked delighted.

Their performance that evening was to be in one of the concert halls of the Hochschule. Other more prestigious

147

visiting orchestras had been allocated use of the Kölner Philharmonie: home of the Gürzenich Orchestra, one of the best in Germany. Organ recitals of Bruckner's music were being held in the magnificent – and magnificently named – Funkhaus Wallrafplatz, which also hosted orchestral and choral works in front of the huge wall of organ pipes. For a week, Cologne thrummed to Bruckner being performed in any and all venues the festival committee could book. Gräfin Friederike von Dürr had flashed her royal connections to pull in any favour she could. It may have been the first year of her Bruckner Festival, but she had grand plans for its future.

Jörg's truck was already parked when they arrived. A Hochschule member of staff met the coach and, after discussions with Ingrid while the musicians retrieved their instruments, led the orchestra through the building to the hall. Ingrid waited outside with Keith, waved Jörg off to park his truck elsewhere until after the concert, and stayed looking out for Max arriving in his van with the timpani.

'How's it going so far?' asked Keith, polishing his glasses with a hanky before wiping the sheen off his forehead with it. His tank top hadn't been seen since the start of the week. 'You look like you've got them all under control.'

'One concert down, two to go,' said Ingrid, straightening her shoulders.

'Or three nights down, three to go,' said Keith, philosophically. 'Halfway. Depends if you like counting in nights or concerts, I s'pose.'

Ingrid flicked him a smile. 'The first concert went extremely well. Musically. I am glad about that.'

Keith returned his crumpled hanky to his trouser pocket. 'Did you, er, hear about last night's little rumpus?'

'I was attending the gala evening with Mr and Mrs Ford-Hughes. There was no... rumpus there.'

Keith, hands still in his pockets, rocked back on his heels and squinted at a bird in the top of a nearby tree. 'Word is Julian didn't get his shiner just falling down the stairs after a few too many Kölsches, if you get me.'

Ingrid looked at him steadily. 'I noted the damage to his eye.'

'Well, the sooner we get him out of Cologne the better, I reckon. Just my opinion though, Ms Bauer.'

Ingrid sighed softly, almost to herself. 'Thank you, Keith. I appreciate your counsel – it is wise. And, please, call me Ingrid.'

Keith nodded to her gravely, which ended up being a small bow. He climbed back onto the coach and prepared to leave. 'I'll be back here before nine-thirty. See you later.'

Ingrid raised her hand and then looked at her watch. Max was late. She checked her phone for messages. Not for the first time, she wished she could install trackers for everyone she was supposed to be in charge of for the duration of a tour. If she wasn't allowed to insert electronic chips under their skin, at least she should be permitted a phone app.

Inside, the orchestra was setting up, appreciating the efficiency of the air conditioning. Even Pearl – who had been a few shades more rosy than normal for days despite the floatiest of garments revealing her preference for midnight blue matching underwear – was slowly returning to her original colour.

Alexander wandered over to Eliot, his horn tucked under one arm and blowing raspberries into his detached mouthpiece to warm up. 'Have you seen Julian's face?'

'Yeah. As long as it's just his eye and not his lip. Do you know? Can he play OK?'

'Think it's just the eye, yeah. Wanker.'

Eliot snorted. 'Well, let's see how it goes. If we need to, can you swap parts with him? We play the Bruckner after your Strauss anyway, so you won't knacker your lip for that. If he's struggling, he might prefer to play some low notes.'

'He won't want me to muscle in on the first part,' said Alexander.

'It's OK,' said Eliot. 'If I need to, I'll pull rank.' He looked round the hall. 'Have you seen Max yet?'

Alexander shook his head. 'Ingrid was waiting for him outside, I think. Do you want me to check?'

'No, don't worry. If Ingrid's there, all will be well.'

Outside, Ingrid was increasingly not convinced that all would be well. Max was nowhere to be seen, and not answering calls or texts. Ingrid reasoned that could be because he was currently driving towards her and couldn't take the calls. She hoped it was that.

Her phone buzzed, and she read a text from Eliot asking if Max had arrived. She replied that he had not, but she hoped he would not be long.

Just then, Max rolled round the corner at a more urgent speed than usual, and stopped with a jerk beside Ingrid. He jumped out, ran round to the back doors of the van and hastily unwound what looked like loops of string from the handle.

'Max!' called Ingrid, stepping forward to help. 'May I assist? Is everything alright?'

'No it bloody isn't!' snapped Max, then looked horrified. 'I'm so sorry, Ingrid. I didn't mean to swear at you. But I could kill those… vandals.' He went on trying to untangle the string, but getting it more knotted because he was rushing. He muttered, more to the handle than Ingrid, 'Come on, come *on*… oh for heaven's sake… there!' He flung both doors wide and leaned in to unstrap the first timp. He pulled it to the edge of the van, turned it round and said to Ingrid, 'There! Look! Look what they've done. Bastards.'

On one side of the gorgeously burnished, copper-coloured belly of the drum, there was an enormous dent.

24

It was roughly the shape of South America, and to Max it seemed to be much the same size.

'Oh no!' said Ingrid. 'Max, what happened?'

'It was those bloody kids. Sorry.' Max looked almost as appalled at his involuntary swearing in front of Ingrid as he was about the damage to his beloved drum. She waved it away and indicated he should continue. 'I mean, I guess it was the kids. Youths, I suppose. When you get to my age, they all look like kids these days.' He smiled apologetically. 'I'd seen a few of them straggling past the hotel when I got in last night – after a few beers, you know? They were yelling stuff – "Nazis out" or some such. I dunno. Apparently there was some hoo-ha down by the river yesterday evening. The guy at reception said it was to do with some of the festival musicians. I didn't see it. And then they did this!' He stroked the dent as if he could smooth it out with his hand.

Ingrid cleared her throat gently. 'Did what, exactly?'

'Legged it over the fence into the hotel car park. Broke into my van. Didn't steal anything – oh no, that would have been too obvious. You can see the timps inside the van, though, right? Through the windows. So they knew I was part of one of the orchestras. Broke the lock, unbuckled the timps and buggered off! So when I take a corner coming here, the door flies open, one timp falls out and to be honest I'm lucky the others don't follow it out onto the road. There are horns blaring all over the place, I slam on the brakes, get out into two lanes of traffic and have to fetch the timp from right in front of a lorry, pack it back in the van and hitch the doors shut at best I can with some string I found in the glove box. Bastards.' He sat down on the edge of the van floor and put his head in his hands.

Ingrid laid her hand on Max's shoulder. He was quivering. Digesting what she had heard, Ingrid was grateful she was merely dealing with a dented drum and not a multi-vehicle pile-up with casualties. She discarded that as being something Max would like to hear, in favour of, 'Are you hurt, yourself?'

'What? No. No, I'm fine. Just a bit, you know. Shaken up.'

Ingrid's phone buzzed again: another text from Eliot. She dialled him directly, thinking it was probably easier to speak.

'Eliot? Yes, Max is here. Could you please send four people outside to help wheel the timps through? I'll bring Max. Yes. I'll explain when we get there.'

* * *

The rehearsal was delayed. Four volunteers brought the timpani to the hall, while Max followed with Ingrid. He carried his high stool and set of sticks.

Eliot hurried forward when he saw them walking into the hall. 'Max! Are you OK? I've seen the timps. Crikey.'

Max raised a weary smile. 'Yes, I'm fine. It's probably playable, but we'll notice the timbre being off.' He walked over to his set of four drums and set about tuning them as best he could. Pearl rushed over to him carrying her tote bag, and over the next few minutes could be seen offering him every kind of refreshment she could produce from her stash.

Eliot turned to Ingrid. 'What happened?'

'I fear Max has been the victim of action aimed at Julian,' said Ingrid solemnly. 'I understand – I have only recently learned – that last night Julian may have been involved in… an incident similar to the one in Amsterdam. But unfortunately we were not there to, how shall I say, ameliorate it.'

'Ah,' said Eliot. 'I too had, um, heard that. I was hoping it didn't have to be taken any further. But why would Max be involved?'

'I don't know, exactly. But perhaps Julian said something about being in this orchestra, and where he was staying? Apparently they were looking for a musician staying at our hotel. And Max's van has a British registration plate.'

'Do you think they'll come back?' said Eliot, now properly worried. 'We're there tonight as well.'

Ingrid smiled. 'I shall deploy Jörg as a deterrent. He has worked for me on this basis before.'

Out of the corner of his eye, Eliot caught sight of Charlie nodding wildly, mouthing 'springy karate!' and trying to do martial art actions around his cello, much to Erin's amusement.

'Brilliant,' he said. 'Jörg's the man we need in a crisis, clearly.' He left Ingrid making arrangements with Jörg over the phone, and turned to the orchestra. 'Right, then. Are we all OK? Max?'

'I'm fine. I'll do my best, but don't be surprised if I give you a duff note every now and then.'

'I'm sure you'll be magnificent,' said Eliot. 'Now, I don't propose to bang through everything this afternoon or we'll be on our knees later. Just a few odds and ends of the Strauss, and a bar or two of *Figaro*. Then we'll spend some time ironing out the hairy corners of the Bruckner, since we are part of their festival and people will be coming along to hear it specially. So, Bruckner players, if you wouldn't mind hanging around for a few minutes, we won't be long before we get to you. Thanks.'

There was a particular moment in the Bruckner that Eliot wanted to iron out. It is a peculiarly written symphony in one – famously niche – respect. For such huge forces (he wrote for triple wind and brass, plus the extra Wagner tubas) Bruckner was very spare in his percussion writing. Max on the timpani had a normal amount of work to do, but the entire percussion section aside from him comprised one pair of cymbals and a triangle, which played for exactly one bar together. Just one bar. In the whole symphony.

Famous stories have grown up around this bar. It occurs in the second movement of four: the triangle and cymbal parts merely say that they are *tacet* (silent) for the first movement, meaning the percussionists can snooze, and *tacet* for the final two movements, meaning they can go to the pub if they can sneak off the stage without anyone noticing. The third movement is where the action is, if you call action having to count more than one hundred and seventy bars' rest before you play your single bar.

There was an additional specific issue facing Eliot, in that it had been deemed too expensive and wasteful to bring along three percussionists for the whole tour simply for two of them to play for one bar in each concert. Percussionists play multiple instruments, often leaping between them with impressive dexterity within the same piece, and even playing them simultaneously if limbs allow – for example, a triangle and a bass drum, which at a pinch can be done with one hand each. In this bar, however, the huge cymbal crash requires one cymbal in each hand, and unless someone can play triangle with their foot, a third player is required.

Flagging this problem up at a Stockwell Park Orchestra committee meeting, David suggested Pearl and Pete might be persuaded to become a trianglist and cymbalist for one bar. After all, they sat at the back of the viola section, which was near-ish to the percussion. Everybody else would be playing in that bar, but he wondered if the lack of one viola desk in a *tutti fff sempre* passage (always *fortissimo*) might not be noticed as much as the lack of triangle and cymbals in their moment of glory. Pearl and Pete agreed to try.

The Bruckner in Amsterdam had not gone entirely to plan. Pearl had marked their viola part with a combination of Post-it notes, stick-on arrows and pencil markings, indicating when she and Pete should stop playing viola and pick up the cymbals, triangle and triangle stick. She had stuck the relevant percussion bar on a flap, so at the right time she could fold it around the music stand so they could see it. Despite being only one bar, she reasoned that stress could render her and Pete unable to remember what to play.

They had put their violas down on the floor in front of them as planned, as the music around them swelled, crescendoing from an already overwhelming *fortissimo* to an *fff* marking: fifty percent more *f*. Pearl had elected to take the triangle part, owing to her fear of trapping a bosom between the cymbals. They checked with each other how many bars to count from the mark in the viola part. Pete lifted the heavy discs from their stand by his chair and sat ready, twisted round to the side, holding them out at shoulder height. His arm muscles, unfamiliar with the weight of a hefty pair of cymbals, trembled slightly like a novice attempting a yoga plank. Ann, playing cello next to him, tried not to hit him with her bowing arm and braced herself for the crash.

Eliot glanced over at them and saw they were ready. He had the rest of the orchestra to herd to a climax: absolutely everyone was playing. The flutes were shrieking up in leger-line-land, oboes too, practically bursting a vein and turning puce, and all the massed brass were giving it enough welly to make the floor shake. Eliot gathered in all four Wagner tubas half a bar before Pearl and Pete's moment. He looked at the back desk of the violas, transformed into nervous temporary percussionists. He drilled them right in the eye and gave them notice that this, *this* was their moment. Pete did his one great clash and held the vibrating cymbals out for a moment, feeling drunk with a power unknown to viola players. Pearl valiantly started her ting-a-ling, but was so overwhelmed by the moment and her enthusiasm that her overheated, sweaty fingers lost their grip on the smooth metal beater, which flew up over her head and away at some speed behind her, landing a glancing blow on Carl's knee before clattering to the floor among the legs of music stands. Luckily the noise of its landing was completely drowned out and, because of the brevity of the part, Pearl hadn't missed much out. She then looked around her in confusion, wondering where it had got to. A few bars further on, when things had calmed down and the trombones had a rest, Carl slid it towards Pearl's chair gently with his foot. Pearl by that time had picked up her viola again and was playing *pianissimo tremolando*, and so didn't notice. She never discovered how it had found its way back to her.

Eliot was keen to run over that moment a few times before that evening's concert. He knew the Bruckner aficionados in the audience would be waiting for it, and wanted it to pass off without a hitch.

He started by congratulating Pearl and Pete on their Amsterdam success. The orchestra shuffled their feet on the floor in quiet agreement while also giggling about Pearl's impromptu ballistic experiment.

Eliot tried to explain how important that bar was to those who loved Bruckner. 'It is a special bar. Let's not undermine Bruckner's subtlety of touch here – and god knows he's not known for his symphonic subtlety the rest of the time. Apparently, this bit depicts the very moment he found out about Wagner's death. You know: big shock, huge loss to music, et cetera et cetera. Whether anyone wants to be remembered by a furiously ting-a-linging triangle is neither here nor there. Personally, I feel one can over-triangle situations, but there we are.' He waited for the laughter to die down. 'The point is, tonight we'll have a roomful of people who know about this bar, what it means, and how often it gets fucked up, so let's all just run it a few times so our *marvellous* temporary percussionists are in tip-top shape. OK?'

He did a few laps round that corner, getting Pearl and Pete to change from viola to percussion and back to viola again, without dropping a cymbal or throwing a triangle beater at Carl, until they felt confident.

Eliot nodded, and finished the rehearsal. There was no more he could do.

25

A lot of the orchestra ended up in the same brewhouse near the Hochschule between the rehearsal and the concert. Even Ingrid was there, but there was general agreement that her primary role was to keep an eye on Julian so he couldn't get himself thrown into any more bodies of water before he had to play. She certainly kept a close watch on him, and sat nearest to the door.

'Is Julian OK to play, do you think?' Eliot asked Alexander. 'It sounded alright. I don't know what your section thinks?'

'Yeah he'll be fine,' said Alexander around the most enormous slice of rye bread and cheese. 'Dunno how much he can follow your beat with that eye closing up on him, but he's not a great watcher at the best of times.'

Eliot laughed and agreed.

Charlie was gazing at Ingrid by the door, his chin in his hand. 'She looks like a coiled panther,' he said. 'Ready to spring at any moment.'

'Julian's not going anywhere tonight,' said Erin.

Ann turned to Max, sitting next to her on the bench. 'So, did you find out what the hell he said last night to set those kids on your van?'

Max looked confused. 'Who?'

'Julian.'

'What did he do?' Max looked at Ann, Eliot, Erin, Alexander and Charlie in turn.

'Oh boy,' said Charlie.

'Well,' said Eliot, 'you know we fished him out of a canal in Amsterdam on Tuesday night?'

Max nodded. 'All three of them were soaked. But what's that got to do with my van?'

'Unfortunately, he appears to be your stereotypical Wagner fan,' said Eliot.

'Racist git,' added Charlie.

'Not all Wagner fans...' murmured Ann. 'But yeah, in his case...'

Alexander leaned in towards Max. 'There's a picture in a local paper of him being chucked into the river here in Cologne, last night. That kerfuffle we've been hearing about: it was Julian. Or at least, he was involved somehow. Dunno if he started it.'

'Though going on our Amsterdam experience, he probably did,' said Eliot.

Max listened open-mouthed, which was unfortunate because he hadn't swallowed all his bratwurst.

'If he mentioned he was here with our orchestra, or maybe where he was staying – I dunno, he's thick enough to boast about anything – they could have come looking for his car,' said Eliot. 'He's proud of it. Those flags!'

'Jeez, those flags,' said Ann, shaking her head.

Max chewed thoughtfully. 'I'm the only other British vehicle in that car park. And Julian's car is hidden round the corner behind Jörg's truck. Maybe they thought...'

'If only there were someone else who could play the Wagner tuba,' said Eliot, 'then we could let him sink the next time someone chucked him in a river.'

'Except he owns all the tubas,' Alexander pointed out. 'I think we're stuck with him. And if I can say that, sounding that magnanimous, after being trapped in Flag Car between London and Amsterdam, I think frankly you lot can suck it up.'

The others laughed, and agreed.

'What about your van, Max?' asked Ann. 'Can Ingrid help with fixing the lock, do you think?'

Max grinned. 'She already has. Arranged for a mobile locksmith to meet me at the hotel later, and Bob's your uncle.'

'God, she's amazing,' said Erin.

'I think she deserves a little something from us by the end of this week,' said Eliot.

* * *

They returned to the Hochschule in good time and peeled off to change in segregated rooms near the hall. Ingrid delivered Julian to the boys' room with a pointed look at David, who nodded and silently took over custody duties. She returned to the main foyer, not requiring a change of clothes herself because she was never not on duty and dressed appropriately.

Mr and Mrs Ford-Hughes were among the first audience to arrive: he stalwart and steady; she flittering around with delight, tethered to his arm. She wore an entirely new outfit – another long dress, this time in bright yellow, with matching feather fascinator and sparkly shoes and bag. She looked like a large Bruckner-loving bird of paradise, bobbing and displaying. The capacity requirements of the Ford-Hughes luggage set were becoming ever more apparent.

Ingrid moved to greet them in the foyer. 'Good evening to you both. You are looking quite splendid tonight, Mrs Ford-Hughes.'

Mr Ford-Hughes amplified the compliment, lengthening the arm she was attached to so as to direct all attention at his wife, gesturing at her with such pride that she batted her lashes coquettishly.

'I think the Schneiders said they were coming,' she said. 'Have you seen them?'

'Not yet, but you are early,' said Ingrid. 'And I believe the festival director herself will be in attendance, Gräfin Friederike von Dürr.'

Mrs Ford-Hughes's eyes widened, and she tried to repeat 'Gräfin Friederike von Dürr' in the hushed tones of one honoured to be graced with the presence of minor royalty, but her Arkansas accent, which had been so helpful in navigating the umlauts and consonant clashes of Strauss's *Four Last Songs* the year before, presented her with its traditional obstacle. She made 'von Dürr' sound more like a fondue.

They swept into the hall down to their customary front-row seat, and slowly the rest of the audience arrived, shown to the hall by Hochschule staff. The Schneiders walked through the foyer greeting the staff with great friendliness as a sort of warm-up act for the real celebrity audience to follow. Gräfin Friederike von Dürr did indeed arrive with her husband, accepting the formal bows and bobbed curtseys with dignified pleasure. They joined the Ford-Hugheses and Schneiders at the front. Yellow feathers could be seen upping their metronome tempo from *allegro* to *presto* with excitement at their royal proximity.

Eliot marshalled the orchestra ready to go on five minutes before their scheduled start time. He peeked round the wings to have a look at the audience.

'How's it looking?' asked Carl.

'Pretty much full to capacity. There's a lot of sparkle happening on the front row.'

Charlie, who had poked his head out after Eliot, snorted with laughter. 'It's heaving. And Mrs Ford-Hughes seems to be dressed in custard.'

'Custard?' said Erin, from behind Carl.

'You'll see in a minute,' said Charlie.

'I believe the correct fabric colour is "mustard",' said Eliot. 'Honestly.'

'No, definitely custard,' said Charlie. 'You know – the really radioactive glowing stuff you get when you make it with Birds powder out of a tin.'

'You two can start your food-fashion crossover programme later,' said Ann. 'Are we going on?'

'Sorry, yes,' said Eliot, laughing. 'After you.'

They filed onto the stage to warm applause, followed as usual by Richard who coordinated their tuning to Gwynneth's oboe.

Eliot turned to Alexander, who had joined them in the wings, warming up his horn with silent breaths. 'See you in five minutes. All set?'

'Sure,' said Alexander.

'I hope Julian and the other Wagner tubas stay on site until the Bruckner this time.'

Alexander grinned. 'I saw Ingrid come backstage just now and take up position outside the men's changing room. They'll be there. See you after the Mozart.'

A hush fell after the orchestra had tuned. Eliot stepped out to his own applause, and started the evening with *Figaro*.

26

Alexander played his Strauss just as superbly as he had in Amsterdam a couple of days earlier. His easy charm and relaxed posture on stage radiated such enthusiasm the audience felt it and were drawn in. The eerie calm of the slow movement worked its magic. Eliot's trick of hypnotising Brian and Amber into synchronised flute hopping was again bizarrely successful, and by the end of the piece Alexander had the entire audience under his spell, musically and otherwise. They erupted into whoops of appreciation along with deafening applause.

Mrs Ford-Hughes's yellow feathers were all aquiver as she turned to Jutta Schneider on one side and Friederike von Dürr on the other, agreeing yes Alexander was marvellous and accepting their gushing praise on behalf of her orchestra. For an audience who had primarily come along for the Bruckner, they were taking to Strauss with striking enthusiasm. There was no control experiment, so it was unclear whether *any* soloist would have garnered the same reaction, but having a soloist with the charisma – and frankly athleticism – of Chris Hemsworth's Thor wouldn't have hindered Alexander's effect. Several ladies fanned themselves, assuring their husbands that yes it was a warm evening but they were feeling very well thank you, never better.

Eliot walked offstage with Alexander, after telling the audience there would be a short interval before the orchestra rearranged itself into Bruckner formation. This news was received with a ripple of anticipation, and a low buzz of conversation swelled as the orchestra filed offstage. A couple of Hochschule staff started to serve drinks at the back of the hall.

Eliot and Alexander walked to the men's changing room. Ingrid was still there on a seat in the corridor: she rose as they approached.

'That sounded excellent.'

'Thank you,' said Eliot. 'All down to our fabulous soloist here, of course. Thank you for standing guard – I assume everyone is still present?'

Ingrid smiled. 'No one has left the room.'

Alexander went in to swap his horn for a Wagner tuba, and in a moment the corridor was filled with an orchestra milling about holding their instruments, passing the time during an interval which wasn't really long enough to do anything else in. Some who might have been tempted to blag a glass of wine in the hall were kept in check by Ingrid's presence.

A short while later Alexander filed out of the changing room with the other three Wagner tuba players, plus all the trombones and other extra brass. Eliot nodded as they walked past. Tracie joined them carrying the triangle and its beater along with her trombone, and the two cymbals and their stand were shared one each between Carl, another trombone player and Leroy, the tuba player. They had been asked to perform these minor stage manager duties because they sat the closest to the back of the violas and could pass them to Pearl and Pete with the least fuss.

Carl winked at Eliot, muttering, 'Nobody AWOL this time,' and followed the rest of them out onto the stage.

'Are you going round the front to listen?' Eliot asked Ingrid.

'Not tonight. I'll liaise with Jörg and Keith to ensure they are both in position when we finish. I imagine I'll be able to hear it from anywhere in the building, in any case.'

The sound of heavy brass enthusiastically tuning up drifted along the corridor. Eliot grinned. 'Are you saying they can't play quietly?'

'Good luck,' said Ingrid, smiling.

Eliot walked out to conduct another hour and ten minutes of Bruckner. Even in the hall's air-conditioned temperature he knew he would lose a lot of fluid by the time he'd finished.

The first movement went well, ending with the kind of *fortissimo* string scrubbing, pointed brass chords and shrieking sustained wind parts that most composers save for the end of a whole symphony, rather than just the first of four movements. Eliot brought them off and put his arms down to give the players a short breather before starting the second movement. There was a frisson of shuffling around the audience as Alexander and the other Wagner tuba players lifted their instruments: the first time they were played in the piece. Eliot looked over at Pearl and Pete to check they remembered this was their hybrid movement, albeit in a few hundred bars. They both nodded.

The second movement, *Adagio*, started in its melancholy way, with the Wagner tubas adding their mournful harmonies to the strings. Julian managed to keep his good eye open and trained on Eliot, and all in all the section held together well. They worked their way deeper into the movement, with gorgeous string interludes sounding more lush than usual because Bruckner kept them in their lower register. Slowly, inexorably, the texture built, in ebbs and flows, still with the lazy pulse but increasingly having more notes to play within each beat, giving the whole effect more purpose. Bruckner managed to do this by alternating slow sections with four beats in a bar and quicker ones with three beats. Some players liken playing Bruckner to living in Groundhog Day. Some say it is a tantric experience. These two groups rarely concur.

By the third time the orchestra had circled back to this slow, four-in-a-bar motion after the brisker three-in-a-bar, the usual *sehr langsam* (very slow) marking was joined by *hervortretend* (pronounced or prominent) for the Wagner tubas, second violins and violas, who all had the repeat of the slow phrase that started off the whole movement. Underneath that, the first violins were given sextuplets, which weren't very fast given the glacial beat. Each set of six notes was a rising motif, but they were instructed to play *In gleicher Stärke, ohne Anschwellung* (in the same strength, without swelling). They were not allowed to *bulge*. With the number of accidentals Bruckner threw into these scales including double sharps, naturals and flats – in a key signature that already sported four sharps – the violins could have been forgiven for allowing themselves a small bulge now and then as a dopamine hit, but *nein. Verboten.*

From this point, Pearl and Pete had twenty bars until they became percussionists. They kept going with the violas for a while, but started sitting more upright in their seats as adrenaline began to flood their bloodstreams. They put down their violas and readied themselves with triangle and cymbals.

Four and a half bars before their entry, the whole woodwind section came in to join the strings and brass in a *fortissimo* chord. The violins jumped up high on their E string and for the first time started at the top of their scale and descended, instead of their usual climbing motion. One might be forgiven for thinking this was the climax, but Bruckner was wily and not to be rushed.

Out of the corner of his eye, Eliot noticed Pearl's head bobbing up and down. He saw the triangle in her hand and wondered what was going on. Pete started bending down as well, searching for something, and they appeared to be mouthing things to each other in increasing panic. Eliot steered the huge orchestral sound steadily on, drawing out a *crescendo* that everyone knew had only one destination.

With two bars to go, Pearl leaned under her chair and unclipped her handbag which always went everywhere with her, even onto a concert stage. She rootled around inside for a second, then straightened just as the Wagner tubas came in again two beats before the great triangle moment. She beamed at Pete, and then at Eliot, and right on time, as Pete clashed the cymbals next to her, she dinged the billy-o out of her triangle for its minim of glory with her emergency travelling teaspoon.

27

Keith had the coach ready by the kerb on Friday morning, engine off and door open before anyone emerged from the hotel. It wasn't even ten o'clock and he was already drinking his second coffee: up early despite his late night transporting the orchestra after their concert. Keith was a natural lark, not an owl. Tours burned the candle at both ends for him, but he loved his job, and could relax in his allotment when he got home, put his feet up in the evenings with a cocoa and reruns of *Morse* and be in bed by nine. This week, Note Perfect Tours needed his overtime, and for Ingrid he was willing. He sipped his coffee through the hole in the lid of his battered insulated travel mug, and waited.

It had been a funny old trip back from the centre of town the night before, he thought. First off it had taken them ages to get themselves out of the venue on account of all the milling around with local dignitaries. Even when the musicians had given their instruments to Jörg, and he had packed them in the truck to his own satisfaction, Mrs Ford-Hughes had held everyone up by hanging on to Eliot and Alexander to present them around her new friends. Quite the celebrities, apparently. Rubbing shoulders with a princess or something, he'd heard. Anyway, once they were away, there was another raucous round of cheering for Pearl: something to do with saving the evening with a teaspoon. Keith chuckled to himself and shook his head. Musicians: daft as a brush, the lot of 'em, but a cheery lot.

Ingrid was first out of the hotel, wheeling her suitcase behind her and taking the curved slope down to the pavement rather than the steps. Her other arm cradled her clipboard.

'Good morning, Keith,' she said, collapsing her case handle and clicking it in to place. 'Are you well?'

Keith left his coffee in its cup-holder and hurried to stow Ingrid's case in the hold for her. 'Yes, thank you, Ingrid. Never better. And yourself?'

'Yes, thank you. And now we are, I believe, what you call on the home straight.'

'Let's not count our chickens,' said Keith, smiling. 'Not with this lot.'

Max was next to emerge. He walked down the steps to Ingrid and fished in a pocket for his phone. 'Morning, Ingrid. Thanks so much again for getting that locksmith out last night. I went round to check earlier and it all seems fine in the car park this morning.'

'I'm very glad,' said Ingrid. 'I know Jörg was keeping an eye out.'

'I'll double-check my van before I set off, though.' Max laughed nervously. 'Could you give me the details of tonight's hotel in Bruges? I'll stick it in my phone for the satnav.'

'Of course.'

While they were bending over Max's phone, other musicians began to make their way out of the hotel in varying states of alertness, carrying or wheeling bags. Ann, holding her own travel mug which she had filled at the breakfast buffet, squinted at the cloudless sky and pulled her sunglasses down from the top of her head.

Ingrid and Keith between them noted who was there and loaded their bags. Mr and Mrs Ford-Hughes arrived in a taxi, which stopped conveniently close to the open doors of the coach hold so Keith didn't have too far to carry their luggage. While he was doing this, Mrs Ford-Hughes practically ran over to Ingrid and greeted her with vastly more enthusiasm than any of the musicians had shown so far that morning.

'Ingrid, honey! I just wanted to tell you how successful our little concert was yesterday. Oh my! The Schneiders and the Fondues were *so* appreciative – they said if we ever wanna bring our outfit over again, they'd be only too happy to arrange something! Mr Ford-Hughes and I went out for a nightcap with them after the show. *What* a delightful place Cologne is! Who knew?'

Ingrid bore the onslaught of relentless excitement, geographical ignorance and mispronunciation stoically, her pen motionless above the clipboard. 'That is wonderful news. I'm pleased the evening went well.'

'Oh, more than well, Ingrid! So much more than well! Now, I must tell Eliot about it, and Alexander of course too. Are they down yet? Are they on the coach?'

Without waiting for an answer, Mrs Ford-Hughes bustled up the coach steps and could soon be heard repeating the glowing reviews to various people inside. Ingrid saw Ann turn her head towards her through the coach window by her seat and drink her coffee steadily. Their eyes met, and both women smiled. Each was, in their own way, grateful for the Ford-Hugheses' enthusiasm, but neither needed it in their faces at this time in the morning.

Julian was one of the last down. The colour of the bruising around his eye was really starting to come through and, although it was clearly getting better, it looked much worse. He was, improbably, wearing yet another rugby shirt over his shorts. This time it was England replica kit.

Ingrid ticked him off her list and looked closely at his face. 'Would you like any painkillers? Are you safe to drive, do you think?'

'Right as rain, thank you,' said Julian, sounding remarkably cheerful himself. 'Pop me over the hotel details by text, there's a love, and I'll get myself there.' And with that, he sauntered towards the hotel car park, pulling his case behind him.

'He looks suspiciously chipper,' said Erin to Charlie, as they were both about to climb onto the coach. 'What's going on?'

'Well he can't be buggering off with the Wagner tubas,' said Charlie, 'cos Jörg's got them in his truck. Guarded by springy karate. Don't look at me like that. You know it's true.'

'Hmm. I don't trust him.'

'Wise. Still, let's just be grateful that we don't have to see him until our rehearsal tomorrow afternoon.' Charlie reached the top of the steps in the coach and had to stop because the aisle was blocked. 'Oh, Mrs Ford-Hughes! Hello. How lovely. You smell delightful this morning. Is it? Well, I like it very much.'

They managed to negotiate past the Chanel No. 5 catchment area and settled in next to Ann and Eliot, as before. The last few stragglers arrived, Keith slammed the hold doors shut, swung himself into the driving seat and switched on his microphone, glancing up at the mirror that showed him the top deck.

'Morning all. Usual drill. It's around three hundred and fifteen kilometres to Bruges, which is about three hours forty minutes' driving time. Who wants lunch on the way?'

There were cheers of support for lunch.

'Right you are. If that's OK with you, Ingrid?' Ingrid nodded, smiling. 'Lunch stop it is. And what do I want you to do there?'

'Go to the toilet!' everyone shouted.

'And what do I *not* want you to do in here?'

'Go to the toilet!'

'Cracking. Let's go.'

Keith clicked the mic back in its holder and smiled. He did love his job.

28

Their hotel in Bruges was not as boxlike as the one in Cologne: right in the buzzing Steenstraat Quarter next to the Concertgebouw.

While their luggage was being unloaded, Eliot wandered over the road and leaned on a wide brick wall.

'Look, we're even right next to a canal!' he shouted, looking down at the water. There were some shallow steps on each side leading down to the water's edge. People were scattered about on them, sitting in the sunshine. 'That's what you need in Bruges. Canals.'

Tracie ran over to see, and jumped up on the wall.

'Tracie Scott don't you dare!' called Kayla from by the coach. 'I've got you this far without either losing or injuring you. Get down.'

'Awwww,' said Tracie, and pretended to overbalance before jumping lightly down next to Eliot.

'Glad you did that,' he said, 'or we'd have been in *Titanic* territory when Jack has to threaten to jump in after Rose if she throws herself off the back. And I don't think Ingrid wants to have to clean any more clothes.'

'Is that another old person's thing?' said Tracie, grinning.

'What? No. It's not that old… oh hang on. Yep, it came out before you were born. Oh god. I *am* old.'

Tracie laughed and ran back to get her bag from Kayla.

Eliot walked back after her. 'How she can run in this heat is beyond me.'

'Right,' said Charlie, picking his bag up. 'It's three-thirty. Anyone who wants a wander round Bruges, meet me here in ten minutes. There's loads to see.'

'But is there a chocolate museum?' said Ann, laughing.

'Why yes, Ann, there most certainly is. Do not doubt me.'

'Of course,' said Eliot. 'We only tour to cities with chocolate museums. Have you managed to see any yet?'

'Well, no,' said Charlie. 'There's been other cultural stuff to do.'

'Like drinking beer,' said Ann. 'I'm in. Ten minutes, you say?'

'Yep,' said Charlie. 'And funny you should say that: apparently we can do a chocolate *AND* beer walking tour if you like?'

'Maybe not today,' said Ann, laughing. 'But I'll meet you down here in ten.'

'Me too,' said Eliot.

'And me,' said Erin.

A few others were interested, so there was quite a gaggle of them who eventually set off with Charlie a few minutes later. They wandered down the narrow cobbled streets, crossing over canals and turning corners to discover a hidden square with cafés and groups of people enjoying the late afternoon sunshine with a cold drink.

'God, this is a pretty place,' said Erin. 'So… curvy and old.'

'Don't talk about Ann like that,' said Carl.

'Oi!' called Ann from the back of the group. 'Rude.'

'Three and a half hours by train from London,' said Charlie. 'We should come back and have a proper look round.'

'Blimey – that's less time than London to Glasgow,' said Alexander.

'Let's make the most of it before the Brexit faff,' said Ann.

There was a chorus of groans and shouts of 'Don't mention the B-word,' and 'Forfeit!'

'I'm allowed to be cross still,' said Ann.

'I've got *more* cross,' said Kayla. 'Didn't think that was possible, but it apparently is.'

'It's funny, you know,' said Eliot. 'There's Julian, with all his flags and patriotism—'

'And wankiness,' said Charlie.

'And wankiness,' agreed Eliot. 'But he's happy to play Mozart and Strauss and Bruckner, and drink delicious continental beers and probably eat delicious continental cheeses—'

'And fall in continental canals and rivers,' said Charlie.

Eliot laughed, but continued with his point. 'It's a very cherry-picked sort of philosophy, that's all I'm saying.'

'Do you think he should refuse to play anything except Vaughan Williams, Britten and Holst, then?' asked Ann.

'Oh god no,' said Carl. 'Holst sounds far too foreign.'

They laughed, but with an edge of sadness.

Neema looked particularly thoughtful. 'You know, he's been sitting right behind me all week, and I don't think he's spoken to me once. Maybe *I'm* too foreign for him.'

Alexander, walking next to her, put his arm round her shoulders for a few steps in a commiserating hug. 'He is, as Charlie so perfectly put it, a complete wanker. I'm sorry.'

They turned off the square and into a very narrow road, shaded by the high wall of a church on its western side that cut off the afternoon sun. A heavy oak door was recessed back from the street, and on a whim, Ann tried the latch. It opened. She turned, raised her eyebrows and entered. The rest of them followed her in.

Inside, the atmosphere was cool and heavily tinged with incense. Shafts of sunlight looked almost solid as they slanted down from high windows, through dust and thick religious air. It was a huge space: deceptively deep from the width of its wall on the road. They walked further in, gazing up at the vaulted brick ceiling high above them.

'Wow!' breathed Eliot.

'This is a nice discovery,' said Ann. 'I don't do religion, but I'm a sucker for old churches.'

'Quite right too,' said Eliot.

'Bet it's got a brilliant acoustic,' said Alexander. He raised his face to the high wall opposite and sang the very opening phrase of the horn solo of Bach's *Brandenburg Concerto No. 1*, very loudly in falsetto.

The sound rang round the space and hung there for a moment before decaying back into silence.

'I was right,' said Alexander, smiling.

'Love that piece,' said Neema.

'Well, of course – it does have a fabulous horn duet,' agreed Alexander. 'I'm doing it next week. It was probably in my head under all that Strauss.'

'I can't sing the second part, or I'd join you,' said Neema. 'It bounces around all over the place. Playing's easier.'

Alexander bit his cheek thoughtfully. 'Well, there's an idea.' He looked round at the musicians who were there. 'What have we got? You and me: two horns. There's Erin, Charlie and Ann: three cellos. Kayla: bass. Carl: no use whatsoever, sorry mate. Violins… we can always find violins. And violas. What else? Bassoon, and oboes.'

Eliot shook his head at him. 'Harpsichord? And you need three oboes, if you're thinking what I'm thinking. We've only brought two. *And* we don't have the parts.'

'Aha!' cried Alexander. 'It just so happens I've got the full set stashed down the side of my horn case for next week. Forgot to take them out. Wouldn't it be great in here?'

'And the missing oboe?' said Eliot.

'Pfft. Can't we get Amber to play it on the flute or something? It's all the same kind of pitch, isn't it?'

Eliot laughed. 'More or less, I suppose. If you're not going for authenticity. And you can forget about the *violino piccolo* too – you'll have to get a violin to do it.'

'What are you plotting?' said Ann, wandering back from where she had been inspecting the altar.

Eliot looked at her seriously. 'I think Alexander wants to do a Brandenburg from scratch. Without some of the instruments.'

'What a brilliant idea!' said Erin. 'We can play German music in a Belgian church and say bollocks to Brexit and we love it here and please don't blame us!'

'Well, that's a lot to put on an unrehearsed piece before we've even found the players to do it,' laughed Alexander, 'but it *is* a brilliant idea. Thank you.'

'Don't you think we ought to ask permission?' said Kayla. 'I mean, we did just wander in off the street. They might have plans.'

'There was a kind of service timetable over there,' said Ann, pointing to a table by a door on the opposite side of the church. 'I'll have a look.'

She returned to report that they seemed to hold Mass every morning and a lot happened on Sundays, but Friday evenings didn't seem to be pencilled in for organised God.

'Right then,' said Eliot. 'We just have to hope it's still unlocked when we get back with our instruments. Speaking of which, how are we going to get them from Jörg?'

'Don't you have Ingrid's number?' asked Erin. 'She'd be able to help, I'm sure.'

They walked back to the hotel while Eliot called Ingrid to plead for her organisational magic for their off-grid surprise, and Charlie marked the location of the church on his phone app so they would be able to find it again later.

'Electronic breadcrumbs,' he said, tapping his head. 'It's not far to walk, but with these twisty streets we could end up anywhere.'

'Glad we've got you on the case,' said Erin, absentmindedly. She was busy putting out a message on the orchestra's WhatsApp asking anyone who wanted to come and play an instant Brandenburg to meet them at the hotel reception in half an hour.

'Can we get Courtney to play bassoon?' asked Kayla. 'Rafael is very nice, but he's a bit—'

'Scary?' said Erin.

'Well, he does make me nervous,' said Kayla.

'Rafael doesn't like solos anyway,' said Eliot. 'He won't want to do this. Let's message Courtney separately and persuade her. And we'll need both oboes and Amber too.'

'I'll text Gwynneth,' said Carl. 'We've probably got another oboe player somewhere, but they won't have brought their second instrument with them, I guess.'

'Nobody's going to mind,' said Alexander. 'This is just us having fun. There won't be an audience.'

They got back to the hotel to find Ingrid had persuaded Jörg to unlock his truck in the underground car park accessed around the side of the hotel. She was in a buoyant mood, surrounded by musicians who were far more keen to go and play something new and unofficial than they ever were to attend a scheduled rehearsal.

'Do you want to come along, Ingrid?' said Eliot. 'You can be one of our human music stands, if you like. Jörg could come too.'

She smiled. 'I shall. I love Bach. But I'm sure we can use some of the orchestra stands, if they are not too heavy to carry? Jörg has them in his truck also.'

'Ingrid,' said Eliot, beaming, 'you are a marvel.'

29

Alexander and Eliot led the stream of chattering people back to the church, being given shouted directions by Charlie further back if they looked as if they were going astray. They drew curious glances from the drinkers at the square's café tables as they snaked through carrying their various instrument cases. The cellos were of course the most recognisable shape and got more people pointing at them and speculating, as well as Kayla's bass which she wheeled on its collapsible trolley. Carl walked next to her carrying a crate of stands as if it weighed nothing.

The church door was still unlocked. They trooped inside and those people who hadn't seen it before exclaimed to Alexander that it was perfect. They spread out into the church and began getting out their instruments.

'Do you want me to wave or just listen?' asked Eliot.

'Waving would be brilliant, if you want,' said Alexander. 'I didn't like to ask, since it's your day off.'

'It's your day off too. If your lip can take it, so can my arms.'

Alexander opened his horn case, unzipped the side pocket and took out the parts, handing them round. 'We'll just have to share them out however we can. Who wants the *violino piccolo* part? Richard? Brilliant. Then we've got some firsts... and seconds... and violas. Courtney – here's the bassoon part. And Gwynneth – you've got three oboe parts and Amber: you can sort it out between yourselves! Here – Erin, cello part for you. Brilliant, we've got three of you! And bass part for Kayla.'

He grinned, looking around at everyone busily putting up music stands and sorting their parts. 'This is fantastic! Thanks so much for joining in. Here, Neema. Horn part for you.'

'Can we move these chairs, do you think?' said Erin, pointing to the front row in the nave. 'We'll put them back, obviously.'

'Don't see why not,' said Eliot. 'I mean, we've barged in here without asking anyway. In for a penny.'

He helped Erin, Charlie and Ann sort how they could have enough room to bow and see their single part at the same time.

'I'll need you to be as crisp as can be, you lot,' Eliot said to them and Kayla. 'You'll have to imagine the plinkiest-plonkiest harpsichord right behind you, and somehow pass it on. In fact... Ingrid?' He turned to where she was standing halfway down the aisle. 'If you could walk up and down the flagstones in time, your heels could add the clack to our continuo? Sorry.' He laughed, gesturing his apology to Ingrid, who took it with good humour.

Everyone else could play standing up, and arranged themselves in a rough semicircle so they could see each other. Gwynneth gave an A and they all tuned.

'OK,' said Eliot. 'This whole thing only lasts about fifteen minutes. Are we ready for our impromptu, non-authentic, added-flute, no-harpsichord Brandenburg? You nutters. Let's go.'

182

The infectious sound of the First Brandenburg Concerto filled the church. It doesn't ease into itself: right from the start it bounces into its rhythm of irrepressible good cheer. Eliot put his weight on one leg and gently leaned on the beat as if he had an invisible dancing partner. Maybe it was because most people were standing up and could move more to the music, or because this was an unexpected ensemble, or because it was the first time they had read it through together, but everyone had more energy and synchronisation than Eliot was used to hearing. But then, he had long believed anyone who could stay still while listening to Bach was already dead inside.

The violins and violas bent forward and dipped their knees, leaned back and turned to each other, passing the melody along the line like a current flowing through kelp. Alexander and Neema sounded as though they were two halves of the same instrument: moving perfectly together in Bach's geometry. Amber's flute didn't sound like an oboe, it was true, but she meshed with the other two as a trio that Bach surely wouldn't have minded.

At the end of the first movement, the horn triplets rang out against the duplet strings, signalling what Alexander and Neema were about to unleash further into the piece. They grinned at each other and tucked their horn bells under their arms as the second movement started without them: an *Adagio* where Gwynneth drew out her beautiful sustained arc of melody before handing it over to Richard's solo violin, playing the part written for the *violino piccolo* baroque instrument, which was smaller and tuned higher than a regular violin. They weaved a duet between their different instruments, often playing the same melody at staggered intervals so it sounded as if it were dragging its own shadow alongside itself.

Alexander tipped the water out of a valve tube and readied himself for the next movement. It exploded out of the calm of the previous one with another dancing pulse, and Alexander and Neema played their harmonies again with absolute synchronicity. Each phrase seemed to be higher than the last, and Alexander's face tightened as he moved the air through his lips at ever greater pressure. A trickle of sweat ran down one temple. Eyebrows working overtime, he seemed to float his notes down on top of the texture rather than strain to force them up, and Eliot grinned at him, enjoying watching his apparently effortless talent. One phrase of Alexander's wound its way up, through Richard's virtuosic violin playing, to a high trill that he had to control through lips alone. No valve help at all: he flipped the note up a tone and down again unbelievably fast, for what seemed like a week. He played it with his eyes closed for concentration, and when he opened them he saw Eliot's awestruck grin. He waggled his eyebrows in acknowledgement. The accompanying string players were all looking at each other and smiling too, leaning into the harmonies. It was at times like this, Eliot thought, that he knew why his life was in music and always would be.

The final movement was split into a suite of seven dances that sounded as if someone on *Countdown* were choosing what letters to have: Minuet, Trio, Minuet, Polacca, Minuet, Trio, and finally another Minuet please, Rachel. Each one foregrounded different combinations of instruments, and it was the penultimate one of the whole lot, a Trio, that Alexander had sung earlier that afternoon. He grinned at Neema just before they started, and then off they went. Two horns pinging around to the top of their range with oboes bouncing about like excited space hoppers below them: Alexander and Neema were matching each other note for note, leap for leap. Every now and then Alexander had a ridiculous stretch up to a high note that boinged out of the texture and then fell back into it again. It is one of the most irrepressibly optimistic pieces Bach ever wrote.

Everyone reprised the final Minuet afterwards, and the whole thing was over less than twenty minutes after they started. To Eliot's shock, the church was suddenly rocked by applause. Loud whoops and cheers came from all directions. He turned to see the entire nave packed with people, many angling phones in front of them to film what was going on. Some were still holding the drinks they had picked up from their café tables when they had followed the sound of the music from the square. Ingrid was standing near the front, also filming, and gave him a huge smile and a thumbs-up.

Eliot laughed, bowed, and moved to one side behind the cellos, clapping the musicians himself, who then awkwardly bowed themselves. Richard, Neema, Alexander and the oboe/flute trio led by Gwynneth got a special whoop each, as they were pointed at by Eliot.

'When did they come in?' he asked Ann. 'You might have said.'

'They just sort of drifted in when we started to play,' she said. 'I think they enjoyed it, don't you?'

The applause was still going on, and it wasn't until the players themselves began to move towards their instrument cases to put things away that it died down. Some people came up to the players to ask who they were and why they were playing in the church. Ingrid, ever prepared, handed out some leaflets for their concert the next day, which were taken with enthusiasm and exclaimed over.

Charlie leaned in to Erin as they were putting their cellos back in their cases. 'You wanna ask Ingrid to send you over that video and get it online. Would be quite a coup for orchestra publicity, don't you think?'

'That's not a bad idea.'

'You'll need a hashtag. *#StockwellParkBruges* or something.'

'Or something.'

'Well, I don't know. You're the bloody expert. Look – go and ask her now.'

Ingrid was delighted to send the video to Erin and, while they were sorting that, Alexander collected the parts and Carl followed him folding up the stands.

'Top work, mate,' said Carl.

'Thanks. Sorry about no trombones.'

'Yeah, well. A failing, obviously. But nice to listen to anyway.'

'I think we all deserve a drink. Let's get these instruments back to Jörg and crack on.'

'Now you're talking.'

They tidied up, shut the church door carefully and wandered back to the hotel in a loose, straggly line, all chatting and laughing. As they walked through the square, a second round of applause followed them from their erstwhile audience who were now sitting back at their tables in the late sunshine.

'It's like a bloody guard of honour,' said Ann.

Eliot beamed and waved. 'I think it's lovely. Look at this, Alexander! You did this!'

Alexander nodded at the quite extraordinary sight of people all round the square grinning and clapping them as they walked past. 'Well, I had to have some excuse to practise it for next week.' He gave one last wave as he reached the far corner of the square, then turned towards the hotel.

30

Around the same time as they had finished playing Bach and were thinking of a drink before dinner, Julian Talbot was parking his ancient car in the centre of Brussels, a hundred kilometres away. He had detoured via Maastricht, and indeed was on a route of entirely his own making. He had always planned his itinerary this way, and would have been willing to take Alexander, Tom and Lamar along with him, but in fact their absence made his Friday peregrination simpler. Persuading people always took such time and energy. He took his phone out of a pocket and replayed part of the last video.

A small, off-centre, black-eyed Julian squinted out of the screen, the shadow of his phone and selfie stick lying diagonally over his chest. He stood on a bridge over a flowing river. His tinny voice squawked out of the phone. 'Greetings, fellow patriots! Excuse my appearance, but it was an injury inflicted in righteous battle and thus something I wear with pride. Where might I be today? Well, behind me, you can see the government building of Limburg Province. This bridge leads to it over the River Maas. Yes, you've guessed. I'm in Maastricht, or as we know it, the First Circle of Hell! [*pause for helpless laughter at own joke and a final snort]* I stand here, resplendent in my ENGLAND shirt, in front of the…'

Inside the car, Julian nodded to himself, turned off the video and straightened his shoulders. Time for the next phase. He got out and strode towards the line of flagpoles outside the European Parliament building, stopping only when he reached the British flag on the end of the row, beside a mini-roundabout. It, along with all the other flags, hung limp in the oppressive heatwave, but seemed to droop ever so slightly further down as Julian approached, almost as if it knew what it was about to be forced to endure.

Julian stopped next to the pole, extended his selfie stick and fiddled with his phone. He put a foot up on one of the low bollards edging the pavement, in what he hoped was an alpha male, territorial stance, as though posing over a vanquished enemy. He was managing to manspread while still standing. He put one hand on his raised knee, pushing his leg ever wider, checked his entire body was in frame together with the flag at the top of the pole, failed to note that the view up the leg of his shorts revealed more than perhaps he imagined, and started recording.

Over the previous few years, Julian had built up a small but dedicated online following of like-minded men and boys, who lapped up his frothing views on a depressingly predictable range of subjects. Brexit had been their coalescing joy, and Julian had jumped at the chance of a subsidised jaunt to Europe in the final few months of Britain's subservience. The orchestra tour had enabled him to record his triumphant thoughts for posterity from a number of major landmarks on the way.

This segment of video was the pinnacle of his series. He threw everything into it: gesticulations, vocal range, pelvic thrusting. He was concentrating so much he didn't notice a small knot of people stopping to watch him from further up the road. As his speech veered from merely distasteful to definitively racist, they grew restless, muttering to each other. A couple of them threw out some heckles, and then, as Julian was taking no notice, some marshmallows from the pack they were sharing. A couple of the pink and white squashy balls hit Julian softly on the head.

He looked round and saw half a dozen people frowning at him. They were youngish men, clearly all knew each other, and were utterly unafraid. This was their city.

'Fuck off,' Julian shouted at them, picking up one of the fallen marshmallows and chucking it back. It fell to the ground before it had made it halfway, and the group of onlookers laughed. Around them, other people hurried or drifted through, perhaps on their way to the nearby station or for an early evening stroll round the lake in Parc Léopold. Most took no notice of Julian.

He tried to continue with his video, but as soon as he resumed his speech, so did the heckling. He raised his voice to be heard over them. So did they, and their numbers were growing.

The situation escalated in a way sadly all too familiar to Julian, but he never seemed to learn from past experiences. It was as if he enjoyed this part, like a performance artist. He was shouting now. There were some chants of 'Nazi out' from onlookers, and as soon as Julian's aggressive body language tipped over into an actual punch, the collective restraint that had been holding the small crowd immobile disintegrated, and they threw themselves on him. He got a few kicks in at first, then turned and ran back to where he had parked his car, followed by a stream of people yelling after him. It was all too easy to identify which car was his. The crowd surged around it, riled up with the excitement of a chase and each other's outrage, and for the next few minutes set about damaging as much of the car as they could, and any bits of Julian that got in the way too. They ripped most of the stickers off the back of the car and stamped them onto the flags in the gutter.

They finally ran out of steam and small flags to snap off, and ran away as quickly as they had arrived before anybody had the chance to call the police. Julian slowly levered himself upright from where he had been knocked over by his front wheel, and looked at the damage. Both headlights had been smashed. All the flags along the roof box had been snapped off, their fabric trodden into the dust in the street. There was a crack all the way across the windscreen, which was fingering smaller lines out along its length. One rear light was smashed and a rear tyre slashed.

'Mate – you alright?' The voice from behind him made Julian turn. 'Saw the British plates and your rugby shirt – you British, yeah? Oh, mate, you don't look so good yourself either. What happened?

A man was walking towards him from the other side of the road with a concerned look on his face. He was in shirtsleeves and linen trousers: still on the formal side of casual but dressed comfortably for the temperature.

'I, er, I'm fine,' said Julian, putting his hand up to his head to discover that his good eye was now bleeding. 'The car though. Fucking vandals.'

'Who was it – did you see?'

'Oh, some randoms. No more than kids, really. Don't know what set them off.'

'Well, look, we should get that eye seen to. And I know a couple of garages we could try who might pick your car up tonight. It looks bad, but if the engine hasn't been touched, it might just be surface damage, yeah?'

Julian looked at the car again. 'Maybe, yeah. I've got to get to Bruges tonight.'

'Oh, man. Well, that's not too far.' The stranger paused. 'For anything special? I mean, time-specific?'

'Well, no, I guess not time-specific. Concert is tomorrow, so I've got to be at the rehearsal tomorrow afternoon at the latest, I suppose.'

'Concert! What kind? You in a band? I play a bit of guitar myself. Took it up again recently. Love it.'

'Orchestra. Classical stuff.'

'No way!'

Julian smiled. 'Yep.'

'Excellent! Well, first things first. Do you want me to call a garage, and you can come back to my office and we can get a dressing on your eye? We've got a first aid box there.'

Julian looked at the man in crumpled linen in front of him, eager to help, knowing nothing except that he needed help. And frankly, getting the hell out of this pissing Belgian dump would be easier with local info. He nodded. 'OK. Thanks.'

The man smiled, and put out his hand. 'Great. I'm Ben. Ben Blackman. Come on, the office is just over there.'

'Where do you work?'

'The Parliament building. My boss isn't sitting over the summer, obviously, but there's always so much to catch up with I usually just push on through August.'

He led Julian over to the building with the flagpoles, and his ID card beeped them in through the door.

31

'Erin, get your face out of your phone and keep up with the drinking!'

Erin raised her head and looked over at Charlie, who was draining his glass of beer and about to get more. 'But this Bach thing – it's taking off. Like, kind of viral.'

They were sitting at a street table at the side of Markt, the square in the centre of old Bruges that looked as if it hadn't changed much for eight hundred years. A lot of the musicians who had played in the Bach were there. All smiling, all chatting, drinking at tables clustered under the huge canvas sunshades as if the orchestra were still in London and this was the pub after rehearsal. Some things really do stay the same. Except this bar was in a medieval town with obscenely picturesque photo opportunities and canals at every street corner.

'That's good, isn't it?' said Charlie. 'Now drink up.'

'Chips,' said Ann. 'I want Belgian chips. Crispy ones. With mayonnaise. Do they do them here? Chuck us a menu.'

'Ugh,' said Charlie.

'Let's not get into a cultural clash right now,' said Eliot. 'Some people like mayo, Charlie. Get over it.'

Erin let out a laugh that was sort of a gasp, and said to everyone, 'That video Ingrid took that I posted? It's had thousands of retweets and loads more likes. And that's in – what? An hour? Look!' She held out her phone to the others, and as they watched, the retweet total clicked round a few hundred more. She took her phone back and tapped another app. 'And it's gone mental on Facebook. This is insane.'

'You must have got some influencers in on it,' said Charlie, taking his own phone out and checking his own feed.

'This is brilliant though, Erin! You're a social media manager now,' said Alexander, handing Ann a menu. 'Loads of chips. Shall we have a chippy tea?'

'I can't keep up with the messages,' said Erin. 'They're coming in too fast.'

The others got their phones out.

'Well, I retweeted it when you sent it through,' said Eliot, 'and I've had a flurry about it too. Ha! Loads of musician friends have picked up on it and shared it – it's going round a lot of professional orchestras now, I see. Good job you sounded so bloody competent, Alexander!'

Alexander laughed. 'Yeah, it went OK didn't it? This could be my audition tape. And you're right, Erin, it's going feckin' nuts.'

'Got your hashtags on there, I see,' said Charlie. 'What a pro. Who we are, where we are. Bruges *and* Brugge! Top work. Inclusive. At this rate you'll soon be trending in three languages.'

Erin looked suddenly worried. 'Oh! Oh god. I hope this is OK for the orchestra? I mean, I didn't check with David or anything before I posted it.'

'Are you kidding?' said Eliot. 'You can't buy this kind of publicity. Ingrid knew what she was doing filming it. David will be delighted. In fact…' He tapped out something busily with his thumbs. 'I'll send the link to him and Mrs Ford-Hughes directly. They'll love it. And Richard should know too – his playing was spectacular! As usual. Is he on Twitter?'

Ann caught a passing waiter and, along with more beer for everyone, ordered an awful lot of *frieten*.

'You've got to do a follow-up reply, so people see it underneath,' said Charlie. 'You know SoundCloud or something. Do you have SoundCloud?' His mouth twitched.

Erin looked at Charlie gravely. 'I do not. As you well know.'

'Tell them about our concert tomorrow,' said Eliot.

'Yes!' said Alexander. 'Then if they're anywhere near here they can come along. It's our last night. Let's make it a good one.'

Erin shrugged. 'OK. If you say so.' She frowned and wrote for a minute. 'Anyone got the actual address of this church we're in tomorrow?'

Ann dug around in her bag and produced one of Ingrid's leaflets. 'There. It's all at the bottom.'

Charlie was looking at Erin with admiration. 'Twitter royalty. Hashtag the hell out of it. Imagine you're on Instagram.'

Erin stuck her tongue out at him, sent the tweet, and put her phone away. 'Enough. Where are those chips? I'm starving.'

'On their way,' said Ann. She leaned back in her chair and laced her fingers behind her head, gazing up to the top of the belfry. 'That really is beautiful. Although it does look like something my kids used to build out of old boxes and loo rolls. A square and then a smaller square on top of that and then a – what? Octagon? But with added balconies.'

'Don't get started on balconies,' said Eliot, laughing. 'That'll give us all PTSD.'

Alexander looked puzzled.

'Eliot did a bit of moonlighting as a singer a few weeks ago,' Erin explained. 'On a balcony. It all took a turn nobody was expecting – Ann, Charlie and I went to watch. You really don't want to know.'

Ann smiled. 'Oh yes. I'd forgotten about that. But I mean, here. Look at it! It's like sitting in a theme park – you can't believe anywhere real is quite this old and pretty.'

'The belfry was built in the thirteenth century,' said Charlie. 'Eighty-three metres tall. Three hundred and sixty-six steps. And it leans about a metre to one side.'

'Oh, here we go,' said Eliot. 'Mr Tourist Guidebook is off.'

'No, no, don't be like that,' said Charlie, and added pointedly, '*It leans to the east.*'

'You sound like you're a Cold War spy having a meet-up on a park bench.'

'One day you'll be glad you're with someone who does their research. I was merely going to go on to say that it's the backdrop to *the* climactic scene in one of *the* best films, and I can't look at it without expecting Brendan Gleeson to come plummeting down through the fog to splat on the attractive medieval cobbles.'

They stared at him in silence.

'Loved that film,' said Alexander. 'Where was it set?'

He flinched as it looked as if he was about to get pelted with an assortment of small mobile objects immediately to hand on a café table. They were all slowly lowered to the table top as he held up his hands, retaining their threat.

Eliot grinned at him. 'Now you see what I mean about their potential violence?'

Luckily at that moment the chips descended from a large tray held aloft by a waiter.

'You'll be OK,' said Eliot to Alexander, leaning in. 'They won't use food as ammo when they're this hungry.'

32

A hundred kilometres away in Brussels, Ben Blackman had finished patching up Julian's new injuries and phoning some garages to see if one of them would come out on a Friday evening to fix a car. One of them said they would, so Ben and Julian arranged to meet him where the car was still parked on the street, to see what could be done.

They walked out of the Parliament building together and over to the car. A street sweeper had been through. There was no sign any more of the various flags that had been snapped off and trodden on.

'It doesn't look as bad as all that,' said Ben, nodding at Julian's car that seemed to be sagging into the kerb. He had the kind of voice inflection that suggested he tried to put a positive spin on any situation, which is exactly the right kind of guy you need in a crisis. That he still had this ability at all spoke volumes about his resilience, working as he had been for the previous few years in a Parliament knowing he and others in the British contingent were on borrowed time. 'Those lights, and the tyre, and the windscreen, yeah. But maybe that's all you need to do to get on the move again.' They walked round the other side to stand on the pavement.

'Well, I mean, you can get all those scratches sorted when you get home, I guess.'

Julian sniffed, put his hands into the pockets of his shorts and stood on splayed legs. 'Bastards.'

To take Julian's mind off his immediate car worries, Ben cast about for something else to mention. 'So, what instrument do you play in this orchestra? Is it in the car?' He grinned. 'You could do some busking while we wait. Raise the money for the repairs? Whaddya reckon?'

'French horn. And no, it's not in there – kept with the other instruments in a special truck.'

'They've got a special truck for the instruments and then make you all drive round on your own?' said Ben. 'Bit of an odd way of organising things.'

Julian laughed mirthlessly. 'Yeah, well. There's a coach too.'

'Ah, brilliant! I love coach journeys. D'you remember school trips, when you'd all fight for the back seat and eat your packed lunch before you turned out of the school drive?' Ben laughed, shaking his head, his eyes bright with warm memories.

'If you like being stuck in a tin can with a load of idiots, they're alright I suppose.'

'Oh. But you don't…?'

'Nah.' Julian took a deep breath and filled out his chest, lifting his chin. 'I like the open road. Master of my own destiny. My own mobile castle.'

Ben looked doubtfully at the old Skoda, leaning towards him onto its flat tyre. Even without its current difficulties, it was a stretch to describe it as a castle. From where he was standing, Ben could see the footwells were littered with crumpled fast food packets and disposable cups, water bottles, and unidentifiable detritus that had silted up the carpet over many journeys. The paintwork and glass, underneath their scratches and cracks, were grimy. Even without getting into it, Ben knew how that car would smell.

'Well,' he said, determined to keep cheerful, 'tell me about the orchestra. What are you playing tomorrow? I love a bit of music, me.'

'We're on a tour,' said Julian. 'Came from Cologne this morning, and doing our last concert in some church in Bruges tomorrow night. Mozart overture, a Strauss horn concerto and Bruckner 7.'

'Wow! And are you playing the horn concerto then?'

Julian pursed his lips. 'Well, no. The solo part is played by some Scottish hotshot who thinks the sun shines out of his arse. Nah, I'm providing the Wagner tubas in the Bruckner symphony. There are four, and I play first.'

Ben's face, which had crumpled like Julian's car's headlight as he heard the misanthropic description of Alexander, lightened as he latched on to what could be a great pub quiz fact if only he could pin it down. 'What on earth is a Wagner tuba? I thought you said you played the French horn? And don't you all play together?'

Julian actually laughed. 'I play the first part in the quartet: the highest part. The one with the tune. The most important part. The leader.' At each iteration, his chest puffed out slightly further.

'And the Wagner tuba bit?'

'They're a weird kind of cross between a horn and a trombone. Don't crop up much. I happen to have a set of four, and so I was the go-to guy for this orchestra when they needed them.'

'Oh, so you're not a regular member of this orchestra?'

'Christ, no.'

Ben raised his eyebrows and smiled politely. Every avenue of conciliatory politeness he tried seemed to flip up in his face. He scanned the road for any sign of the mechanic to rescue the car and the conversation, but saw no one. 'So… what? You decided to stop off in Brussels on the way past to Bruges? Have you got a special interest in the European Parliament?'

Julian's mouth pressed into a thin smile. 'Yeah. Yeah, I have actually. I'm what you might call a specialist. I was recording a piece to camera when… I noticed those vandals attacking my car.'

Luckily, Ben was saved any further details about Julian's afternoon philosophy lectures by a pick-up truck rolling alongside. The driver, wearing a baseball cap over greasy hair, leaned out of his window and called out in Flemish.

Ben replied fluently, and proceeded to translate for Julian as the mechanic climbed down from his cab and walked round the Skoda, kicking its wheel and poking the cracked glass with an oil-ingrained finger. The windscreen bowed in alarmingly as he pressed the crack. He crouched down onto the road and looked underneath, pointing and shaking his head at Ben. Standing up again, he settled the baseball cap more comfortably on his head and wiped his hands on the front of his overall.

'Oh,' said Ben, rather more soberly than his entire previous conversations with Julian. It sounded as if the news had been bad enough to take the wind out of the sails of even the irrepressible Blackman optimism. 'He says that apart from all the stuff we can see – the tyre, the lights and windows and so on – you've also got a crack in your fuel tank. It's leaked out all over the road under the car.'

'What?' said Julian, crouching himself and peering underneath. 'Shit. *Shit.*'

Ben and the mechanic looked at each other. The mechanic didn't need any translation for that.

The mechanic said something quietly to Ben, who nodded.

'What's he saying?' said Julian, standing up.

'Um, he can take your car back to his garage, but with the fuel tank it's not going to be a quick fix, I'm afraid. Certainly overnight. Maybe into next week.'

'Shit,' said Julian again, and then, just when Ben thought Julian's vocab had got stuck, he surprised him. 'Bollocks.'

'Well, yes,' Ben agreed. 'What do you want to do? He says he can fix it. He'll need a credit card number and some details, obviously.'

Julian walked round in a tight little circle, running his hand through his hair. But there was nothing for it. 'Yeah, OK. Fine. *Bollocks*.'

Ben translated the gist of Julian's acceptance and, after Julian had retrieved his luggage from inside and passed on his card details and contact number, the mechanic set about winching the Skoda onto the back of his truck.

'What are you going to do now?' Ben asked.

'Head for Bruges, I suppose. Is there a train?'

'Well, yes. But, um,' Ben paused, weighing up Friday evening, Julian's predicament and his own altruism limit. He let a long breath out with puffed-out cheeks. 'Look, I could give you a lift. If you like?'

'To the station? Great, thanks.'

'To Bruges.'

Julian stared at him. 'What?'

'It's not that far, really. Just over an hour. And you've had a bump to your head – I don't think you should be taking public transport on your own.'

Julian didn't need more persuading: in his view, a car was preferable to any kind of public transport. 'Decent of you. Thanks.'

They waved the mechanic off and Ben showed Julian the way to his flat, where he sorted what he needed for a surprise trip to Bruges. Less than half an hour after leaving the Skoda, they were in Ben's Nissan Leaf heading north-west.

33

Ingrid's phone buzzed as she was drinking her after-dinner coffee with Jörg. They had just finished their meal at the restaurant adjacent to the orchestra's hotel, at one of the small tables arranged in neat geometry on the street. She looked at the text. It was from Mr Ford-Hughes.

Deciding it would be easier to speak, she dialled his number. 'Mr Ford-Hughes? This is Ingrid Bauer. I received your text. Shall we meet to discuss? Yes of course. You are less than ten minutes' walk from me. I'll come to you. Goodbye.'

Jörg looked at her and raised his eyebrows: no mean muscular feat given the amount of metal pierced through them. She shrugged, paid the bill and asked him to keep his phone to hand in case she required assistance. He nodded, and they walked in different directions: he to a bar and she to the Ford-Hugheses' suite at the Hotel Dukes' Palace.

Mr Ford-Hughes opened the door to Ingrid's knock and gestured that she could choose any of the chairs or sofa in the plush sitting room. Their suite occupied a good part of an upper floor of the five-star hotel, and expressed its opulence through the medium of thick carpet in neutral tones, stripy wallpaper, and a surprising number of silk scatter cushions.

'Is that Ingrid?' called Mrs Ford-Hughes, bustling in from where she had been trying to catch a warm evening breeze on the balcony. In one hand she held half a glass of champagne. 'Hi, honey. Thanks so much for scooting round. Isn't it exciting? Oh, darling?' She turned to her husband. 'Pour Ingrid some champagne, won't you?'

'I don't think—' started Ingrid, but Mrs Ford-Hughes was having none of it.

'Oh, come on! We're celebrating!'

Ingrid smiled. 'Well. Perhaps a small glass. Thank you.'

While Mr Ford-Hughes poured more champagne from the bottle leaning in an ice bucket, Mrs Ford-Hughes sat on the sofa and patted the seat next to her. 'Let's decide how to play this thing, shall we? Do you think we need to get anyone else here? Eliot, maybe? Or Alexander?' She couldn't help the eyelash flutter as she suggested him, which was immediately doused by her next name. 'Or David, I suppose? He is the chairman.'

'Or Erin, perhaps?' said Ingrid. 'She is doing the orchestra's social media, I believe?'

'Now, tell me,' said Mr Ford-Hughes, bringing Ingrid a glass of bubbles and sitting down on a chair opposite, 'you were at this ad hoc performance earlier, weren't you? Whose idea was it?'

Ingrid sipped. 'Yes indeed. It is my video that Erin used. I am not sure who had the original idea: the first I heard was when Eliot asked me if Jörg could let them get their instruments from the truck. They had only just found the church, I understand.'

Mr Ford-Hughes had opened a laptop on the coffee table in front of him and tapped a few keys. 'It just keeps going and going. Over a hundred thousand shares now. There's the full version, and also short clips people are sharing and linking through.'

'Well, I thought the Bach was enchanting! I do so love Bach, as you know,' said Mrs Ford-Hughes, inclining her head towards her husband, who smiled at her indulgently. 'This sure as sugar is gonna put our little orchestra on the map!'

Ingrid sat up straight, put her drink on the table in front of her and got her phone from her bag: movements signalling a transformation that revealed her nature as visibly to Mr and Mrs Ford-Hughes as if she had changed her clothes. Ingrid Bauer was in the room, and was taking charge. 'Note Perfect Tours has a media division with press contacts and so on. Local news teams will want this story. We can handle that side of things, if you like? I would need the orchestra's social media passwords and authorisations, of course. I suggest we ask David and Erin here for a catch-up and strategy meeting, with perhaps also Eliot and Alexander in case the media want interviews. Do you agree?'

Mrs Ford-Hughes beamed at her, one hand to her own heaving décolleté. 'I just *knew* we should call you. Look, honey, Ingrid can handle everything.'

Mr Ford-Hughes nodded. 'Absolutely. Always happy to delegate to a professional. Ingrid. Let us know how we can help.'

* * *

Erin didn't hear her phone because by that time they had moved to a much noisier bar and were in a crowd of Friday night drinkers. The first she knew about it was Eliot elbowing his way to her in front of Charlie, beckoning for her to follow him a little way down the street away from the noise. He had his phone clamped to his ear.

'Sorry, Ingrid – say that again?' he said. 'I've got Erin with me now. Bit noisy.' He put her on speaker.

Ingrid's voice rose from the phone like a calm palm tree signalling an oasis in a desert. 'Please would you and Erin come to meet me and Mr and Mrs Ford-Hughes? I am with them at the Hotel Dukes' Palace on Prinsenhof. It is about five minutes' walk from our hotel. I don't know where you are now.'

'Are we in trouble?' asked Erin, leaning into the phone in case anyone else on the street could overhear the conversation.

'Not at all,' said Ingrid. 'Quite the reverse. We need to talk media strategy for your Bach video. It is performing extremely well.'

'You mean it's gone viral,' said Eliot, grinning. 'We know – we saw. It's had tens of thousands of shares.'

'Your information is out of date,' said Ingrid, a smile pouring down the line. 'Hundreds of thousands, and counting. When can you be here?'

'Bloody hell,' said Erin.

'That's why she needs to meet,' said Eliot, and then louder into his phone. 'Not sure quite where we are, Ingrid, but I can pull up a map on my phone and we'll be on our way. It can't be too far: Bruges is only the size of a stamp. Dukes' Palace, did you say? What street?'

Ingrid spelled the address, and went on, 'Ask for Mr and Mrs Ford-Hughes's suite and they'll show you up. Is Alexander with you?'

'Yep,' said Eliot. 'Do you want him too?'

'It was his idea, after all,' said Erin.

'Please bring him, yes. See you soon,' said Ingrid, and disconnected.

Eliot and Erin stared at each other, and started to laugh.

'*Suite*?' Eliot said, before giggling again. 'Oh, god.'

They walked back to the bar and found Alexander in a crowd of people, talking to Charlie and Ann.

'We've been summoned,' Erin told him.

'Whattoned?' he said.

'Summoned,' said Eliot. 'Your Bach is going mega-viral and the big guns want some of the action.'

Alexander drained his beer. 'Neither of you is making any sense. Can you not hold yer drink?'

'We've gotta go,' said Erin. 'Ingrid is with the Ford-Hugheses and apparently we need a media strategy or something.'

Alexander looked at his watch. 'Now?'

'And you're all a bit pissed,' Charlie pointed out. 'Mind you, so am I.'

'I'm not,' said Ann.

'Legend,' said Alexander.

'Can we come?' said Charlie.

'No,' said Erin, 'and you won't like where we have to meet them. You'll come over all socialist and disapproving.'

'Yikes, have they gone somewhere as posh as their Amsterdam gaff?' said Alexander.

'Posher, by the looks of it,' said Eliot, who had brought it up on his phone. He showed the pictures round. 'They have a suite.'

'You'll have to stay with me, Charlie,' said Ann. 'Let them do the publicity grunt work.'

'Grunt work? Thanks,' said Erin, and then turned to Alexander. 'We really do have to go.'

In the end, they all left the bar together. Erin, Alexander and Eliot followed the dotted line on Eliot's phone map to the Hotel Dukes' Palace, with Charlie shouting after them as they turned a corner, 'Try not to act too pissed!' He and Ann decided to have a nightcap at the bar next to their hotel.

Just as the slightly pissed trio rode up in the Dukes' Palace lift to the Ford-Hugheses' suite, Ann and Charlie were ordering a whisky called The Belgian Owl, which Charlie refused to believe existed until Ann asked the waiter. They sat at a street table enjoying cool evening air after the relentless heat of the day. Ann idly watched passers-by as she sipped her whisky, but sharpened her attention on something behind Charlie's shoulder.

'Christ.'

'What?'

'I wondered why we hadn't seen Julian all day,' said Ann. 'Not that I wasn't enjoying it. Looks like he's been up to his usual tricks.'

Charlie turned round to see. Julian was getting his bag out of the back of Ben's car while Ben climbed out of the driver's side, stretched out his back and looked up at the tall red-brick walls of the Concertgebouw opposite. 'But where's his flagtastic car? Looks like he's brought a minder.'

'Turn back around,' said Ann quickly, but it was too late. Their table was right next to the hotel entrance, and Julian saw them both, lifted his hand and walked towards them.

34

'Charlie! Ann!' he called. 'How's it going?'

He came right up to their table while Ben hung back looking doubtful.

'Julian,' said Ann, sounding neither friendly nor inviting.

'Where's your car?' asked Charlie, and then nodded at Ben a few feet away. 'Hello.'

'Oh, yeah,' said Julian, waving an arm back towards Ben. 'This is Ben. Had a spot of trouble with my car, and Ben gave me a lift. Top man.'

Ben smiled the weak smile of one who had just spent over an hour in a car with Julian. Ann correctly identified this expression, and took pity.

'Julian, Ingrid has been looking for you for ages.' She glared at Charlie, daring him to say anything. He wisely drank his whisky and kept watch over the brim of the glass. 'You'd better go and check into the hotel before they give your room away to someone else, and then find out which room she's in and tell her you're here.'

'Oh. Well, I'm sure she can wait a minute or two longer.' Julian hovered, unmoving, looking thirstily at the menu on the table.

'Honestly, you don't want to rile her any further,' said Ann. 'Especially with your track record. We'll look after Ben, won't we, Charlie?'

Charlie nodded, still holding his glass in front of him like an alcohol shield. Julian looked from one to the other, sniffed, and nodded. 'Right. Cheers, Ben. Back in a sec.'

Ann watched Julian's back view disappear into the hotel, and grinned at Ben, pushing out a spare chair with her foot. 'Hello. Take a seat. You look as if you've earned it. I'm Ann, and this is Charlie.'

Ben smiled weakly and sat down. 'Hello. Are you in the orchestra too?'

'We are,' said Charlie, sticking his hand out round his glass and shaking Ben's. 'Cellos. Did Julian's car get beaten by the drag from all those flags in the end? Is it just round the corner, panting?'

Ben frowned. 'Flags? No. What flags?'

'The ones that make his car look like a second-hand car dealership at a Brexit jubilee,' said Ann. 'Where is it?'

'In Brussels. I didn't see any flags.'

Charlie coughed into his whisky. '*Brussels*?'

'You've driven from Brussels?' said Ann.

'Er, yeah.'

'Fuck me,' said Charlie. 'Ben, I think you'd better have a drink and tell us all about it.'

Ben smiled. 'I'd quite like something to eat too. I'm famished. Didn't get a chance before we left.'

Ann passed him the menu. 'Start at the beginning. This is going to be good.'

Ben chose a local beer and *moules frites*, drawing a broad smile from the waiter as he ordered in Flemish. Ann and

Charlie raised their eyebrows at each other. They let Ben take the first swallow of his beer before leaning forward and quizzing him about the whole story.

'So, Julian was in Brussels?' said Charlie. 'Was he lost?'

'No – he said he was doing some reporting or something. Recording videos. I think he wanted to do one about the European Parliament.'

'I bet he did,' said Ann.

'Well, he spent a fair bit of time in the car on the way here uploading stuff to his site on his phone,' said Ben. 'I think it was what he'd been recording. He said it was a bit of a rush job though. I'm not sure what it was about – I was driving.'

'He's got a site?' said Charlie. 'This I have to see.' He got his own phone out and started googling.

'Go on,' said Ann. 'So how did you meet him?'

The waiter arrived with Ben's food, and he started eating hungrily. 'I didn't see what happened, but there had been some sort of scuffle and Julian was sort of… slumped by his car, so I went over to help. My office was nearby, so I patched his eye up in there, then we got a mechanic out to see if he could fix the car, but it turned out to be a bigger job than we thought, and then, well, here we are.' He put another chip in his mouth and chewed happily.

'Tell you what, Ben,' said Ann. 'You are a knight in shining bloody armour and Julian didn't deserve you.'

Ben smiled and shook his head. 'I just did what anyone would have.'

'Driving a stranger a hundred miles—'

'Oh, it's not that far,' Ben protested.

'Whatever – to a different city, just because he got beaten up. Again. Honestly. None of us would have lifted a finger.

He keeps getting pushed into canals and rivers. He's a git. And you are clearly lovely.'

Ben covered any embarrassment he might have been feeling by eating more chips. 'Well, I wanted to come and meet the orchestra, too,' he said. 'It sounds brilliant. I don't know any classical musicians. Play some guitar myself, but nothing like you lot.'

Charlie let out a long whistle, and said 'fuck me' softly to himself. He looked at Ann and Ben, and showed them his phone. 'Let's not have the volume up too much, eh?' he said, so they huddled round the small screen. Charlie tapped 'play', and immediately the frame was filled with a crotch shot of Julian in his shorts, with his face looking small by comparison because of the wide angle lens. Behind him the Union Flag flew on its pole in front of the European Parliament building. The camera angle ensured that the image any viewer would have seared onto their brain was that of Julian's comfortably slack shorts revealing underwear completely failing to disguise the shape of, well, anything.

'Oh god, no,' said Ann. 'Absolutely not. Nobody needs to see those undercrackers.'

'It's horrifically mesmerising,' said Charlie. 'I mean, it almost takes your mind off the drivel he's spouting.'

'I may have to bleach my eyes,' said Ann.

Ben was watching with a horrified expression. 'That's in front of the EU,' he stammered. 'This must have been just before we met – look, his eye is OK there.'

'We may be able to see what happened,' said Charlie, as the film jumped to audible heckling. Julian's grip on the selfie stick was clearly wobbling.

'Anything that will change that camera angle works for me,' said Ann, still trying not to look. 'That must be an indecent image, surely?'

'He did say something about not having time to edit it properly,' said Ben.

The film ended with Julian throwing something at the hecklers and then starting to run away, before cutting to a black screen.

'What did he throw?' asked Charlie.

'Looked like a marshmallow,' said Ann. 'Nothing is making sense any more.'

Ben took a long swallow of beer and put it back on the table slowly. 'He's horrible, isn't he?'

Ann and Charlie nodded, not unkindly.

Charlie put his hand on Ben's shoulder. 'Sorry. We're not horrible, though. Are you staying for our concert tomorrow? We might be famous by then. We've gone viral, apparently.'

Ben brightened. 'Well, I wondered if I might. I did sling in an overnight bag. I fancied a weekend of culture. It's been quite a week at work.' He looked at the hotel next door. 'Do you think they have a room?'

'I'm sure you could charm one with your Flemish flair,' smiled Ann. 'And I know for a fact they've got a car park underneath. You get in round the side. By the way, what do you do in that office of yours, apart from patch up gormless Brexiteers?'

Ben laughed. 'I work at the European Parliament. For an MEP. Who is definitely *not* a Brexiteer.'

'A toast,' said Charlie, formally. 'To the forbearance of the EU faced with numpty Brits.'

They clinked their glasses together, grinning.

'Julian's such a slimy hypocrite,' said Ann.

'All we need to do now,' said Charlie to Ben, 'is get you booked into the hotel and the car hidden before Julian gets back, and we can bugger off to another bar without him. Eat up. We'll see if we can find you some other musicians to meet.'

35

Mr Ford-Hughes opened the door to Erin, Eliot and Alexander, and waved them inside. Mrs Ford-Hughes and Ingrid were already sitting on the sofa beside a low coffee table. David was perched in one of the three armchairs.

Mrs Ford-Hughes leapt up as they came in and hurried over to Erin to envelop her in a bosomy embrace. 'What a clever girl you are!' she cried. 'Just the perfect combination of zip and online know-how.'

Erin spluttered her thanks from inside the Ford-Hughes floaty sleeves, and staggered free as Mrs Ford-Hughes moved on to kiss Eliot and Alexander. They didn't get the full wraparound experience, but a champagne-fuelled Mrs Ford-Hughes was not easily deflected.

'Come over and have a drink,' she insisted, taking Alexander's hand and guiding him to the middle of the sofa in between her and Ingrid. 'Do we have another bottle, darling?' Her husband, on cue, offered a glass of champagne to him, as well as to Eliot and Erin, before sitting in the second armchair and turning his attention back to his open laptop on the table in front of him.

'Thank you for coming,' said Ingrid, looking up from her phone. 'To take full advantage of this, we need a strategy for tomorrow. I'm already getting interview requests from radio stations, and a breakfast television station has reached out.'

'I've given Ingrid the social media passwords, Erin,' said David. 'You were brilliant, but maybe Ingrid might have more contacts and experience now it's, um, hotted up. As it were.'

Erin nodded her agreement. The champagne on top of beer was giving the whole late-evening party a glow and she wasn't about to argue.

'Hang on,' said Eliot, running his hand through his hair. 'Is all this just from the Bach we did earlier? What's happened?' He sank into the third and last chair, stood up, dropped a couple of cushions over the side like a balloonist ditching ballast, and tried again.

David's lips twitched. 'It appears that a performance that nobody knew was happening, which had no rehearsal time or planning, turns out to be the performance everyone wants more than one we spend weeks preparing.'

Eliot put his head on one side, shrugged and nodded. 'Of course. Of course.' He sipped his bubbles.

'But the video Erin uploaded isn't the only one online,' said Ingrid. 'Several of the tourists who came into the church also started recording, and have shared it, adding their own stories of how they found us. You have become, as unpredictable as this may seem, an internet sensation.'

Ingrid Bauer using the words 'internet sensation' with no hint of irony made Alexander laugh. 'There's a first time for everything.'

'So what happens now?' asked Eliot. 'Why are we here, exactly? I mean, apart from drinking your excellent champagne.' He inclined his head towards Mrs Ford-Hughes.

'In your excellent suite,' added Alexander, doing the same.

Erin perched on the arm of Eliot's chair. 'Well, I don't want to have to do any interviews. Alexander can do that. It was all his idea.'

'And a bloody good one,' added Eliot.

'May I suggest a timetable?' said Ingrid, looking round at the forces she had available to her. 'We put Alexander and Eliot up for the breakfast television show. They are confident, extrovert, and will be able to talk fluently about the Bach and Stockwell Park Orchestra. Agreed?'

Eliot and Alexander looked at each other in shock.

'Fine by me,' said Eliot. 'If it's fine by him?'

'It's fine by me,' said Alexander, laughing.

'You sound like *The Two Ronnies* already,' said Erin. 'Watch out, or you'll come out of this with a double act and nobody will remember you do music at all.'

'Excellent,' said Ingrid, typing details into an emergency spreadsheet she had created. 'That will be live, of course. I can arrange wake-up calls for you both, and transport to the studio. Do you each have reasonable clothing left in your packed wardrobe?'

'Oh blimey,' muttered Eliot.

'Serves you right for being so keen,' whispered Erin at his shoulder.

'We'll be fine,' said Alexander.

Ingrid was already on to the next agenda item in a brisk meeting nobody else quite realised was occurring until an action point hit them right between the eyes like a low-flying alarm clock. Guerrilla meetings of course, are the ones that get most done on account of springing tasks onto those who hadn't prepared any defences.

'Two local radio stations so far want to do pieces,' Ingrid continued, 'and of course those may be able to be recorded in advance. It is unclear from the details I currently have. David, I suggest you take at least one of those, and perhaps Erin?'

'Oh no,' said Erin. 'That's not part of the deal at all. I'd be awful.'

Ingrid gave her a penetrating look and a small smile. 'I think you would not be awful, but so be it. Perhaps Alexander or Eliot will be available by then. Obviously I can field any other queries while the scheduled items are in progress. And then you have your regular rehearsal at two o'clock, so we would need to leave the hotel by one-thirty.'

'Oh yes,' said Eliot faintly. 'I'd almost forgotten about that. More Bruckner, anyone?'

'In addition,' said Ingrid, and they all sat up straighter and tried to give her their renewed earnest attention despite it being the end of a long evening and they had been drinking for many hours of it, 'my team at Note Perfect Tours will draft regular social media posts and a longer piece we can upload to the orchestra's site first thing tomorrow morning. Subject to your approval, of course, David.'

David nodded. 'I'm sure it will be superb.'

'This may generate additional interest in tomorrow evening's concert, so Jörg and I will be on hand to deal with issues arising from that.'

'Thank you,' said Mr Ford-Hughes. 'If Maryanne or I can assist you in any way, please do call on us.'

'I shall, thank you. Finally,' Ingrid looked round at faces that were hanging on but clearly at the end of their stamina, and she softened. 'Finally, it might be a good idea to get a picture of those people who played in the Bach together, to use going forward. However, I suggest that might be done at the start of tomorrow's rehearsal, when the players will be assembled in any case. I can take that myself. Any questions?'

There was a shell-shocked kind of pause, tinged with awe.

'No questions, but massive thanks,' said Eliot, raising his glass to her. The rest of them joined in.

'Ingrid, you are a marvel,' said Mrs Ford-Hughes, leaning across Alexander to pat Ingrid's knee. Alexander tried to keep out of the way, but there was a certain amount of torso proximity he couldn't help, on account of the immutability of the back of the sofa. He stared at Eliot and Erin in silent and immobile embarrassment as the Ford-Hughes bosom nestled heavily in his lap. Erin and Eliot had to bury their noses in their champagne glasses, trying not to laugh too obviously at his discomfort.

36

Charlie, Ann and Ben hurtled round a corner and came to a breathless halt, leaning against a brick wall that pressed some faint retained heat into their backs.

'Oh god,' said Charlie, leaning down to put his hands on his knees. 'That was close. Christ, I'm unfit.'

'Well, you did set off at a stupid pace,' said Ann. 'It wasn't a race: we just had to get out of view. And you're about half my age – if I can do it, you should be able to.'

Ben started to giggle. 'I had this idea that classical musicians were kind of – serene?'

'Common mistake, mate,' puffed Charlie.

'Wait 'til you meet Carl,' said Ann. 'We're nothing.'

They started walking again slowly, having got their breath back. Ben had successfully got a room at the same hotel, and managed to check in at reception and spirit his car round the side to the underground car park before Julian had reappeared. In an unfortunate coincidence, Julian had started walking towards the centre of Bruges on a parallel street, and they nearly ran into him as they rounded a corner on their way to the bar to meet Carl and Kayla.

'If we'd led Julian to the same bar as the others, Carl would have gone ballistic,' explained Charlie. 'I think we've all had about as much of Julian as we can take this week.'

'Oh, I dunno,' said Ann. 'Bruges is full of canals.'

Ben let that go, bemused.

'Come on. This way.' Charlie led the way, looking at the map on his phone. They went round a few more corners until they saw familiar faces sitting at tables outside a bar.

Catching sight of them, Carl stood and raised his arm in greeting. 'Finally! Where did you get to?'

Kayla turned and smiled too. Tracie was next to her, and beyond them a few others from the orchestra. 'Hi. Last time I saw you, you were with Erin and Eliot. What happened to them?'

Carl leaned in to deliver a slightly drunk stage whisper to Charlie. 'And, you know, I don't mean to make a big thing of it, but you seem to have picked up a stranger. Either that or Alexander has shrunk. And changed his hair somehow.' He squinted at Ben.

'Oh, no – this is Ben,' said Charlie. 'He came with Julian.'

Carl straightened, looking immediately more threatening. Ben shrank away from his bulk, stepping behind Charlie.

'Back off, matey,' said Ann. 'Ben is the lovely Good Samaritan that Julian definitely did not deserve, and we have all just escaped by running like teenage idiots to get to you without leading Julian here, so be nice to Ben and let's have a drink.'

Carl laughed. 'Oh well, in that case,' he said, and held out his hand to Ben, who shook it.

'Pleased to meet you,' said Ben.

'This is Carl. He plays trombone,' said Ann, taking on the persona of a society hostess at a cocktail party giving guests snippets about each other that they can then use to kick-start a conversation. 'And this is Kayla, double bass. And Tracie, also trombone. She's not supposed to be here, but that's a long story. Everyone, meet Ben. Ben has arrived in Bruges in an electric car for a weekend of cultural excitement that only our orchestra can provide.' She turned to Ben. 'Our kind of cultural weekend sometimes involves alcohol.'

'Sometimes,' snorted Charlie.

'Not always,' said Kayla. She put her arm round Tracie. 'I let her have one beer at the start of the evening – I mean, she's sixteen, right? There has to be some relaxation of rules. And now she's on alcohol-free lager. Before you report me to Ingrid.'

'Top work,' said Charlie. 'Let's get some of the real stuff.' He picked up a menu from a nearby table and they found some spare chairs.

A cheer, led by Leroy, erupted from the table behind Kayla, and there was a flurry of glasses being drained. Charlie and Ann looked over at them, then at each other, and shrugged. Kayla rolled her eyes.

'They've been doing that all evening,' she said. 'Someone's following Erin's tweet's progress about our Bach thing, and every time it ticks past another thousand or ten thousand or whatever squillion it's up to now, they get another round in.' She glanced over her shoulder. 'They're quite drunk now.'

Ben ordered beers for himself, Charlie and Ann, impressing everyone else with his facility for language.

'Useful chap,' murmured Kayla.

'You have no idea,' said Ann. 'If it wasn't for Ben here, Julian would still be lying in a gutter in Brussels, possibly exposing himself, while his car is scavenged for parts by local urchins.'

Ben was instantly the rather self-conscious centre of attention.

'Brussels?' asked Kayla.

'In a gutter?' said Carl.

'Flashing?' said Tracie, unerringly honing in on the most pressing item of the list. 'Ugh. I bet I could play one of them Wagner tuba things. They should let me try and then Todger Talbot can fall in as many canals as he likes and we can leave 'im there.'

'You probably could,' said Carl. 'But Todger Talbot – and don't think for a second that name isn't going to stick to him like shit to the arse he is – owns the Wagner tubas.'

'You see?' said Charlie, nodding owlishly. 'The capitalist that owns and controls the means of production holds all the cards.'

Ben had been following this conversation round the table like a kitten after a laser pointer, but was flummoxed at the latest swerve into Marxist dialectics.

'It's beginning to sound as if I should have left him in Brussels,' he said. 'Sorry.'

'Don't be daft,' said Charlie. 'Then we'd never have met you. Or got the good beer they always seem to bring you when you don't order it in English.'

'It's not *just* beer,' said Ann, glaring at Charlie. 'We really do need both Julian—' She was interrupted by Carl saying 'Todger Talbot' quietly, but she carried on, '—and his Wagner tubas. As you'll hear at tomorrow's concert. Do you like Bruckner?'

'Um, I don't know? Can't remember ever hearing any?'

'You'll get used to him. He plays everything at least three times, so you'll get the hang of the tunes by the end. We're doing a little bit of Mozart too, and Alexander's got a Strauss horn concerto.'

'He hasn't met Alexander yet,' Charlie pointed out. 'Stop confusing him.'

'He's not as drunk as you,' said Ann. 'You are the most confused.'

'I am *quite* confused,' Ben assured her.

'Don't worry,' said Tracie. 'You get used to them.'

37

Saturday arrived far, far too early for Eliot and Alexander on top of the after-effects of their previous evening. As promised, Ingrid made sure they were up, and conjured coffee for them in takeaway cups from a nearby café.

'I hadn't really clocked that to be on a live breakfast show means being awake before anyone else,' yawned Alexander.

'She did get us to agree when we were pissed,' agreed Eliot. 'Charlie tried to warn us.'

Ingrid was kindly but brisk as she put them in a car that would take them to the television station half an hour away in Roeselare.

'The interview will be conducted in English,' she said as they walked to it waiting in the road by the hotel, 'so there is no need for me to attend as translator.'

'Crikey – I hadn't even thought of that,' said Alexander. 'And another thing. I haven't got my horn. They don't want me to play anything, do they?'

'No. Five minutes' talk and then back here. The car will wait and return you to the hotel.' She smiled. 'Drink your coffee. You will be great. Remember to talk about tonight's concert too.'

The driver looked round at them from the front seat of the aggressively patchouli-scented car and nodded, and Ingrid shut the door.

David was able to do the first of the radio interviews over the phone from his hotel room. Ingrid sat with him, the interviewer on speakerphone between them, offering translations of various phrases when required. It was conducted in a hybrid of English and French, and if David's tic started jumping, nobody heard it.

Ingrid sent Jörg straight out after their regular breakfast catch-up meeting, clutching a handful of flyers for that evening's concert. He went to the church where they had played the Brandenburg, and surreptitiously laid a small pile of them on a table just inside, then attached some to any amenable surface he found nearby outside: bike stands, drainpipes, road signs. Note Perfect Tours had already arranged for some larger posters to be displayed, as they always did, but Ingrid was not going to let any opportunity slip through Jörg's nimble fingers.

By the time the rest of the orchestra straggled into breakfast, Jörg had returned and was sneaking in a second coffee. Eliot and Alexander sat with a hungover Charlie, making up for a definite lack of breakfast earlier, and reported on their brief moment as television celebrities to anyone within earshot who wanted to know.

Alexander waved at Erin as she came in, so after she had collected her breakfast she walked over to sit with them. Charlie raised his mug at her in salute and carried on eating in silence.

'How was telly-land?' she said to Alexander, and then looked closer. 'Is that *make-up*?'

'I told them to contour me properly,' he said, 'but they claimed the beard did that. Eliot's been done too, look. We are both utter tarts.'

Eliot looked round and grinned, looking slightly more tanned than he had been the previous evening. 'I'm thinking of keeping mine on all day. Whaddya think?'

Erin munched her croissant thoughtfully, then spoke through it. 'Nope.'

'Harsh.'

'What happened then?' she asked again. 'Apart from being tarted up.'

'Oh, it was a laugh,' said Alexander. 'Ingrid had already emailed them with a whole load of info—'

'There were *bullet points*,' said Eliot. 'I saw the page. Bullet points.'

'Ha! Why doesn't that surprise me?' said Alexander. 'So anyway, they knew stuff about the orchestra and why we were on tour and everything, so the woman just asked me specific stuff about why I'd chosen a Brandenburg, and about the horn part. And she asked if maybe we should be playing in the Concertgebouw now we were so famous. But I think that was a joke.'

'He bigged Richard up too,' said Eliot. 'Quite right too. He's such a great violinist.'

Erin licked croissant crumbs off her fingers. 'He is.'

'And then she came to me,' said Eliot, 'and was asking about how it felt to be a British orchestra touring Europe, you know, now, so close to the final…'

'Rift,' said Erin, looking glum.

'Yes, exactly. But then they played another clip of the video, when it pans round and shows your cello case – you know, where you've got that old EU flag sticker on the front – and she was asking all about that, and I made a bit of a speech about solidarity and not wanting to leave and loving Bach and European culture and blah-di-blah.

Anyway. Yeah.' He ran out of words and drank more coffee.

Alexander nodded. 'You were great!'

'You should have added that we'd captured an MEP's assistant and were keeping him as our mascot for tonight's concert,' said Charlie, gently and deliberately, as though every word hurt. His eyes were barely open. 'That would have been a USP nobody was expecting.'

Erin blinked at him. 'I thought you were hungover, but are you still drunk?'

'Unfortunately not. The drugs will kick in soon. S'true though. He's called Ben. He picked Julian up after he – Julian not Ben – had been beaten up in Brussels and drove him here.' Charlie waved a vague arm towards the door leading to the lobby. 'He's staying here. You'll prob'ly meet him in a minute when he wanders down for the buffet. Lovely chap. Actually, maybe not lovely.' Charlie frowned. 'He ordered my final beer last night and I think that was the killer. Don't know what it was, because Ben speaks ninety-seven languages and I didn't understand.'

Erin patted Charlie's arm sympathetically and made 'I've no idea what he's talking about' faces at Alexander and Eliot.

'Did you know,' said Alexander conversationally, 'that poor-quality beer was nicknamed "whip belly" in eighteenth-century English?'

'You,' said Eliot, 'are good value. Meanwhile,' he continued to Erin, 'how are your mentions going?'

Erin laughed. 'Well, since I handed over the professional bit to Ingrid, much better, thanks. Though – this'll tickle you – I got a message from Noel Osmar saying he'd noticed some "ripples in the ether" about us. I think that's how he described it.'

'Noel! Bloody hell,' said Charlie.

Eliot turned to Alexander and explained. 'That's DCI Noel Osmar to you, my friend. But, you know, a friendly one. He drinks with us sometimes… solves crimes… that sort of thing. He's got a soft spot for Erin.'

'He has not!' said Erin.

'You should get him to have a look at Julian's video,' said Charlie. 'Borderline porno. Surely breaking all sorts of rules. He should collar him on either the unsavoury underwear bulging or the words.' For the second time in two minutes everyone else looked at Charlie as if he were unhinged. He was unrepentant. 'Even I, socialist that I am, would rather have hobnobbed it with the Ford-Hugheses last night than have Julian's political willy-waving branded onto my retina. There are some things one cannot unsee.'

At that moment, Ben wandered into the breakfast room. Charlie waved at him. 'Ben! Get some food and come over here. My friends think I've invented you.' He turned to them and said earnestly, 'Ben's seen what I've seen. He will back me up. But on no account search it out for yourselves.'

Charlie returned to his coffee and the rest of his breakfast, leaving the rest of them to introduce themselves to Ben.

38

The church they were using for their concert was close to their hotel, so Ingrid asked Jörg to take the instruments there in his truck while the orchestra walked through the narrow cobbled streets. Keith, having parked his coach overnight in a larger car park on the outskirts of Bruges, had some well-deserved time off. Max and his timpani followed Jörg round a twisty route to arrive at a turning area with a few parking bays by one of the dusky red church doors. The truck and the van tucked themselves next to each other with their back doors facing the church, which rose in tall Gothic splendour, its red bricks warm in the sunshine. Pale stones contrasted with the brick up every available corner, and there were turrets, weathervanes, crosses and unidentified spiky-arm arrangements all across the roof, lifting their individual prayers to heaven in a haphazard ecumenical chorus. Tall mullioned windows of clear glass swept up the vast walls, promising half a chance of enough natural daylight for the musicians to be able to read their music inside.

Jörg opened up the back of the truck, lowered the tail lift to his customary halfway point and lounged on it like a cat on a windowsill, swinging one leg in the sunshine, waiting for the players to arrive. Max tugged his van doors open with a protesting creak.

Jörg watched as he lifted the first timp onto the cobbles. It was the one with the dent. 'I am sorry for your drum,' he said quietly, in the voice of one whose entire job revolved around keeping musical instruments safe. The precise wording of this second-language phrase gave more away than perhaps he realised.

Max nodded, grunting, leaning down to stroke his palm over the dent again, as if he could heal it by being more attentive. 'Could've been worse, I suppose. And it can be repaired when we get home.'

Jörg nodded. At the sound of a heavy rattling, they both turned to see one of the huge church doors swing open, and a small wizened man who looked about eighty stepped out of the gloom, putting up his hand to shade his eyes. He wore formal trousers and a collared shirt with the air of someone who had worn formal trousers and a collared shirt every single day of his eighty years, irrespective of day of the week or seasonal temperature.

'Stockwell Park Orchestra?' he called, in heavily accented English.

'*Ja*,' said Jörg.

The man beamed a twinkling smile, raised his other arm in acknowledgement and turned to open the second door. He fixed it fully open, sketched another wave in farewell over his head as he retreated inside. After looking at Jörg for a moment, Max trundled his timpani after him.

Ingrid and David arrived before Max reappeared. They were deep in conversation, well ahead of the rest of the orchestra. Jörg poured himself off the tail lift and straightened up to greet them.

'Hello, Jörg,' said David. 'I'll just pop inside first with Ingrid and have a quick check round before getting my horn, OK?'

'For sure,' said Jörg, leaning back on the tail lift. 'Max is in the church. Also, a man opened the doors and went back in.'

'Ah yes, that will be Diederich,' said Ingrid, nodding. 'He arranged to open up the church for our rehearsal.'

She and David walked in through the heavy doors. Jörg stayed motionless, looking down the street with a steady gaze. It was a quiet road, away from the main swirl of tourists that eddied through Bruges every day. The cobbles and God had been communing there for centuries. He listened to the distant sounds of a summer city, far enough removed to let him imagine he was waiting outside a church in a small village.

Before he could meditate for too long, he heard voices approaching, and hitched his hip off the tail lift. By the time the musicians appeared, he was standing in the back of the truck, ready to unload the first instrument.

Within twenty minutes, everyone had collected what they needed and brought it into the church. True to their promise, the windows welcomed in the sunlight. As well as the tall full-length ones, there was a row of shallower windows above the arches and pillars on either side of the nave, running its full length. The light fell on white walls and a pale stone floor, diffusing up to a white vaulted roof.

'Blimey!' said Charlie, looking up. 'Very clean and bright. Like living in a bar of soap.'

'It's to cleanse our souls,' said Ann, walking past him to put her cello case to one side. 'You wait. By the end of the rehearsal you'll have guilt feelings about things you can't even remember doing.'

'Blame Ben. He got that last beer in.'

'What's Ben doing on his own this afternoon?' asked Erin.

'I think he's going to visit Choco-Story,' said Charlie. 'It may only be to get me a present. He said I was going on about missing every single chocolate museum on our tour. Me! "Going on".'

'Well if you hadn't had quite such a banging hangover this morning you could have gone yourself.'

'Alright, alright, Little Miss I'm Visiting The Posh Suite.'

'Children,' said Ann, not that saying that ever made any difference to Charlie and Erin.

'Sorry, Mum,' said Charlie. He ducked out of the way to avoid Ann's slap to his head.

Eliot was sorting scores on his stand in front of an orchestra-shaped arrangement of chairs that was slowly being populated. Diederich had been most particular where they got their chairs from: apparently they had to sit on completely different ones from those used for any congregation, and it involved carting them from a distant store room accessed only via a spiral staircase in a turret. Diederich had twinkled and smiled and delegated and done absolutely none of the chair shifting himself.

'Hello everyone,' said Eliot, as most people had sat down. 'I think it's Saturday. Seems a long time ago since our last concert. Was it only Thursday? And what a lot has happened since! We've come over all famous, for starters.'

There were laughs and a few cheers. Several members of the orchestra had managed to find the breakfast television interview with Eliot and Alexander online, and everyone had been sharing the clip on social media.

'Who knows how that will affect tonight?' Eliot carried on. 'Anyway, we'll just do our thing and let everything else sort of wash over us. First things first: do we have a pair of cymbals and full complement of triangle equipment?'

Pearl flushed a deep red, and held up both triangle and its official stick to beat it with, to enormous applause.

'It weren't my fault,' said Tracie. 'I definitely handed both over on Thursday night.'

'I'm sure you did. Did we ever find out what happened to it?' asked Eliot, grinning broadly.

'I think that was my fault,' said Pete. What he was about to say was drowned out by a chorus of 'oh *Pete*' and general good-natured groaning. He tried again when it had quietened down. 'It had fallen on the floor and I must have kicked it away when I was getting ready to play the cymbal clash.'

'It ended up somewhere under the second violins, I think,' said Marco.

'Ah, I see,' said Eliot. 'Well, let's hear it again for Pearl's emergency teaspoon, and hope we won't have to use it again.' He grinned again as she again received a round of applause. 'Right, then. I suppose we'd better start. Let's do it in the reverse order this time, so we can let people go after we've worked on the Bruckner if they don't play in anything else.'

'Excellent,' called Carl, to a few foot-thumps from other brass players.

'On one condition,' said Eliot, swinging round to look at Julian and the other Wagner tuba players. 'I'm only letting you out of my sight if you *promise*, on an aged relative's soul, that you will not start a fight, incite riots or fall into any canal between now and the concert. OK?'

Julian nodded. Alexander looked along the row at him, past Tom and Lamar, and said quietly, 'Or we'll set Carl loose on you.'

Julian flicked a look of annoyance at Alexander, who gave a thumbs-up to Eliot. There was nothing more they could do.

As the final players got into the right seats, and any remaining turf wars of where a music stand should go were being settled more or less amicably, two women walked on silent shoes through the main doors, squinting as their eyes adjusted away from the harsh glare outside. Ingrid stepped up to greet them, and had a quiet conversation in Dutch. They came over to Eliot, where Ingrid made some introductions.

'Eliot, this is Lise and Noor. Eliot Yarrow, conductor of Stockwell Park Orchestra.'

Eliot shook hands with both Lise and Noor, turning an enquiring expression to Ingrid. Lise said something that sounded as if she was clearing her throat of a fur-ball ready to speak.

'Sorry?' said Eliot.

'They are from the Vlaamse Radio- en Televisieomroeporganisatie,' said Ingrid, sounding only marginally less furbally. 'It's the Flemish public broadcaster here in Belgium.'

'Oh! Sorry. Right.' Eliot wasn't going to go near a phlegmish pun out loud, but that didn't mean he wasn't thinking it.

'VRT,' said Noor, smiling. 'It's quicker to say.'

'We work at Klara, VRT's classical radio station,' added Lise. 'I'm a producer, and Noor presents a topical arts magazine programme.'

'If it's OK,' said Noor, 'we'd like to make a programme about you and your orchestra.'

39

Eliot looked dazed.

'I asked them along this afternoon,' explained Ingrid. 'Klara would like to do a piece covering Stockwell Park Orchestra's final day on tour – you know, capturing some of the more informal moments and so on, as well as what we are playing.'

'I see, yes,' said Eliot. 'Of course. Lovely. Help yourselves. Is it alright if we just crack on?'

'Please,' said Noor. 'You won't know we're here.'

She and Lise walked over to a chair near the side wall to unpack their bags, bringing out notepads and a digital microphone.

'As I said,' Eliot said to the orchestra, 'fame. Let's all try to rise above it and concentrate.'

'Says the man in make-up,' muttered Erin from just underneath Eliot's right elbow.

'Shh,' said Eliot. 'Come on. Bruckner top and tail. Third movement, please. There were a few hairy corners I'd just like to finesse our way around before we get to the Wagner tuba bits, if that's OK. Can we remember that it's *da capo* when we get to the end of the *Trio*? Write it in, in big letters. I know you lot: even when you've remembered you have to go back to the start of the *Scherzo*, you look at those three bars' rest at the end and think "oh we're fine, I'll just turn the page then", but all the strings need to be there. Everyone else can faff, but not us. Stick a paperclip in the page you need to get back to, or something.'

'We don't have a paperclip,' said Maureen, from her customary stance of gloomy criticism. In her case, since she sat on the outside of the desk, she had no responsibility for the page turns at all: that was Marco's job. Marco was counting the rehearsals until he could be upgraded from being Maureen's desk partner.

'It's OK,' he said quietly. 'I'll manage.'

Eliot looked at Marco kindly. Everyone had been Maureened at one time or another and he knew Marco put up with more than most people. 'Maybe Pearl's got a spare biscuit you can stick in the place. Something nice and flat, like a… Nice.'

'Or those lovely almondy things they give you with a coffee here,' said Charlie.

'Neither of those would stick in the part though,' Erin pointed out. 'You'd need something with chocolate.'

'Don't mind us,' said Eliot to the wind and brass. 'Strings just having a biscuit discussion. It's like bowing only with more calories.' He winked at Marco, and raised his baton. 'Shall we?'

The strings started their insistent motif, in a quick three-four tempo marked *sehr schnell* (very fast). Eliot was never going to attempt to show all three beats, but set off giving them the speed of each bar and leaving them to subdivide the crotchet pulse for themselves.

Lise, whose microphone had picked up all the previous conversation, crept closer to the orchestra and extended the boom.

When the horns, trombones and trumpets all joined in to beef up the sound, Eliot called, 'Save it, save it!' He didn't want to get to the evening's performance with a whole section of knackered lips.

There were a couple of bars in that movement that Max had to fill with a moment of solo timpani work, which happened to be on his dented one. He grimaced as he got through it, perfectly timed but sounding, to his ears, very off indeed. Eliot saw the face he pulled, and stopped conducting.

'It probably sounds worse to you than it does to us, Max. Don't worry.'

'I could try tuning one of the others for it?' said Max.

Eliot flicked through a few pages of his score. 'Honestly, for the faff, it won't be worth it. You've got those couple of bars on your own, but then the rest of it is with everybody. Don't worry about it.'

Max did look worried still, but nodded.

Eliot took them round some of the awkward corners, including making the strings turn back for their *da capo* several times until he was sure they wouldn't leave him hanging that evening. 'OK, great. Thanks. Now a few bits with the Wagner tubas, then they can go.' He took a quick glance behind him to see if Lise and her boom microphone were still hanging on his every word. 'Subject to our earlier agreement, yeah?'

They nodded, and Eliot went through some stops and starts and tempo changes, including Pearl and Pete's bar of triumph, which they managed without any cutlery-based incidents. One thing an orchestra at the end of a tour doesn't want or need is to be forced to play swathes of loud music they know well, just to tire themselves out. Eliot knew it, and – up to a fairly well-defined, Julian-shaped point – trusted them to be there for him later.

As some brass and the other Wagner tuba players packed away their instruments and got ready to leave, Carl called to Eliot, 'Are we OK to leave our instruments here until later?'

Eliot looked at Ingrid for confirmation, who stopped tapping out emails on her phone and nodded.

'Jörg will be in attendance,' she said.

Alexander swapped his Wagner tuba for a horn and took a swig from his water bottle. Noor approached him. At barely five feet tall, light on her feet and slightly built, she looked like an elf approaching a giant.

'Ingrid tells me you are the soloist in the Strauss?'

'Yes.' Alexander put out his hand. 'Hello. I'm Alexander.'

'Noor. If it's OK with you, I'd love Lise to get some recording of you rehearsing some bits of this?'

'Fine by me, but I'm not sure how much of it Eliot will be doing now. I know he's not keen on tiring us all out before this evening.' Alexander smiled, not knowing how far to push his luck. 'You could always come along again tonight and get the whole thing?'

'I'd like to very much,' said Noor. 'I've heard your performance of the Bach, and am looking forward to hearing you play the Strauss. But I'll have to see what resources are available.'

'Of course.' Alexander raised his water bottle to her as if in a toast.

Over in the cellos, Charlie and Erin were leaning back in their chairs and, like most of the rest of the orchestra, drinking water too. The church may have been cooler than outside but it was still ludicrously warm.

'Looks like Noor's in the charm zone,' said Charlie, nodding over to where she and Alexander were talking.

'Who wouldn't be?' said Erin, smiling.

'Oh, not you as well.'

'What? No. He's a lovely guy.'

'Who just happens to look like a *Ragnarok*-era Chris Hemsworth. You know, before fat Thor in *Endgame*.'

'Someone's been overthinking this.'

Charlie poked his tongue out at her, which handily saved him from articulating any of the thoughts which he had indeed been, privately, overthinking.

Eliot looked round and raised his eyebrows at Alexander to see if he was ready to start the Strauss. He excused himself to Noor and walked over.

'Just a few bits and pieces,' said Eliot. 'Not much to polish. Let's just remind them of what to do and we can set it running tonight.'

'Sure,' said Alexander. 'Um... Noor said something about wanting to record some of this rehearsal. I told her it was OK by me – is it?'

'Absolutely. In for a penny. When Mrs Ford-Hughes hears about all this showbiz stuff she will be beside herself.'

Alexander gave him a steady look. 'I'm going to get hugged again, aren't I?'

'Yep.'

'Let's do this.'

Eliot checked Lise was ready, threw down the first orchestral chord and let Alexander take the church's fine acoustic for a test drive.

* * *

After the Strauss had been put through its paces, and there had been several intense exchanges of looks between Noor and Lise, Eliot let the trumpets go so he could dust off the *Figaro* overture.

'And I guess you can go too, if you want,' he said to Alexander, who was emptying out his horn and rubbing the bell over with a soft cloth before putting it away.

'Would you mind waiting for a few minutes more?' said Ingrid. 'I would very much like to take a picture of all the musicians who played in the Bach. Perhaps at the end of the rehearsal?'

'No problem,' said Alexander, and sat on the front row of seats in the nave, leaning his elbows behind him over the backs of the chairs and crossing one ankle over his knee. Noor went to sit next to him.

'Shall we just run this?' asked Eliot. 'It's only five minutes. Let's remind ourselves how it goes. Think of it as a palate cleanser.'

Pete blinked hard to ready himself for the quavers, and they were off.

40

While Ingrid arranged the Bach players together to take their picture, the rest of the orchestra took their instruments and cases into a side room. Diederich stood beside the open doorway, smiling and nodding and waving them through, exclaiming cheery-sounding things in Flemish that nobody understood.

Ingrid grouped the remaining musicians in front of the carved wooden pulpit: a structure that looked as if the seventeenth-century wood carver had drunk an obscene amount of Trappist beer and accepted a bet to cram as many figures as he could onto every surface. It was a spectacularly crowded, writhing, indoor treehouse. An overwritten, adverb-heavy character sketch in pulpit form.

'Wowzer,' said Charlie, peering over the rope strung around the pulpit to keep people out. Or the pulpit in. 'That's quite something.'

'Imagine having to climb up into that to deliver a sermon every week,' said Erin.

Ann cast her eye over the lumpy figures. 'Carved by a man, no doubt. Nightmare to dust.'

'Maybe it was to keep people occupied daydreaming while they had to sit through a couple of hours of boring finger-wagging,' said Eliot.

'But you complain if we get distracted in rehearsal…' said Erin.

'Oi! That's not the same thing at all.'

Their attention was called back by Ingrid, lining up her frame. 'Can we look over here, please? Kayla, can you bring your bass in closer on the left? Alexander, your horn higher, please. And Richard, stand closer to Alexander. Violin up. Perfect!'

She took a few shots, declared herself satisfied and looked over to where Diederich was still manning the door to the side room like a liminal museum attendant on the cusp between galleries. 'Your instruments and cases can be left in that room. Either Jörg or I will be in attendance at all times between now and the concert.'

Near the main door, Lise was standing close to Noor, who was on the phone. There was a lot of gesticulation and nodding going on.

Charlie nudged Alexander on his way to put his cello case away, nodding to where Noor was talking with animation. 'Do you think you've blagged your way into being a major international feature?'

'Dunno. I did get the distinct impression our rehearsal was some kind of audition.'

'Wonder if we passed.' Charlie grinned. 'You did, obviously. We might hold you back, I'm afraid.'

'No finer cello section,' said Alexander.

'Well, I meant "we" in the "Pete" sense more than us, but thanks.' Charlie laughed and walked off.

242

Alexander laughed too, and shook his head. He was bending to put his horn away in its case when Noor touched him gently on the shoulder.

'Alexander? Lise and I have just got off the phone to our manager. We pitched an idea to him, and I'm very pleased to say he agreed. We're going to do a much longer feature on you, and this orchestra, than the short item we had planned, and if it's still OK with you we'd like to record the concert tonight? Not to broadcast live or anything – we can't change the station's output like that! – but in a few days when Lise has edited a full programme together, we'll put it out with some or all of the concert material. How does that sound?'

Alexander straightened up. 'That sounds... brilliant. Thanks very much! Um... should we be speaking to Eliot or maybe David the orchestra manager too? I don't know how much is up to me.' He looked round to see if either of them was still in the church.

'Of course.' Noor smiled. 'I thought I'd ask you first. I'm sure Ingrid can help to sort details.'

Ingrid turned at the sound of her name from where she had been in discussions with Diederich, and walked over. She was delighted to hear about the plans to record the concert for broadcast, and promised that she and Jörg would help set up when the sound engineers arrived. Eliot and David had already left the church, but it was the work of a moment for Ingrid to dial up a conference call with them and Mr and Mrs Ford-Hughes, for Noor to outline her plan and get enthusiastic assent. Noor's face implied she hadn't been totally prepared for the decibel level of a Mrs Ford-Hughes enthusiastic assent, but Ingrid's speakerphone coped admirably and it was all good.

Ingrid finished the call, and added another page of notes to her clipboard tally. 'On behalf of Note Perfect Tours, I'm so pleased to be able to work with you and Lise,' she said, shaking Noor's hand. 'You have my number. If you require anything else between now and this evening, please contact me.' She left them and returned to Diederich and Jörg in the instrument room.

'One last request,' said Noor to Alexander. 'May Lise and I shadow you for the rest of this afternoon? We can record a few snippets to use later instead of a formal interview. More like a casual conversation. I think everyone will be more relaxed that way. We'll come back here early to meet our sound engineers and then obviously stay for the concert.'

'Of course,' said Alexander. He left his horn with Jörg, and they walked back towards the hotel in search of a bite to eat.

Charlie, Ann and Erin had already met Ben at a bar, and were ordering food and soft drinks.

'Is this a mid-afternoon snack or early supper?' asked Charlie. 'I never know on concert days.'

'Your stomach is a law unto itself,' said Erin.

'I suppose it must muck your timetables up,' said Ben. 'Just when everyone else normal would be going out for dinner, you're putting on the entertainment.'

Ann laughed. 'We're definitely not normal.'

'And we drink after, not before,' added Erin, accepting her sparkling water from the waiter with a smile.

'I'm having one beer,' said Ben. 'It's still early, and I'm not driving 'til after the concert. Which I don't have to play in.'

'Anyway, Ben, what have you been up to while we've been working?' said Charlie.

'You mean did I manage to get you something from the chocolate museum?' said Ben, leaning down and reaching into a bag at his feet. 'Yes. Though in this heat you might need a spoon.'

'Ah, cheers man,' said Charlie. 'How much do I owe you?'

'Don't worry about it,' said Ben. 'I've been having a great time pretending to be a tourist. It's mad, isn't it? You live somewhere and you don't do any of the tourist visiting stuff. Like – did you know there's a brewery here that has built a *pipeline* to get its beer off site, because their delivery lorries can't really fit in all these tiny, crinkly streets? Man alive.'

Ann looked at the pure pleasure on Ben's face. 'This is why we needed you, Ben.'

'Did you manage to see that dog?' asked Charlie. He looked at the blank faces. 'You know, the golden Labrador who spends all his time lounging around in the window seat above a canal, saying hello to everyone going past? He's famous!'

'Um, no,' said Ben. 'Sorry.'

'I think you're making it up,' said Erin, getting her phone out.

'Am not,' said Charlie. 'He even got a cameo shot in *In Bruges*. He's famous!'

'So famous you don't know his name,' said Ann.

'Ah. Bad news on the dog front,' said Erin, frowning at her phone. 'He died in 2016. Called Fidèle. Looked like a handsome chap.' She showed the pictures on her screen to Charlie. 'Sorry.'

'Damn,' said Charlie. 'I should have come here earlier.'

They had a short moment of quiet mourning for Fidèle.

'Well, Ben, while you were off being a chocolate and beer fiend,' said Erin, brightening up, 'our orchestra was being sussed out by a local radio station. Soon our fame might not be just internet-based.'

'Oh yeah? Which one?' said Ben. 'And in which language? It's a minefield.'

'Did anyone catch what those women said?' asked Ann. 'I didn't hear.'

'Klara, I think,' said Charlie. 'Part of something else bigger that I can't remember or attempt to pronounce.'

'Ooh,' said Ben, taking a sip of his beer and raising his eyebrows. 'Hit the big time.'

'I can't tell if he's joking,' said Ann to the other two in a stage whisper. Ben just laughed.

'Blimey,' said Erin, and looked up from her phone. 'Guess who's coming to our concert.'

'Petroc Trelawny,' said Ann.

'You're making that up,' said Ben.

Ann laughed. 'Well, it's a real – rather splendid – name, but I doubt he's coming. Presenter on Radio 3.'

'Nope,' said Erin.

'Alexander's wife?' muttered Charlie.

Ann gave him a sharp look. 'He's single, as far as I know. We give up. Who?'

'Noel Osmar,' said Erin.

'Good grief,' said Ann. 'That's dedication.'

'Who's this?' asked Ben.

'That policeman we mentioned before,' said Charlie. 'Our tame one. Nice guy.'

Erin scanned the message she had received. 'He says he's got the weekend off – that must make a change – and since we're now famous he thought he'd get on a train and come and say hello. He gets in at five o'clock.'

'About now, then,' said Ann, looking at her watch. 'He's not one to build up anticipation, is he?'

'Remember how he always sneaks up on us in the pub and just appears?' said Charlie. 'He's doing the same thing, only on a continental scale.'

'Is he staying over?' said Ann. 'Tell him which hotel we're in.'

'One in, one out,' said Ben. 'I'm back to Brussels tonight.'

'Aw, just when we'd made friends,' said Charlie.

'You can come and visit me any time. All of you,' said Ben. 'Except Julian. Not him.'

Erin tapped a reply. 'I've told him where we are now too, but that we'll be back at the hotel by around six to change and get out again.'

'But there's no crime for him to solve,' said Charlie. 'Unless we count Julian's video. Maybe that'll do.'

'Leave him alone,' said Erin. 'Let the bloke go on a minibreak and relax.'

The waiter appeared with their grilled sandwiches, and they thankfully put all thoughts of Julian's Y-fronts out of their minds.

41

When Alexander, Noor and Lise walked back to the church shortly after six o'clock, the quiet street was not as deserted as it had been earlier. Jörg's truck was still neatly parked alongside Max's van, and another van had drawn up in the next available parking space. The row of bike racks to the right of the church doors was now full, with more free-form bike-parking spilling against the brick wall. People milled about, taking pictures of the church, the truck, the vans and, as he approached, Alexander himself. They allowed themselves a small surge in his direction.

'Ah – the VRT engineers are here,' said Noor, looking at the new van. She smiled at Alexander. 'Setting up the mics for you.'

'Not just me,' said Alexander, looking at the small crowd in bemusement.

Noor followed his eyes. 'You think?'

Lise peered into the open doors of the empty VRT van before leading the way into the church. Inside, two sweating men in T-shirts and shorts were adjusting microphone stands and taping electrical cables to the stone floor as the wires snaked underfoot. Diederich had climbed up to the organ loft and was looking on from the balcony, nodding and appearing just as delighted as he had been all afternoon. Jörg, now transformed into his front-of-house clothing rather than his usual vest, was giving the sound engineers a hand.

Ingrid looked over to Alexander from where she was trying to speak calmly to a group of people clustering round her, all jabbering questions at once. As if directed by her gaze, they immediately detached themselves from her and clattered over to Alexander. He smiled at them, but shrugged at Ingrid. She too came close, and stopped just beyond his bobbing admirers.

'Hello, Ingrid,' said Alexander. 'Um, guys, please – can we have a bit of hush and we'll see what's what?'

The crowd stopped jostling and fell mostly silent. They were a mix of young people with daypacks slung over their shoulders, and couples who slung their arms over each other's shoulders, and a group of teenage girls who had been the loudest of the lot and even now were trying to suppress giggles and squeaks.

Ingrid smiled at Alexander's almost magical effect on them. 'Good evening, Alexander. As you see, we have an audience that is both keen and early.' She addressed the group crowding round him. 'This is Alexander Leakey, our French horn soloist for tonight's Strauss concerto. You may also have heard him play a Brandenburg recently online—'

The teenagers erupted into high-pitched cheering and started jostling again, but Alexander flapped his hands at them as if he were Neptune calming turbulent waters, which was more or less effective. He could see it would only be temporary.

'I'm sure Alexander would be only too happy to speak with you after the performance,' Ingrid continued, 'but please allow him now to continue to our room "backstage", as it were.'

There were general groans of disappointment.

Noor spoke up, in English as Ingrid had. 'Hello everyone. I'm Noor. That's our VRT van outside – we're recording tonight's concert for our classical music station, Klara. This is Lise, my producer. While Alexander goes to get ready, I would love to interview some of you for a feature we're running? I don't know where you're all from, but we can do it in English, Dutch or Flemish, or anything else we can work out, if you like!'

Ingrid nodded her grateful thanks to Noor as the crowd followed her outside as if she were the Pied Piper, with a mic instead of a flute. Jörg walked over from where he had been tightening the last boom. He and Ingrid had a short exchange in German; Jörg nodded and went to staff the table by the door to take money for tickets and sell programmes.

'*Gut*,' said Ingrid, smoothing her already smooth hair and checking her clipboard. She looked at her watch, and then at Alexander. 'Your Brandenburg seems to have had even more of an effect than anyone anticipated. Congratulations. I am delighted.'

'Thank you. Believe me, I'm more surprised than anyone.'

'I imagine those people are only the earliest arrivals of the extras we are to expect tonight. May I suggest you go into the side room until the performance?'

'Of course,' said Alexander, glancing back to the door where the silhouette of Jörg could be seen dealing with some of the crowd previously outside, who now wanted to come in. 'I'll get out of the way. Thank you for,' – he gestured around the church, to the microphones, cables, and general sudden popularity of the place – 'all this.'

Ingrid nodded, smiled and blinked slowly, as was her custom. It was almost a bow. In an increasingly wild evening, Alexander felt he could rely on her lodestone nature, and slip into an easy orbit around her steadfastness. He went to sit quietly with his horn until the rest of the orchestra turned up.

He didn't have to wait long. Ingrid had delegated to David the task of getting all the players out of the hotel on time, but because they were all walking instead of arriving on a coach, they drifted along to the church in twos and threes. Eliot was one of the first to arrive, and close behind him came Charlie, Erin, Ann and Ben. Walking easily as a cat next to them was Noel Osmar, recently arrived at Bruges station and even more recently booked into a room in the same hotel as them. He carried a lightweight jacket hooked on a finger over his shoulder; the other hand was in his trouser pocket. He had opened the neck of his shirt to catch any breeze that was going, and had a definite air of one who was determined to enjoy his weekend off. His lined grey eyes, as quietly observant as usual, moved between Erin and Charlie, who were speaking in cascades trying to squash the events of six days into the ten-minute walk they had available before the concert.

Charlie broke off in the middle of trying to explain about Julian getting his second dunking of the week, and saw the crowds of people surging around Noor and the VRT van. 'Bloody hell. Look at this!'

They stopped walking.

Noel looked at Erin. 'I said you were famous. Are you going to be on the telly too?'

'There were some radio people here earlier,' said Erin. 'But I don't remember that van being here.'

'It's VRT – they do both, but I don't see any cameras,' said Ben. 'She looks like she's doing some vox pops.' He pointed to where Noor was surrounded by a group of young people all leaning in to talk into the microphone she was holding. 'In Dutch by the sound of it. Shall I go and join in and big you up? I could be a "friend of the celebrities".'

Ann laughed. 'You can work your way up to some proper ones via us.'

'We ought to be getting inside, I suppose,' said Erin. 'Ben, do *not* leave afterwards without saying goodbye. Noel, we'll definitely see you for a drink after.'

'You'd better go and get a ticket from Jörg,' said Charlie. 'Before it's sold out. Given that one of you has come from another city, and the other from a whole different blimmin' country, it would be a shame if you didn't get to hear us. After all that.'

'We could sneak them in as our new percussion section,' said Ann.

Ben looked alarmed. 'I couldn't!'

'Some might say you were overqualified, given the current incumbents,' said Charlie.

'They're kidding, don't worry,' said Erin. 'Come on. Let's go. Look after each other.'

Noel sketched a wave and watched as she, Ann and Charlie ducked in through the door past what was now a substantial crowd of people. He turned to Ben and gestured to the door, smiling. 'Shall we?'

They were just about to follow the others through the door when there was a shriek behind them. They turned to see the vision in fuchsia flower-printed silk that was Mrs Ford-Hughes shimmering towards them, like a sentient trellis. She had paired that evening's gown with another matching fascinator, this time with artificial blooms instead of feathers, and was bearing down on Noel with her arms outstretched. His nostrils began to tickle as the outrider perfume molecules arrived.

'Well, I declare, as I live and breathe! Noel Osmar! It *is*! Come here, honey.' With the inevitability of an oncoming tornado, Noel was enveloped, spun around and deposited slightly more dishevelled a bit further along the pavement. Mrs Ford-Hughes looked back for her husband. 'Look, darling! I said I thought it was Noel.'

Mr Ford-Hughes shook Noel's hand to try to coax some formality back into the proceedings. 'Indeed you did. Good evening, Inspector.'

'Oh, I'm off duty tonight,' said Noel with a smile. 'And I don't think I have any jurisdiction over here in any case.'

Ben looked from Noel to Mr and Mrs Ford-Hughes with the air of someone out of their depth, as if they had started reading the third book in a trilogy without knowing what went on in the first two. Noel cleared his throat.

'Ah, Ben. I'd like you to meet Mr and Mrs Ford-Hughes, sponsors of orchestras and, in the case of Mrs Ford-Hughes,' he bowed gallantly to her, 'a fine singer in her own right.'

Mrs Ford-Hughes giggled. The flowers on her fascinator wobbled in sync.

'Hello,' said Ben. 'I'm Ben. Rescuer of Wagner tuba players and, um, not a bad guitar player, if I'm honest.'

Noel raised his eyebrows at him. 'I hadn't heard about the rescue. Never a dull moment this week, apparently.'

'And now it's got even more peachy for our last night,' cried Mrs Ford-Hughes, 'with this radio programme wanting to record the whole caboodle, and Alexander being a superstar over all the social medias! Have you heard?'

'I caught the edited highlights,' said Noel. 'I've just arrived. Erin was telling me.'

'Oh, she was the one who got the whole thing started! She's smart as a whip.'

'She's just gone inside, if you need her.'

'Oh! Well, we must get in! Let's find Ingrid, darling, and see if we need to speak to any of these radio folk!'

She bustled into the church, technically on her husband's arm but actually propelling him herself, leaving scattered exclamation marks behind her.

Noel looked at Ben kindly. 'You never forget your first Ford-Hugheses. Come on. Let's go in and bag a seat.'

42

They found themselves two seats near the front and sat there together as the space around them filled rapidly. Mr Ford-Hughes had stationed himself on the front row. He was defending the seat next to him for his wife, who was nowhere to be seen, and had already moved through the ultra-polite gracious head shake in response to an 'is this seat free?' enquiry to blocking moves Bruce Lee would have approved of. The last few members of the orchestra walked down the side of the church with stunned expressions, having had to fight their way through the crowds outside and those pressing round the table by the door to buy a ticket. Jörg and Ingrid were performing gate-keeping duties with both warm hospitality and iron resilience as they let the audience swell through the doors in a controlled way.

Noor finished her interviews outside and, with Lise, rode the surge of extra people over the threshold, as people who had been hoping to speak on the radio now switched their priority to getting a seat close enough to see Alexander. Ingrid told them quietly which door led to the steps up into the organ loft, where they could join their sound engineers. Noor and Lise melted away in what they hoped was an unobtrusive fashion, in case any excitable fans decided to follow them.

In the side room, the orchestra was doing their usual instrument twiddling and warming up in a space that was slightly too cramped to do that comfortably. They were interrupted by Mrs Ford-Hughes, who had burst in past Diederich (standing outside the door as a wizened sentry) and flung her arms wide. People nearest to her tried to ride the perfume wave without obviously choking.

'Don't mind me! I just wanted to come back here to wish you all the very best,' she cried. 'And I can honestly say that my husband and I have never been prouder of Stockwell Park Orchestra. Have you seen the crowds out there? This tour has been all we'd hoped, and so very much more. Eliot, honey,' she reached out her hand toward him and grasped his, 'thank you so much.'

Eliot smiled and squeezed her hand, wondering how much champagne she had already drunk.

'And Alexander – where are you?' she said, dropping Eliot's hand and scanning the room for him. He waved from the far corner, over the heads of the rest of the orchestra. 'Well, I can't reach you over there, honey, but I wanted to thank you too, and everybody, and to say how much I appreciate all your hard work!'

Just as Eliot was trying to work out how to get her to reverse out of the room and let them get on with the concert, she twirled, blowing kisses to them all, and swept out.

There was a slightly stunned silence.

'Think of it this way,' said Eliot. 'We could have been doing Strauss's *Four Last Songs* instead of the horn concerto.'

People broke down into laughter and groans in about equal measure, and Ingrid put her head round the door.

'Ready?' she said.

'As we'll ever be,' said Eliot, and stepped aside to let the players who were in the Mozart file out, hearing the swell of applause fill the church.

While they were tuning, Ingrid turned to Eliot and Alexander, keeping her hand on the door handle and letting them see through a small crack into the church. 'We have people standing at the back and along the sides. I have never seen such demand for a concert.'

Eliot grinned and flicked a look at Alexander. 'Well, we know who they've come to see. What does it feel like to be an international icon?'

Alexander snorted with laughter. 'Bugger off.'

'OK. See you in five. Get ready to wow your young fans.'

Carl looked up from where he was sitting with the other trombones. 'We'll keep his feet on the ground, don't you worry.'

'Great. Nobody go anywhere.'

And with that, Eliot walked out past Ingrid and Diederich to another roar from the crowd that would have been more familiar at a rock concert. He raised his arm in acknowledgement and grinned.

'Good evening, Bruges!' he called out, enjoying himself hugely as they answered back. He turned to look up at the organ loft behind the orchestra, where Noor, Lise and their two sound engineers were checking levels with concentrated faces. Noor smiled and gave him a thumbs-up.

'Thank you all for coming out to hear us play. We're going to start you off with Mozart: the overture to *The Marriage of Figaro*.'

He turned back to the orchestra and raised his baton. For all that they were playing it for the third and final time that week, the players' attention was sharper than ever, perhaps because of the crush of people and the anticipation that brought, or maybe it was the pheromone level generated by hundreds of teenagers waiting for Alexander. Either way, the quavers raced along, somehow conveying the infectious good cheer Mozart packed into the music. When Eliot stepped back and invited the *tutti* sections to let rip, the horns and Max on his dented timpani beefed up the decibels with such sudden alacrity the first few rows were blasted as if by an oven door opening. Ben and Noel's faces broke into smiles, and they exchanged a glance of shared excitement.

Eliot wound the tempo up as much as he dared without any viola wheels falling off, and conducted the last few bars locked in eye contact with Pete to stop him crashing into the rest. When he lowered his arms, the applause shot forward over him and the orchestra, and he nodded at his players, knowing they were experiencing a rare moment of teamwork that night and it could turn out to be something very special.

He bowed his thanks, winked at Mrs Ford-Hughes and walked off to fetch Alexander.

'Sounding great,' said Alexander, standing by the open door. 'Good crowd, is it?'

Eliot laughed quietly and nodded. 'It's quite something out there. You OK to go on?'

'Let's do it.'

As Alexander came into view from behind a pillar, the reaction was overwhelming. As well as the solid wall of applause, several teenagers stood up and screamed, waving and jumping in their excitement. A couple of hundred phones tracked his movement, and more flashed as they took his picture. Alexander grinned at the audience in general, and waved a few times at the knots of students bobbing above the

258

level of their seated companions like a volcanic archipelago in a superfast chain reaction. The noise was deafening.

'I think they like you,' said Eliot.

'This is unreal. Hey – maybe you'd better say something about flash photography, or they'll be popping all the way through.'

Charlie leaned over to Erin. 'Look what you've done. This is all your fault, you know.'

Erin laughed in disbelief. 'I just don't think things through, do I?'

Eliot put out his hands to quieten the crowd, and spoke once he could be heard. 'Thank you – again – for giving us such a warm welcome. May I present our soloist, whom I *think* you know about already: Alexander Leakey.' He waited to let the new eruption die down before speaking again. 'Just one thing, if you don't mind. Please don't use any flashes on your cameras during the performance. It will be distracting for our players, and I want them all to be looking at me.' As they laughed, Eliot looked over to Ingrid who was watching from the side wall. 'I can't say that in Dutch, so maybe I could ask Ingrid to translate that so everyone knows?'

Ingrid nodded, and while she was repeating that in Dutch, French and German, just to make sure, Alexander checked his tuning to Gwynneth's oboe.

'Thank you,' said Eliot, as Ingrid returned gracefully to the sidelines. 'So, now: Richard Strauss's first horn concerto.' He waited a moment for the restless shuffling to subside, checked with Alexander that he was ready to start, and threw the first chord down like a gauntlet.

Alexander, always a pretty mobile performer, inhabited the space in that church in an instant: totally and without fuzziness or decay at the edges. He was like an actor crackling with power in a character that can deliver a charisma hit right into an onlooker's brain. No nerves, no apprehensiveness, just pure enjoyment of living in the music at that time, in that place. He almost danced.

Up on the balcony, Noor watched him tease the audience into a conversation, luring them in before whipping round to lock himself into the next *tutti* section with the orchestra. Mrs Ford-Hughes was not the only woman on the front row who found herself swaying forward as if pulled in his slipstream. It was like watching the frontman of a band at a festival. It was elemental.

As in Cologne, Alexander and Eliot centred on each other as the concerto guided itself in to dock with the start of the slow second movement. Alexander became very still, paring back any distractions from the sound he was about to make, and, when it came, it shivered up the hairs on people's necks as it had done before. Alexander played his entire first long phrase without moving his feet from their place on the stone floor, somehow managing to fill the entire church with a *pianissimo* sound that still carried effortlessly to the very back of the space. Nobody in the audience moved. They appeared to have stopped breathing, as if Alexander had cast an ice sheet above their heads and was pouring moonlight over it. Even those people who were filming on their phones were rapt, silent and utterly still.

When the phrases warmed up a little and colour returned to the music, there seemed to be a breath given to the audience: permission to enjoy it as normal mortals instead of in rigid suspended animation. They passed from the gloom of seven flats in the key signature to a short interlude of four sunnier sharps, when Eliot had to get two flutes, two oboes and two clarinets to play their six-note *staccato* chord ensemble exactly as written, as sextuplet demisemiquavers. On his score it looked like lines of extremely cross ants marching through ink blots on the page. While the wind were dealing with that, the strings had to coordinate *pizzicato* chords that cantered up to a bar line in triplet semiquavers and landed on the other side of it in a duplet. Through all this, Alexander sailed his confident melody as if he were carrying on a conversation on horseback with a friend when one of their horses kept limping and the other was learning to tap dance. Eighteen-year-old Strauss was having a laugh.

When Alexander had had enough of his tune, he switched back to seven flats and gave it to the cellos, who started in the tenor clef and climbed until they reached the treble. Erin leaned round Eliot to look at Alexander as she played, since he had a few bars off and was appreciating the giddy heights the cellos were having to ascend. She arrived on her last note and handed it back to Alexander, who started his next phrase on exactly the same pitch. Baton passed, Alexander wiggled his eyebrows at Erin and took a few steps backward to fit himself back into the reprise of the earlier tune, and closed the stillness around himself again.

Then, with a shake of the reins, Eliot had eight bars as a bridge without Alexander to get them from the second into the third movement. Alexander took the opportunity to empty out his horn quickly before starting the *Rondo*. The orchestra bounced over the rhythms without running away with them, which was just as well, as the hiccoughing flute section was approaching. Brian had a fighting chance, having delivered twice that week already, but not if the tempo had got away from him before he started.

Eliot braced his feet apart and leaned back like a carriage driver hauling on the reins to stop his horses bolting, fixed

Brian and Amber with a look that was both confidence-inspiring and daring them to waver from his beat. Alexander half-turned towards the flutes and kept his eyes riveted on Eliot, ready to alter his timing at a micro level if required. Brian, against all odds, made it three out of three, and again when it came back later with the trick accidentals. Once they'd made it through the second time, there was an air of triumph among the players that made Eliot wary, but he needn't have worried. As soon as Alexander had his book-ending call echoing the very first of the concerto, the one that fell all the way through the horn's range to the very bottom then leaped up again only to pause, revving up on the start line with the rest of the players, Eliot knew he could let them kick off.

The horn part is marked *con bravura* (with skill, or brilliance), and Alexander left no one in any doubt that evening. He had more notes than anyone else; they tumbled out of him, with all the added grace notes thrown in for good measure, with what seemed like effortlessness that is the happy product of years of practice and natural talent. Eliot let Alexander lead the tempo, and together they wound the orchestra tight and let it rip.

They all landed on the final *fortissimo* note together, and Alexander had barely started to take his first breath in again when every single person listening was on their feet cheering, clapping and whooping. Eliot blinked involuntarily as the sudden whoomph of noise crashed over his shoulders, then he turned and acknowledged it for Alexander and the orchestra, standing to one side and letting Alexander accept the accolades. They walked off towards the side room, but the applause thundered on, so Eliot pushed Alexander back on by himself to take another bow. Alexander walked off a second time, but the audience started stamping their feet in time with each other, demanding another. Eliot grinned and shrugged, and they went back on together. This time the orchestra joined in the applause, and Alexander beamed at them, clapping back at them himself to say thank you.

Finally, he and Eliot walked off for a final time, people began to sit down again, and the noise level dropped.

Eliot gave Alexander a hug. Some things were worth more than a handshake.

43

Ben turned to Noel, his eyes shining. 'Wow.'

Noel smiled. 'They're good, aren't they?'

'Have you been coming to their concerts for years, then?'

'No. Happened upon them by chance last year. Caught up with something at work, and I sort of stuck. Hooked, you might say.'

Ann looked over at them as the orchestra filed off into the side room, and gave them an enquiring thumbs-up. Ben lifted both his thumbs, and then, not wanting to leave any doubt about his enthusiasm, alternated between a double OK sign and thumbs-up for a while. Ann laughed and nodded.

Mrs Ford-Hughes was twisting around in her seat to look at the size of the audience, a lot of whom were still snapping pictures and obviously putting them online. Over by the wall, Ingrid was doing the same on her phone before walking to the rear of the church. From her vantage point, Noor took the picture of the audience that would define the concert afterwards, packed to the brim with mainly young faces, many of them taking selfies. Ingrid and Jörg got busy at the refreshment table Jörg had set up near the main doors, while the noise level stabilised at an excited thrum that lasted the full twenty-minute interval.

After Ingrid had given the audience a couple of warnings the second half was about to start, the side door opened and the players walked out to play Bruckner. Carl and Tracie were again helping to ferry the percussion to Pearl and Pete. Alexander had swapped his horn for a Wagner tuba, and Julian led his quartet over to their section. His face was a mess of bruising and half-healed scabs, miraculously nowhere near his mouth.

'Crikey,' said Ben, leaning towards Noel. 'Julian's face looks awful.'

'Who?'

'Julian – the guy leading the Wagner tubas on.' Ben enjoyed sounding like the expert on a subject he had known nothing about twenty-four hours earlier. 'He's the one I rescued.'

'Ah.' Noel studied Julian's face. 'Charlie mentioned he wanted to show me a video of his.'

Ben shuddered. 'It's not pleasant. I mean, I just want to make it absolutely clear in the hearing of the law that I didn't know he'd been doing that when I offered to give him a lift.'

Noel raised an eyebrow and filed away what that character note revealed about both Julian and Ben. On the whole, he found himself warming to Ben.

After Richard had led the tuning for the whole orchestra, Eliot came on again to more applause, which he waved down.

'Lovely to have you so keen,' he said, grinning. 'I'm glad you seem to be enjoying yourselves. Our final piece for you tonight is Bruckner's Seventh Symphony. Are you OK with me speaking in English here?' There was general assent. 'Well, maybe I could ask Ingrid to summarise afterwards.

As you can see, we've beefed up the orchestral forces with all the brass we could think of. Over there behind the horns,' he gestured, 'we have four Wagner tubas, which is basically a made-up instrument that doesn't get out much. You may recognise one of the players.' He waited for the cheering to die away again. 'Let's hope he has some lip left for this. In the spirit of letting you know what you're about to hear so you can gauge how far we've got through it, this symphony is in four movements: *Allegro*, *Adagio*, a *Scherzo* and *Trio*, then the *Finale*. Not quite your classic fast-slow-dance-fast arrangement, but mostly. Basically, once that lot,' – he waved at the Wagner tubas again – 'come back in after the strings have been jumping about, we're on the home stretch.'

The audience laughed again. Eliot was not being what they thought of as a normal classical music conductor. A celebratory festival air had invaded the whole evening. Eliot and the orchestra were on their final night and had decided to enjoy themselves.

'Ingrid?' Eliot said, looking over to where she was standing. 'Could you just give them a quick "this is Bruckner and it's in four movements" kind of summary? Thank you!'

Ingrid smiled, unflappably provided her usual linguistic brilliance and returned to her place.

Eliot turned to the orchestra and let out a long breath, inviting them to be calm and focused with him. They had a long way to go. He checked with Erin and her cello section, and first horn Neema that they were ready, lifted his arm and started the violins with their barely audible *tremolando*. Neema and Erin watched each other across the orchestra to coordinate as Eliot brought them in with their first phrase, and the solo horn and cellos asked Bruckner's climbing question in unison, the cellos soaring up to a fourth leger line by their third bar. As Neema dropped out the violas took over, and the entire opening of the symphony masqueraded as an intense, inside-out string orchestra, with the violins relegated to scrubbing the scrunchy harmonies while the violas and cellos sang their glorious melody. The fact that Beatriz was playing along with the tune on her clarinet was a mystery: nobody can ever hear it over the strings having a string-fest. Bruckner being Bruckner, everyone – except the Wagner tubas, who weren't needed until the second movement – was giving it *fortissimo* welly by the time they were forty bars in, before retreating. One felt it was a muscle flex to get ready for what was to come.

Alexander sat back easily and watched the orchestra. He could relax, knowing he wasn't needed until the next movement and didn't even have to count bars. His eye was drawn to Erin and the cellos, since they were opposite facing him, and Bruckner was partial to giving the cellos a lot of the juiciest tunes. Given that this symphony could have taken double the number of string players than Stockwell Park could throw at it, they were making a gorgeous, rich sound. Alexander smiled and enjoyed himself. By the end of the movement, when Max was making the air distort with his timpani rumble under the rest of the brass ramping up layers of sound over the entire string section scrubbing as hard as they could, Alexander could feel the sound physically hit him. He let it wash through, blowing air silently into his Wagner tuba to warm it up. They were on next.

Eliot brought the orchestra off and let the chord ring into silence before he put his arms down and wiped his brow. They all needed a moment. Behind him, the audience stirred, shuffling into a different position, some tentative clapping from people who didn't know there are unwritten rules about not clapping in between movements, but Eliot's quick smile meant it didn't matter at all.

He looked over at the Wagner tubas to check all was well, and then at Pearl and Pete. Pearl nodded, and pointed to her triangle beater that was safely resting on her stand. A slow upbeat and the other-worldly, solemn sound of the odd brass quartet filled the church along with the violas, who shared their tune. Pearl and Pete really were getting their money's worth in that movement.

At the back of the church, on the very last row of seats, a reporter sat with his iPad propped on his knees, a small keyboard connected wirelessly as he silently typed up his report in real time for his online news outlet. His cameraman sat beside him, dozing gently. They had got a few interviews with some of the fans before the concert, who, like themselves, got swept up in the online interest without ever hearing Alexander or the orchestra before. The reporter had already described the ecstatic reception Alexander had got in the Strauss, and now was trying to capture the full essence of the Bruckner without maybe needing to listen until the very end. The earlier he could load his piece, the more topical and therefore more potent it would be.

The cameraman jerked awake at Pete's cymbal crash, looking quickly around to see if anyone had caught him napping. Before Pearl's triangle tinkling had dissipated, he was already slipping back under. Sometimes heat and unfamiliar music combine to be an irresistible sleeping draught.

During the third movement, the reporter noticed there were a lot of bobbing heads, caught up in the dancing rhythm. Some people were swaying in their seats. He even found his own foot tapping as he typed. This orchestral stuff was infectious.

Eliot grinned at the orchestra at the successful end of the third (foot-tapping) movement, nodding his congratulations to them for their exemplary page turn back to the *da capo*. He didn't bother mopping his face. This was the home straight. As the ringing echo of the last note of the third movement decayed, he started the violins off on their surprisingly jaunty phrases at the beginning of the fourth. The symphony stretched itself fully and comfortably back into E major: a happy and relaxed key. The violins sounded like someone kicking a stone ahead of them down a path; someone who has discovered they have an unexpected afternoon off and it's a lovely day. It developed into a determinedly pastoral symphony, with the strings striding about on their path getting some fresh air, and the flutes twiddling about in the trees being birds, which is what all flutes have to do in a pastoral bit. It's the law. Even the Wagner tubas submitted to the general air of merriment. When they could have pretended to be dark thunder clouds arriving to spoil the day, instead they had more an interjection of 'well, it's probably raining over that hill, and we can hear Max pretending to be thunder but he's really far away, and generally the forecast is dry, and what with the prevailing winds you'll be grand carrying on down that path, you have a great day'. Sort of thing.

Of course, being Bruckner, it didn't carry on in that careless way: the heavy brass jumped in, but even when they all got going together, the jaunty dotted rhythm conveyed that it would all turn out alright in the end. It was E major, for heaven's sake. By the time everyone's part was marked triple *forte* and the cellos had started scrubbing on an E until the last syllable of recorded time or until their arms fell off, whichever came sooner, it was a race to see who could out-blow each other in the brass and wind. The flutes had four leger lines but the trombones had accents: that ancient hand-to-hand combat composers insist on, despite the only result ever being tinnitus and numb lips.

They all finished together, in the right key, and Eliot stood there for a moment, sweat dripping off his face, breathing hard, before he let his arms drop and released the applause from behind him. He turned to face it, and took the first of many bows.

44

The scrum inside and outside the church afterwards was extraordinary. Alexander was completely mobbed as he tried to leave the church by noisy fans demanding selfies with him and throwing yelled questions and excited hormones in his direction. He obliged them all with great patience and humour, trying all the while to inch closer to Jörg's truck to stow his horn. The TV reporter and his cameraman also stalked him, hoping for a moment on camera. In the meantime, they shot ample footage of his crowd-pleasing attraction. For background filler, they assured each other. Even they were not immune to the Leakey image being incredibly easy on the eye.

Erin, Charlie and Ann came out of the side room into the church and leaned on their cello cases, waiting for the crush to clear.

'I'm not sure if I'd prefer all our concerts to be like this or not,' said Charlie. 'It's a bit… squeaky.'

'The more the merrier,' said Erin.

'And we might even have made a profit from tonight,' said Ann.

'What, you mean we can upgrade to a posh suite tonight?' said Charlie.

'Not that much profit,' said Ann, laughing. 'Though I reckon if you wanted anything from the Ford-Hughes coffers, now might be the time to ask.'

Mrs Ford-Hughes could be seen bobbing about in the crowd, her silk flowers indicating where she was like a snorkel above the waterline.

'Wow!' called a voice from behind a pillar. 'That was a-mazing!' Ben appeared, grinning. 'You were amazing. The whole thing. Blew me away. Amazing!'

'I think he liked it,' said Charlie.

'We both did,' said Noel, following Ben. They had fought their way out of their row of seats and past Mrs Ford-Hughes, and had managed to pop out of the current in a corner eddy. 'Very glad I came.'

'Well, if we can ever leave this place, it's time for a drink,' said Ann.

'And some food, I'm starving,' said Charlie.

'You and your stomach,' said Erin, rolling her eyes.

'That symphony must take it out of you,' said Noel. 'It's quite long.'

'Like a bloody workout,' said Charlie, and nodded at the sea of people between them and the main doors. 'Shall we just shove our way through?'

Eliot had poked his head out of the side room and heard Charlie's last comment. 'There's a door to the outside through here – Diederich showed me. He's unlocked it to make it easier for us to take our instruments round to Jörg.' He looked over at the throng around Alexander. 'I was going to let him know but it doesn't look like he'll be getting away from his groupies any time soon.'

'Hadn't you better get out there and give him a hand?' said Erin. 'After all, you're half the Breakfast Telly Team.'

'Oh… he seems as if he's coping fine so far,' said Eliot, grinning. 'I'm not nearly that photogenic. Come on.'

'Can Noel and Ben get out that way too?' asked Ann.

Eliot realised who was standing there, and shook hands. 'Ben – hi. And Noel! You made it. I didn't know if the rumour was going to be true. Great to see you.'

'Fantastic concert,' said Ben, pumping Eliot's hand with great enthusiasm.

'Thanks. It *was* good, wasn't it? This blimmin' orchestra, always pulling out all the stops and being brilliant.'

Eliot led the way through the side room and out of an external door hidden behind a fold in the brick wall, out of sight of the main doors. They walked up the deserted side alley and arrived at Jörg's truck on the other side of the crowd spilling out of the church. Jörg was standing in his usual place on the tail lift: half guard, half porter. He took their instruments and strapped them in safely.

'Christ, there's a TV camera now,' said Erin. 'What's happening?'

'I think we're going to be a Note Perfect Tours staff training video,' said Eliot. 'How to Get Your Orchestra Going Viral.'

'In three languages,' added Erin. 'This is unreal.'

'You can't buy this kind of buzz,' said Ben. 'Well, you can, but it's really expensive. Trust me. This is great.'

They watched as Mrs Ford-Hughes and David were interviewed together by the journalist with the cameraman, while Alexander tried to drift ever closer to the truck, orbited by animated selfie-seekers.

The two VRT sound engineers appeared from the same alley leading to the side room, with coiled cables looped over their shoulders and hands full of equipment. They glanced at the melee, skirted it unobtrusively, stowed their gear in their own van and returned the way they had come. They soon reappeared carrying much the same kind of kit, with Noor and Lise following them. Lise got into the van with the engineers and they drove quietly away.

Noor stood next to Jörg's truck with the others. 'Do you know where I might find Ingrid?' she asked nobody in particular.

'No – haven't seen her,' said Eliot. 'She's probably still—'

'There she is,' Charlie broke in. 'Oh, this'll be good.'

Without so much as raising her voice, Ingrid parted the crowd with her clipboard like one with God on her side, and marched through the dead-straight cleared path towards them. Behind her, in a docile row like ducklings after their mother, came four timpani being wheeled in a neat line. Max was first, guiding his dented drum over the cobbles carefully, followed by Carl, Kayla and Leroy, each steering their charge in Max's wake. Ingrid led them directly to Max's van and stepped aside to let Max open the back doors and load them.

'Bravo,' cried Charlie, and started clapping. All the nearby musicians joined in, and then, in the crowd-think of the moment, it suddenly spread to everyone loitering outside the church, until Ingrid was the surprise recipient of a warm round of applause for efficient logistics.

'You are a complete star, Ingrid,' said Eliot warmly, and leaned in to kiss her on the cheek. 'Thank you.'

Ingrid hugged her clipboard to her chest with pride and smiled. 'You are all most welcome.'

While Noor finalised some details with Ingrid, and the timpani-wheelers nipped back round the side of the church to retrieve their instruments, the rest of them tried to decide if they could go for a drink while Alexander was still embroiled in his showbiz lifestyle.

'Come on – I've got his number,' said Eliot. 'We can text him where we are.'

'They could try and follow him,' said Erin. 'He might never get away.'

Slowly the crowd thinned, and most of the orchestra made it over to Jörg with their instruments and drifted away to their evening's well-earned drink. The TV camera stopped filming, and the cameraman and reporter shook Alexander's hand and were about to leave, when they were intercepted by Ingrid who was not allowing anyone to go without taking one of her Note Perfect Tours cards. Mr Ford-Hughes walked over with David, with Mrs Ford-Hughes wafting florally beside them.

'We were thinking of going for a drink,' said Eliot. 'Would you like to join us?'

'Eliot, honey, that would be the most heavenly end to the most heavenly concert,' said Mrs Ford-Hughes, laying her hand flat over the diamonds round her neck, which were probably worth a small country's economy. 'In a heavenly week, while I'm in lyrical mood! It's been just…'

'Peachy?' suggested Charlie.

She laughed. 'Exactly. Just peachy. But we can't go without the star of the show!'

They turned to look at Alexander and waved for him to hurry up.

'Has Julian been over to put his horn and Wagner tubas in the truck?' asked David. 'I said we could take them back with us, since he has to fetch his car from a garage, I understand?'

'Not seen him yet,' said Eliot.

'Thank god,' breathed Charlie. 'Which reminds me, Noel, I've got something to show you.'

Noel raised his eyebrows. 'So I've heard.'

Jörg spoke from his perch above their heads. 'No Wagner tubas yet, David.'

'If Alexander doesn't get a bloody move on, I'm going anyway,' said Ann. 'There's no way I'm going to risk Julian coming for a drink with us.'

There was general agreement on that. Max got into his van and drove away. Erin had an idea. She leaned over and touched Ingrid's arm.

'Ingrid, may we ask a favour, please?'

Ingrid turned. 'Yes, of course. How may I help?'

'Could you please work your magic and extract Alexander for us? We need him. And, of course, you – and Jörg – are very welcome to join us for a drink.'

'Genius,' said Charlie.

'Thank you, but I must wait with Jörg for the final instruments, and take my leave of Diederich in the church. But, one moment.'

She walked over to Alexander and simply waited on the other side of the small crowd that still surrounded him. He saw her, and smiled. Nobody watching quite understood what happened next, but one minute Alexander was being asked noisy questions and having to lean down for selfies, the next a dignified calm had settled on everyone. They thanked Alexander nicely for his time, and walked away in twos and threes, nodding at Ingrid as they did so.

'How does she do that?' said Eliot.

'Witchcraft,' said Charlie. 'Magic clipboard.'

'I love her,' said Erin.

'She's awesome,' agreed Kayla.

'Watch and learn, girls,' said Ann. 'We are in the presence of a mighty power indeed.'

Alexander bowed to Ingrid, and they returned across the cobbles together. Ingrid looked as if nothing out of the ordinary had occurred.

'I am delivered,' said Alexander, handing his horn up to Jörg. 'Let's drink.'

45

They spilled out of the bar, most of them sitting around tables, some on a wall with their feet dangling over the canal, which was a daring position given the alcohol percentage of a lot of Belgian beer. Ben and Tracie were the only ones left sober: one on account of an imminent drive; the other because of her age and Kayla's lingering sense of in loco parental responsibility.

Charlie was showing Noel extracts from Julian's video on his phone and eating chips with the other hand. 'Can't you get him on indecent exposure, or maybe his awful borderline illegal politics?'

'Maybe both?' said Ben. 'I'm still feeling guilty about helping him, knowing what he'd been doing.'

'There must be something,' said Eliot. 'He's an awful man, and we've had to put up with him all bloody week.'

Noel smiled and sipped his beer. 'Are you asking me to see if I can retrofit a crime onto someone because you're tired and you don't like him?'

'No!' said Erin.

'Well, yes,' admitted Ann. 'He *is* truly awful, Noel. You haven't met him. But he really is.'

'Awful and illegal are two different things,' said Noel gently, chuckling. 'But I'll take a proper look at that video later and see what transpires.'

'"See what transpires" – it's working!' said Charlie, waving a chip and flinging a blob of centrifugal mayonnaise on to Noel's lapel. 'He's slipping into policeman-speak already. Ooh sorry – I blobbed you.'

'I didn't believe you had a tame policeman,' said Ben.

'I keep trying to be off duty when I'm around them, but it keeps slipping,' said Noel.

'Last time he came to one of our concerts, he arrested a load of kids shooting acorns at us,' said Carl to Ben. 'We spent the next few weeks wondering if our insurance claims citing "acorn-based assault" would be thrown out.'

'That evening was insane,' agreed Tracie.

Ben laughed.

'You think we're joking,' said Charlie. 'It was a load of lunatic posh kids.'

'God, you're *not* joking?' said Alexander. 'I thought you were joking too.'

'They won't be trying anything like that again,' said Erin. 'And if they did, Carl would probably find out where they lived and torch the place.'

'Maybe not their whole house. The east wing, say,' said Charlie, who was getting happily pissed. 'Or the stables. Stables are nice and combustible. All that chaff. What is chaff? Is it – like – the bobbles from elderly relatives' cashmere jumpers they use to bed down polo ponies?'

Nobody knew.

'Christ,' said Ann, looking at something over the rim of her glass.

'I know that tone,' said Charlie, without turning round. 'Is he?'

'He is.'

A couple of people did turn round, and groaned.

Sure enough, making his unsteady way towards them was Julian, whose weaving gait suggested he had already made a stop or two along the way.

'The man himself,' murmured Noel.

'It's too late to hide,' said Erin.

'Todger Talbot,' said Carl.

Julian caught sight of them and raised his arm. 'Greetings! Wondering where you'd all got to.'

'Away from you,' said Erin, too quietly for Julian to hear.

'What are we drinking?' Julian said, leaning in to their group with his arms round Ben and Erin's shoulders. Erin tried to squirm away from him.

'Actually, Julian,' Ann began, but was cut off by Julian noticing whom he had draped his arm around.

'Ben, me old mate! Didn't know you were still here. Did you like the concert? Bloody Wagner tubas are the business, yeah?' Julian belched in Ben's face for emphasis. Ben looked as though he might be sick.

Ann tried to speak again, but Julian wasn't listening.

'Wanted to ask you a favour, mate,' he said to Ben, breathing beer fumes. 'My car, right? Still in Brussels. Can I have a lift back over to pick it up?'

'Um, well, I'm going back there tonight, after this,' said Ben, still clinging to politeness despite any evidence of it being reciprocated. 'And I don't think your car will be ready until Monday?'

'S'not a problem, mate. I can bunk on your sofa, yeah? Just for a day?'

Ben looked terrified. Carl was just getting to his feet to fix the situation in a Carl sort of a way, when Erin tried another tack. She untangled herself from Julian's arm, walked round to the other side of Ben and put her arm round his waist.

'Actually, Julian, I think you've rather missed the boat on going back to Brussels to stay with Ben,' she said, smiling up at Ben with as much flirtation as she could muster. 'Isn't that right, darling?'

Ben looked as if he couldn't speak, so Ann quickly filled the gap. 'Yeah, Julian. You're late on the news, my friend.'

Behind Erin's back, Eliot lifted Ben's arm so it rested on Erin's shoulder. He leaned round to confess to Julian, 'We all think they make a super couple. Don't you think? It was chemical attraction. Unstoppable. Just like that.' He snapped his fingers.

Ben grinned. 'Well, who wouldn't fall for Erin?'

'Who indeed?' said Charlie, still grinning, perfectly prepared to share his crush on her for such a good and – crucially – pretend cause.

Julian stopped leaning on Ben's other side and stood upright, swaying slightly. 'Oh yeah? Well, in that case…' He curled his lip and made obscene gestures to Ben. 'Enjoy her, pal.'

'Oh, please,' said Ann.

'Maybe I could get a lift on the back seat anyway?' Julian went on, in a wheedling tone into Ben's ear. 'If Erin's that quick and easy, maybe you could share her when we get there?'

'Right, that's it,' said Carl, getting to his feet.

Alexander also stood up. 'Time for a reverse Amsterdam procedure, do you reckon?' he asked. Their combined bulk was persuasive.

'Great minds,' said Carl, reaching for Julian's arm.

Alexander took hold of the other one, and together they marched him over to the canal wall. Julian tried to dodge them, but his half-hearted scuffling wasn't going to dent the resolve and, frankly, torque of the four biceps propelling him. They sat him on the wall; Carl grabbed his ankles and twisted them across the wall to the other side so they hung over the water. Alexander moved his grip on Julian's shoulders so they could share the final push.

They grinned at each other.

'Been a pleasure working with you,' said Carl.

'Pleasure's all mine,' said Alexander.

'Get on with it!' shouted Eliot.

With a gentle nudge, Julian toppled into the canal, to a huge cheer from the onlookers. Ben laughed, not really able to believe what he had just witnessed.

Erin gave him a squeeze. 'That's my virtue defended, then.'

Ann finished her beer. 'Anyone want another? God, I love tours.'

Acknowledgements

As always, my immediate and most enduring thanks go to Abbie Headon, who is the first person to read the Stockwell Park Orchestra adventures after they fall out of my head. Editor, musician, giggler, and so much else besides, Abbie is the reason you're reading this.

It was copy-edited by Jayne Lewis, a process that always saves me hideous embarrassment later.

Clare Stacey at Head Design produced this glorious cover.

Huge thanks – as always – to Pete, Matt and Fanny at Duckworth Books, for continuing to publish books that make us smile as the world tries its best to do the opposite at the moment. We've never needed humour more.

Ben Blackman is not in these acknowledgements because I've done him a new and improved deal.

About the Author

Isabel Rogers writes poetry and fiction, but never on the same day. She won the 2014 Cardiff International Poetry Competition, was Hampshire Poet Laureate 2016, and her debut collection, *Don't Ask*, came out in 2017 (Eyewear). She has written two previous novels in the Stockwell Park Orchestra Series – *Life, Death and Cellos* and *Bold as Brass*.

She had a proper City job before a decade in the Scottish Highlands, writing and working in the NHS. She now lives in Hampshire, laughs a lot and neglects her cello. She is on Twitter @Isabelwriter.

Also available

Classical music can be a dangerous pastime…

What with love affairs, their conductor dropping dead, a stolen cello and no money, Stockwell Park Orchestra is having a fraught season.

After Mrs Ford-Hughes is squashed and injured by a dying guest conductor mid-concert, she and her husband withdraw their generous financial backing, leaving the orchestra broke and unsure of its future.

Cellist Erin suggests a recovery plan, but since it involves their unreliable leader, Fenella, playing a priceless Stradivari cello which then goes missing, it's not a fool-proof one. Joshua, the regular conductor, can't decide which affair to commit to, while manager David's nervous tic returns at every doom-laden report from the orchestra's treasurer.

There is one way to survive, but is letting a tone-deaf diva sing Strauss too high a price to pay? And will Stockwell Park Orchestra live to play another season?

The Stockwell Park Orchestra Series, Volume One

OUT NOW

Also available

**Community music projects always spread harmony…
don't they?**

When players in Stockwell Park Orchestra fear they may
be getting out of touch with the community, they invite
children from two nearby schools to join them for a season.

Supercilious, rich Oakdean College pupils have never
mixed with the rough Sunbridge Academy kids, and when
things go missing and rumours spread, the situation threatens
to turn ugly. DCI Noel Osmar has to tread carefully: after
all, he's off duty. Step forward, Carl the trombonist.

Can music heal social rifts? Who has been stealing and
why? And will the orchestra's newly composed fanfare turn
out to be fantastic… or farcical?

The Stockwell Park Orchestra Series, Volume Two

OUT NOW

Note from the Publisher

To receive updates on new releases in the Stockwell Park Orchestra Series – plus special offers and news of other humorous fiction series to make you smile – sign up now to the Farrago mailing list at farragobooks.com/sign-up.